The Girl In Apartment 10B

Sept/22

To: Margaret

From Dave

David Tylor

The Girl in Apartment 10B

ISBN 978-1-7782474-0-8

I acknowledge my many friends and family whose help and encouragement made this work possible.

To my wife Carol

DTH + CRY

Always

O, what a tangled web we weave

When first we practice to deceive!

Sir Walter Scott

1771 -1832

Chapter 1

Sunday November 10th
9:20AM
Roxworth Towers Apartment 10B

She could have been anyone. She could have been the girl next door, one of his friends' sisters, perhaps someone he passed by every morning on the subway on his way downtown to his office. But she wasn't.

She could have worked anywhere. Maybe as a nurse, or even a doctor. Maybe a barista in the coffee shop where he picked up his mandatory skim milk latte every morning. But she didn't.

Ken didn't know. Try as he might, he couldn't remember. All he knew for sure, and there was no mistaking it, was that she was dead. Lying sprawled out on his white tiled bathroom floor, she was definitely dead. Ken stood frozen in the bathroom doorway, numb, devoid of any feeling, staring down at this woman. He realized that he should be feeling something: some shock, some revulsion, some sense of horror, but all he felt was the pounding in his head and the pressure in his bladder that had brought him here to his formerly clean white bathroom.

As he stood there gaping, his bladder demanded action. What could he do? He couldn't just walk over her, step in the puddle of blood, say excuse me, but I really need to pee. He'd have to pee in the sink. Gross! His bladder was in control now, calling the shots, giving him no choice. A slight chuckle of a hazy memory formed in his fogged-up brain. It was just like college, years ago, hungover, peeing in someone or other's sink.

Finally relieved, he stood there, trying to take it all in. As he looked down at the woman, he could see she must have been in her early twenties. Slim body, small breasts: he liked those. High hips leading to two long slender legs. He noticed her toenails were painted green, a light pale green, very tasteful, and he wondered if they were painted to match her eyes. He couldn't tell. Her long hair, stringy with bright red blood and splashed across her face, wouldn't let her eyes shine through. Her eyes would be open; he knew that. He was smart enough to know that a corpse's eyes always stayed open. But there would be no shining, no life in these eyes. There would be only the dull blank forever-stare of a corpse, lying there on his floor with a face he couldn't see.

So much blood! Where did all the blood come from? More importantly, where did she come from? And even more important than that, why was she dead on his bathroom floor? He didn't remember anything about a girl in his bathroom. Alive or dead.

He knew he'd have to call the police. Knew they'd come charging in, big-footed, crushing his carpets. They would be pushing their way into his bathroom, hungry to claim their prize. Then the questions would start: Who? Where? Why? He knew he'd be asked the same questions over and over. Every movie he had ever seen told him exactly what was going to happen. Over and over, they'd demand who...where...why? And over and over, all he would be able to say would be he couldn't remember.

He needed to think. Needed to try to put the pieces together. Try to remember what possibly could have happened to lead him to be this hung over, with a reasonably attractive young woman sprawled naked in a pool of blood, on his once-clean bathroom floor.

First, he had to get out of these clothes. He had got up from his bed bleary-eyed, to find he was still fully clothed from last night. Traces of dried blood were on his shoes. Taking them off, he threw them without thinking into the kitchen trash. The clothes he had on were sticking to him, reeking with the stink of overindulgence. Dismissing them to the hamper, he pulled on one of his tracksuits, the monogrammed blue one with white piping. Not that he was an athlete, by any means. He just liked the slimming casual look the outfit gave him. Nothing unusual about that!

Now a coffee, strong and black. Yes, that would help. He needed to sit down, drink his coffee, soothe this pressure building in his head and think. Boy, it had been a long time since he'd been this hung over. His thirty-sixth birthday yesterday must have been a real doozy. He didn't remember any of it. Hopefully, it would come back to him once he got himself straightened out enough and the dull insistent pounding in his head would ease.

But the girl. Panic started to build. He could taste it, sour, over the coffee in the back of his throat. There was a dead girl in his bathroom, covered in blood, and he couldn't remember anything.

Oh God, he couldn't remember anything.

Chapter 2

Saturday November 9th

6:55AM

Roxworth Towers Apartment 10B

Buzz.....Buzz....Buzz

In the dark of his bedroom, Ken could hear his phone buzz, yanking him up from his warm comforting sleep. Who in the world would be calling him at this God-awful time of the morning? Christ, it was still dark outside, and he was not eager to rouse himself to start and face another gray morning.

Buzz.....Buzz....Buzz

His phone vibrated insistently: Come on, Ken, answer me.

Buzz.....Buzz....Buzz

Reaching up, he fumbled to find it in the dark.

"Hello."

"Morning, baby," chimed in his ear. "I wanted to be the first to wish you Happy Birthday."

Moan.

It was Vivian, his recent conquest. His on-again off-again girlfriend, as usual trying a little too hard.

"Do you know what time it is?" Ken groaned.

"It's birthday time, and you need to get up and get ready. We have a lot to do today. It's not every day my good-looking man has his thirty-sixth birthday," she said with a chuckle.

Moan.

"I'm pretty sure my birthday doesn't start until at least ten."

"Oh no, you're not wasting your birthday in bed...at least, not without me."

Moan.

Definitely trying too hard. Why did she always have to try so hard? Why couldn't she just relax and chill? Let life happen. Let it move forward or not in its own time.

"I'm picking you up at eight-thirty sharp for your birthday breakfast. Be ready; we can't waste any of this day."

Click, and she was gone, leaving him no time to argue or try to delay this morning madness.

Ken wasn't a morning person. He despised early morning people. Always bubbling, smiling, forcing their "Isn't it a great morning?" onto you. He had his comfortable morning routine. He started the morning off the way any sane person should with a routine he had developed back during his college days. His roommates would be up, scurrying around, trying to get ready for their early morning class, while he would burrow down deeper into his blankets. He was smart. He always picked his classes, so nothing interfered with his morning. A civilized morning, starting at ten o'clock.

With a touch of resentment, he rolled out of bed and opened the curtains. Normally, he enjoyed spending his first couple of minutes looking down on the city, seeing all the little people bustling about starting their day. He enjoyed the feeling of having the luxury of time afforded to him as the nephew of the company president. It was not quite smugness, but definitely a sense of superiority. The comfort of the routine. Today, however, because it was so early and still dark, he was denied his little pleasure of looking down on those less fortunate than himself.

Buzz.....Buzz....Buzz

Who was it now?

Buzz.....Buzz....Buzz

"Hello."

"Happy Birthday, old man. I didn't wake you, did I?" It was Jeff from work.

Had it not been for Vivian, of course he would have woken him. "No, Vivian called earlier."

"Damn, I wanted to be the first."

Jeff Hughes was the talented and quick-thinking young accountant from the office. Ken knew that Jeff had aspirations of moving up quickly in the company, perhaps a little too quickly. Jeff was good, the type of good that made sure everyone else knew he was good. He also knew, given half a chance, that Jeff wouldn't hesitate to take advantage of anyone standing in his way. Yes, around Jeff, Ken always had to watch his back. He knew he had to be careful with how he used Jeff in some of his wheeling and dealing. He thought of Jeff as the kind of friend you kept at arm's length, never close enough to have that arm bitten off. Ken was careful that Jeff only knew enough to do his 'special' biddings, but never enough to be able to slip between him and his uncle.

"What're your plans for later today?" Jeff was saying.

"Well, right now, I have to get ready. Viv says she's taking me out for a morning birthday breakfast."

"No, I mean later tonight. I thought you and I could go out for a real celebration. Maybe that club over on State Street. I think it's called Envy. I hear it's got good food, good drinks, and plenty of single women prowling around. We could make a real night of it. What'd you say?"

"Thanks for the offer. Let me think about it. I never know what Vivian might be planning. I'll get back to you."

"Ken, why don't you dump her? You know you're going to; you always do. Then we can go out and have a real night. A night to remember."

Ken had dumped a lot of women, as Jeff had so elegantly put it, but with Vivian, something was different. He couldn't quite put his finger on it. She was interesting, stroked his ego, was good looking and good in bed, and had a fun side she wasn't afraid to show and share with him. Sure, she constantly tried too hard, but she still had a lot of life in her for him to enjoy.

"I'll let you know."

"Okay, don't wait too long. Call me later." Jeff hung up.

Now, hopefully, there would be no more interruptions. Ken had his morning routine to get to, and Vivian would be here all too soon. Pulling on his slippers, a gift from one of his past girlfriends (he couldn't remember which one), he made his way to the bathroom.

When he'd first viewed his apartment over a year ago, he was struck by two features that he knew he wanted right away. First, the amazing view he would have from his bedroom being up on the tenth floor. A view that stretched over the majority of the city's downtown area. Second, the crème-colored deep plush carpet blanketing the apartment floors. Rich, warm, and sensuous as you walked on it.

There was one drawback, though, that Ken would have to deal with and change. The bathroom was adequate, and he wasn't an adequate type of guy. The whole bathroom would need to be gutted and upgraded as soon as he took possession. He could imagine it as a clean, stark white, uncluttered bathroom with a heavy glass-doored white-tiled shower complete with adjustable power jets and a large rain shower head. That would suit his personality. A bathroom that would make a statement to anyone lucky enough to be allowed in. He liked it, he wanted it, he got it. True, it pushed his budget a little more than he had planned, but he had dealt with that.

He almost always got what he wanted. After all, wasn't that what smart, savvy businesspeople did. A little adjustment here, a little trick there, maybe even a little sleight-of-hand, if required.

Now as he stood naked in front of the full-length bathroom mirror, he took a minute to look at himself. 'Look' probably wasn't the right word, he admitted to himself. It was more like admire himself. Yes, that's it, admire himself. Hey, you're doing pretty good, old man, as Jeff had called him. Height six foot even, not too tall as to be thought of as gangly. Just right. Brown hair with a hint of a curl, and brown eyes. Eyes that girls he met claimed could look right through them. Firm stomach, no paunch here, no way as he patted his abs. He didn't go to the gym. He had tried that once and immediately knew it wasn't for him. He didn't like the vibe he got being around a bunch of strange people, all sweaty and grunting. He kept his firm abs through healthy eating.

He turned on the tap. As the hot water ran, it created a slight steam on the mirror. The perfect temperature. Ken stepped into the shower, and right away the stream of hot spray bounced off his smooth chest. Too bad Vivian was coming so soon. He liked it when his mind drifted as he immersed himself in the warmth of the steam.

So relaxing. But no time now, too rushed. He frowned.

Chapter 3

Sunday, November 10th
6:30AM.
Hedge Street, Eastgate, the suburbs

Homicide Detective Russell Cravers was awake and sitting downstairs at the kitchen table in his bathrobe, reading the Morning Harold and drinking coffee. He always woke early. He treasured the short half-hour of solitude before the house erupted into a whirlwind of chaos, as his time. His to enjoy the quiet, read the paper, sip his coffee, think his big thoughts, and generally brace himself for the day ahead. He was particularly interested in the morning paper's reporting of the previous day's crimes in and around the city. Although promoted only two months earlier to become the youngest member of the Homicide Force at twenty-nine, he found it amusing when the paper tried to pump unknown facts and innuendo into the latest mundane random drug-deal-gone-wrong stabbing. Usually it was reported by a not-so-clever reporter trying to boost his profile and hoping to be lucky enough to have the story picked up by the newswire. Or perhaps the story was about some wife, who, after fifty years of marriage, finally had enough one evening of the cheating bastard sitting opposite her at the dining room table when he complained the soup was too salty, and got up and shot him, then sat back down and finished her soup.

But there were also those times when reading the articles got him worked up and annoyed. Those times when things weren't going well on the job. When a murder case dragged on for months. Surely the smart readers of the paper must realize solving murders that involved more than the average cookie-cutter solution took time, a lot of time. No Sherlockian feats of logic here: 'Elementary, Watson, it was raining so the butler with the wet shoes was the culprit.' No, solving a crime took daily hard, grinding, frustrating work. Endless repetition of studying the crime scene, reviewing the grisly photos over and over again, hoping to find something this time that might just pop out at you. Some little thing you had missed, although God forbid if it turned out to be something obvious that the lieutenant spotted before you did. Countless interviews trying to make sense out of the ever-changing witness statements, trying to sift through the mire of the stories for that one lie that the suspect would eventually slip up on.

And then having to deal with the overwhelming weight of the justice system. People's rights had to be protected. Justification for warrants had to be put together. Phone records, business records, photographs and videos had to be obtained. Stacks and stacks of paper had to be combed through. And on top of all this, there was the endless parade of lawyers to deal with. Boy, he had developed a real loathing for lawyers. Yes, it took hard work, assisted more often than he'd like to admit by a detective's two most valuable partners: Gut Feel and Blind Luck. Newspaper readers had to realize, or so he hoped, that the whole legal system was laid out in favor of the unknown suspect and that the homicide team members were little more than lowly mice looking for that elusive morsel of cheese.

Seven o'clock now, and Russ could hear Mary, his wife, calling for their eight-year-old twin boys, Jamie and Jerry, to come to life. His quiet time was now drawing to an end.

Mary was up, dressed, and acting as traffic warden for the morning bathroom rush. "Come on boys, get moving. Don't forget to brush your teeth." Jerry was particularly fond of 'forgetting' his teeth; last month, Jerry's two cavities had cost Russ $150 to get filled.

Shortly after his promotion from street constable and his passing the required exam to become a detective, Russ and Mary had decided it was time to move. They had been living in a bottom-floor apartment in Mary's parents' home. It was cramped and lacked privacy, with Mary's mom having a knack for sticking her nose into what Russ felt was really none of her business. But the price was right—free—so Russ had to bite his tongue and keep his mouth shut.

With the promotion and accompanying pay raise, combined with the money they had been able to save, it was time for Russ, Mary, and the twins to finally get out on their own. They purchased a sprawling two-floor, four-bed, one-bath, clapboard farm-style house on the edge of Eastgate. It was close enough for Russ to commute to the city each day, but also far enough out to provide some green space where the boys could play.

Granted, the house was a little the worse for wear, but as the realtor said, it had good bones and just needed some paint and a bit of tender loving care. The price was right, and Russ, being handy with tools, knew he could do most of the repairs himself. He had fun on his days off and in the evenings using his skills to slowly breathe life back into the old beauty.

"Kate, time to get up, sleepyhead." Kate, the youngest of the clan, arrived two years after the birth of the twin boys. Russ had been all for calling it quits after the twins. He couldn't imagine trying to raise more than two boys on his pay as a first constable, but Mary was insistent. She wanted a girl, and that was that. So Russ climbed back on the horse for one more time. Two years later, Kate was born. And now, it was Russ who was insistent: no more!

Getting the vasectomy was supposed to be easy, at least that's what his doctor said. A quick snip, five maybe six days of recovery at home, and it was all done. Easy-peasy, lemon-squeezy. Who was the doctor kidding? After five days of excruciating pain, Russ had spent the next ten days walking around the house bow-legged with a grapefruit hanging in his pants. The twins, although they didn't understand why their dad was walking around the house so strangely, loved it and couldn't stop laughing every time he waddled by. A hard way to learn never to trust doctors.

"Russ, can you get the boys' jeans out of the dryer? I didn't have time last night to finish them."

"Yes, dear. Coming right up, dear," Russ shouted, followed under his breath by, "I live to obey."

8:00AM.

365 Maple Row, Eastgate, the suburbs

Homicide Sergeant Karen Langdon bustled around the house, trying to get ready for her turn at once-a-month weekend duty. She was running a little late. When Matt, her husband, woke this morning, he had been feeling surprisingly good and even a touch romantic, very different from the month-long silent downer he'd been experiencing. God, she was glad that was finally over. Maybe some work pressure or problem had finally resolved itself. But a little snuggle here, a little touch there, and before you knew it, the morning had quickly turned into an all-out, no-holds-barred love-making session.

Nearly forty years of marriage, complete with one unplanned pregnancy at seventeen in high school, hadn't dimmed Karen's fire. Karen and Matt still regularly and eagerly enjoyed each other's company. Quite often in the morning, instigated by Matt in bed, but also when the mood hit, by Karen on the couch in the den when Matt thought he was going to be watching TV. Foolish boy.

"Matt, where are my keys?"

"I don't know. If you can't find them, take the truck. I don't need it today," her husband bellowed from the upstairs bedroom. The truck? Nope, Karen wanted her recently purchased SUV. She liked the high, smooth ride it gave her and absolutely loved its dark-tinted windows.

"You know I don't like driving that truck through the city. Can you come down here and help me find my keys?"

Matt and Karen lived a respectable middle-class life in Eastgate. Their daughter, Joyce, grew up here, went to school here, left for college from here. Joyce, now married with a family of her own, lived in another part of the country and rarely came home to visit. Sometimes Karen missed her daughter.

Karen stopped searching for her keys to watch Matt come lumbering down the stairs in his jockeys and dangling old housecoat. He still had that subtle manly look that had first caught her eye so many years ago that morning at Greg's Grill, where she worked as a waitress part-time. A little facial stubble, short messy hair, and a smell. A smell that warmingly surprised her. Plaid shirt, well-worn jeans, sitting there in the booth by himself reading the breakfast menu.

"Good morning, what can I get yeah?" At the time, Karen had wished she had said something witty, maybe a little spicy, something like, 'Morning, you see anything you like, we serve everything here Hot!' But that just wasn't her style. She didn't know it then, but she needn't have worried. For with Matt, Matt Langdon, she had him at 'good morning'.

Matt was the complete opposite of Karen, and the attraction was immediate. From the minute he saw her, he had fallen head over heels in love with this woman.

"Where'd you put them when you last used your car?" Matt now asked. But he knew where the keys were hiding: they were still in his coat pocket from when he had used her car last night. He had forgotten to replace them on the key hook behind the back door when he had slipped in late. Now he quietly pulled the keys from his coat that was hanging by the door and placed them on the small corner table in the hallway.

"Here they are, Karen. I found them right where you left them. You know, if you'd put them back where they belong, you wouldn't have this problem all the time."

"I thought I did," she replied. But she was late and didn't have time to get into a discussion about keys. She had to get on the road. It was a good thirty-minute commute to the city. Luckily, it being Sunday, she wouldn't have to deal with the regular stream of plugging along traffic holding her up.

CHAPTER 4

Sunday, November 10
Noon
Roxworth Towers, Apartment 10B

Ken was sweating. Sitting there on his couch surrounded by his plush carpeting, sweating, and he hardly ever sweated. He had always prided himself on being able to keep his cool and use his head to think, sweet talk, maneuver, or dance his way out of just about any situation. Except this time, he could feel the squeeze happening, forces beyond his control were going to be brought down on him, and there was nothing he could do about it. He knew he had to call the police; he had delayed the inevitable long enough. It had to be done and it had to be done now.

But first he needed to talk to someone to gain some advice and maybe even a little courage before triggering the avalanche that his call to the police would set in motion. He reached for his phone, and with shaky fingers automatically speed-dialed his uncle's private line.

"Simon here."

"Uncle Simon, it's Ken. I—"

Before Ken could utter another word, Uncle Simon exploded.

“Where in the dickens are you, boy? It's noon already and you were supposed to be here first thing this morning to make sure the Ryson order was completed and ready for shipment tomorrow. I explained to you the substantial penalty we’d face for not meeting the deadline in the contract.”

“But wait, Uncle Simon, let me explain, I’m in real trouble here, and I don’t know what to do.”

Trouble again! Simon Spirling, seventy-nine, president of Spirling World Supply didn’t know how much more of this he could put up with from his only nephew. He unconsciously started grinding his teeth.

Ken was the son of his youngest sister, Peg. Simon and his wife, Molly, had never been blessed with children. For Simon, it had been a matter of time and energy, and all his energy in the early days had been focused on building his company. Through endless long nights of single-minded determination, he’d built the company up, stick by stick, into one of the East Coast’s premier supply companies. If a product existed anywhere in the world, Spirling World Supply could get it for you.

Throughout Ken’s childhood, Simon and Molly had spoiled the boy. Molly had doted on the child, and Simon had made sure that Ken wanted for nothing. Hadn’t he paid for Ken to attend college? And not just any college. No, it had to be the best damn college for business management he could find. Granted, it did cost him a pretty penny of a donation to the academic building fund to get Ken admitted, but it was worth it. Ken would graduate with a sound knowledge of business and join the family firm where he would be trained in the ins and outs of the operation. Simon himself groomed Ken to eventually take over the reins when he finally retired.

Uncle Simon had Ken's future all mapped out, but it didn't turn out the way he'd planned. At first, he had felt a little guilty for how things had evolved. Perhaps Molly had spoiled Ken a little too much. Perhaps Simon himself was wrong in giving Ken everything and not allowing his nephew to fight, as he himself had done, for the things that mattered.

Ken had coasted through college, putting in just the barest amount of time and energy. Just enough, combined with another hefty endowment to the school, to graduate. Simon shuddered when he thought of his poor company eventually in Ken's less-than-capable hands. He had given Ken the showcase title of Manager of Business Development. It was a made-up position that would allow Ken to wine and dine and schmooze with customers and suppliers. A position suitable for Ken to make the required contacts and to nurture the relationships necessary to bring in the big-dollar contracts.

But it wasn't long before it became obvious to Simon that instead of Ken having the upper hand in bringing in the deals, the deals were slanted in favor of the other side. With Ken's ever-so-clever, or so he thought, wheeling and dealing and under the table maneuvering, the savvy customers and suppliers were quick to realize they had a good thing going.

Simon knew Ken tried to use his pawn in Accounting, Jeff, to keep his shady numbers hidden in the business books. Unbeknownst to Ken, the pawn, Jeff, had other plans. With running shoes on, he made a regular beeline to the President, informing Simon of every mis-step Ken took.

Ken's voice broke into Simon's thoughts. "Uncle Simon, did you hear me? I'm in real trouble."

"I heard you, Ken. What have you gotten yourself into this time? I can't keep bailing you out every time you screw up, you know."

"There's a dead girl in my bathroom."

"WHAT? What do you mean, there's a dead girl in your bathroom?"

"I woke up this morning, went into the bathroom, and there she was. Sprawled naked on the floor, covered in blood. And the worst thing is, I can't remember any of it. I have no idea who she is or how she got here. I can't remember anything."

"My God, what have you done now? Think, boy, think. People don't just miraculously have a dead woman appear on their bathroom floor. You must remember something."

"I've tried—believe me, I've tried—but it's all completely blank."

"Have you called the police yet?"

"No. I was just about to, then decided I wanted to call you first."

"Okay, good. I'm going to get in touch with our firm's lawyers. Don't do anything or touch anything until you hear from them!" Simon slammed the receiver down.

"Betty, Betty," he hollered to his personal secretary. "Betty, get in here."

Betty picked up her notepad, straightened her skirt, and ventured into the lion's den.

"Yes, Mr. Spirling, you called me?"

"I need you to track down one of our lawyers. I need to talk to one of them right away."

"But it's Sunday, Mr. Spirling. Lawyers don't work on Sundays."

"I know it's Sunday. I'm working Sunday; you're working Sunday. I didn't ask you what day it was. I told you to track down one of those high-priced leeches we keep on retainer. I don't care how you do it, I don't care what they're doing, I want it done now. Do you understand me?"

"Yes, sir."

"Well, get moving. When I say now, I mean now."

Betty hated her job. Simon Spirling was a workaholic. Saturdays, Sundays, late nights: it didn't matter to him. And the rule was whenever Mr. Spirling worked, Betty had to work. She often wondered if it was worth it. Although the pay was good, she worked her butt off for it. At twenty-eight, her prime years were passing her by. How was she ever going to catch a husband if she was always stuck in the office? Now she had to disturb someone else's Sunday off. Looking through the company database, she found the number of Peters, Peters & Cohan, Attorneys at Law.

"You have reached the office of Peters, Peters & Cohan, Attorneys at Law. Our office is now closed. Please call back Monday through Friday from 9AM to 5PM. If this is an emergency, at the beep, please leave your number and someone will get back to you as soon as possible. Have a nice day. *Beep.*"

Betty left her number and waited, and waited, and waited.

"Have you got hold of them yet?" Simon shouted from his office.

"No, sir. I've called their office and left my call-back number, but they haven't responded yet."

"Dammit! Call Jeff Hughes from Accounting at home. He's always dealing with them. See if he has a home number for any of them."

Betty called Jeff. "...and he's insistent that he wants to talk with one of the company lawyers right away. He was on the phone with Ken when he suddenly went ballistic. Do you have any way of contacting one of them?"

"Yeah, no problem. I used to date one of the typists a while ago. I picked up the home number of Cohan from her. I knew it would come in handy one day. Make sure you tell the old man that I was able to help."

Waiting on his couch, small flashes of recall began to take shape for Ken. He had gone to the club with Jeff, he remembered that. There were some women there, he remembered that. Then it got all foggy. Vivian had been there, he couldn't remember why. She wasn't supposed to be. He remembered she had gone crazy, and made a horrific scene, screaming something about how she had to save him. The last thing he vaguely remembered was being thrown in the back of a crowded cab, dragged into his apartment, then waking up this morning.

1PM

Roxworth Towers, Apartment 10B

Buzz…Buzz…Buzz

Ken gingerly picked up his phone. "Hello"

"Hello, is this Ken Harris?"

"Yes."

"Mr. Harris, my name is Jonathan Cohan, from the law firm of Peters, Peters & Cohan. We're lawyers for Spirling World Supply. Your uncle mentioned you were in a little bit of trouble and that I should contact you. Well, Mr. Harris, what can I do for you?"

A little bit of trouble thought Ken. Boy, that's the understatement of the century. He dutifully went through his story for the lawyer, describing finding the body but remembering nothing.

After interjecting a few times to clarify some key issues, Cohan said, "Mr. Harris, listen very carefully to what I am about to tell you. After we hang up, I want you to call 9-1-1. Do not, I repeat, do not tell them what you have just told me. I want you to say that you want to report that there is what appears to be a dead body in your bathroom. Give them your address and nothing more. Remember all 9-1-1 calls are automatically taped. When the police arrive at your apartment, let them in. No matter what they ask you, say only that I am your attorney, and you are waiting for me to arrive before you answer any questions. Is that clear?"

"Yes, I think I understand."

"Good. Now give me your address and I'll be there as soon as I can."

No sooner had Ken hung up when his phone started to erupt with pings. One...two...five text messages from Vivian, pleading with him. Remembering bits of the spectacle she had put on last night at the club, he was in no mood to deal with her now. She had made a complete fool of herself and embarrassed him in front of everyone within earshot. Worst of all, he certainly wasn't thrilled to have had her ridiculous performance played out in front of Jeff of all people.

Ping, I'm sorry, I don't know what came over me.

Ping. Seeing you in the middle of that group, I guess I lost my head.

Ping. Some bad memories swept over me.

Ping. I'm sorry, I didn't mean it. We got a good thing going, let's not throw it away.

Ping. Ken, why aren't you answering me? I said I'm sorry. Please, baby, answer me.

Right now, the dead woman in his bathroom occupied all of Ken's thoughts. Vivian would have to wait. He took a deep breath and dialed 9-1-1.

"9-1-1, what is your emergency?" a calm male voice answered.

"I think I need the police."

"Yes, sir, can I have the nature of your emergency?"

"I woke up this morning and found a dead girl in my bathroom."

"Please stay on the line, First, can you tell me your name?"

"It's Ken Harris, or rather Kenneth Harris," Ken said nervously.

"Thank you, Mr. Harris. Now can I please have your address?"

"Roxworth Towers, Number 10B."

"Thank you, Mr. Harris. You say you found a dead woman in your bathroom. Is that right?"

"Yes, just lying there on my floor."

"Mr. Harris, how do you know the woman is dead? Did you touch her, possibly attempt to take her pulse or check if she was breathing?"

"No, of course not." Now Ken was starting to get upset, being questioned by some unknown voice as if he were some kind of idiot. Everyone knows you're not supposed to touch anything at a crime scene. "I told you, I woke up this morning and just found her there on the floor. I never touched anything!"

"Please stay calm, Mr. Harris. I just need to know how you know the woman is dead."

"Because she's covered in blood, you fool!" Ken's voice rose in frustration. "Of course, she's dead!"

"Okay, Mr. Harris, I'm sending help now. Please stay on the line; the police should be arriving in less than three minutes. Is that okay, Mr. Harris?"

"Fine," Ken said and hung up. He had done enough talking to this oblivious civil servant. The woman was dead. He had found her on the floor covered in blood. He had never touched anything. How much clearer could he be?

Ping. I'm sorry about the note if that's what's bothering you.

Ping. You got to understand, I didn't mean it.

Ping. Forgive me. Please, baby, please.

Ken shut his phone off and tossed it to the other end of the couch. It was bad enough he didn't remember anything about how the dead girl ended up in his bathroom, but he also had no idea what Vivian was all worked up about. Too much was happening. He needed time to think.

As Ken sat on his couch and waited for the police, he looked down and noticed what appeared to be a trail of reddish-brown footprints originating at the bathroom door. They started out dark, then became faded and faint. Stunned, he stared at them. He thought the prints had to have come from his shoes. The same shoes he had just thrown out in the kitchen trash because they had traces of dried blood on them. Now the carpet, his beautiful carpet, was ruined. He had to do something. He couldn't just leave the stained footprints on his beautiful carpet for all to see. What would his friends and guests think? He got up, went to the kitchen, and reached under the sink to pull out a bottle of some kind of cleaning solvent stored there by his housekeeper. On his hands and knees, he scrubbed as hard as he could, but it only seemed to make matters worse. The whole carpet would now need to be replaced. Money, he'd have to think of some scheme or maybe his insurance would cough up the required money. Replacing this carpet wasn't going to be cheap, but it would have to be done.

Hearing the sound of the pulsating sirens in the distance, growing in intensity as they approached, snapped him back to reality. This wasn't a dream or some vision. This was all too real, and he was firmly stuck in the middle of it all.

The sing-song chime of his doorbell was followed by repeated banging on the door.

"Police, open up!" someone shouted loud enough to wake the dead, but it didn't.

Barefoot, Ken went to open the door.

"Are you Mr. Ken Harris?" asked one of the two imposing policemen outside his door.

"Yes."

"My name is Sergeant Killens," the officer carried on. "And you called 911 claiming to have a body in your bathroom?"

"I'm not claiming to have a body. I *do* have a body, and it's not mine."

"I think we had better come in, Mr. Harris, if you don't mind." In reality, it didn't matter one bit whether Ken minded at all, they were coming in.

"Davis, you stay outside and secure the door."

"Yes, Sarge."

"Now, Mr. Harris, can you show me where this body is located?"

Ken raised his arm and pointed, "In there, in my bathroom, lying on the floor, and she's covered in blood. I found her there, I know nothing about her, I can't remember anything. I don't even know her, I have nothing to do with her, I simply can't remember anything about her." Ken knew he was babbling, but the words kept spewing from his mouth. He couldn't stop himself. He had completely forgotten the clear precise instructions that lawyer Cohan had given him.

CHAPTER 5

Sunday, November 10
8:30 AM
Police Services

The city's Homicide Division resided on the second floor of the brown brick four floor building affectionately known as the 'Cop Shop'. The building was old, worn and gave the appearance to the untrained eye of tiredness, hiding the hustle and bustle and often chaotic energy going on behind the secured interior doors.

Lieutenant Tom Melnyk, 48, a twenty-four-year veteran of the force, quickly scanned the events from the last 24 hours. Finding nothing major, only a couple of minor car thefts committed by a group of too much to drink juvenile joyriders, now sleeping it off in the basement holding cells. If luck was on his side, it would continue to be a quiet day ahead for the homicide group.

Melnyk could use a break. His desk bulged with overdue reports scattered across its' top, waiting to be completed. A rising rustle of noise could be heard sweeping through the second floor as the day shift started coming to life. Detective Russ Cravers began settling into his small cubicle workspace that he shared with his partner Sergeant Karen Langdon. The cubicles were a part of the maze of portable area dividers snaking over the center of the open room.

Looking around he couldn't see Sergeant Langdon yet. As the senior detective of the team, it was not like her to be late. Melnyk made a mental note to talk to her later quietly on the side. Now on to the reports, it was wishful thinking they would get done by themselves.

At 1:45 PM, Lieutenant Melnyk's hope of being able to see the top of his desk was brought to an abrupt end. Coming out of his office as a man with a purpose he strode directly over to Langdon and Cravers. "Listen up, 911 just got a call from Roxworth Towers, that upscale apartment block over on Hanover Street. A man named," pausing to look down at the scrap piece of paper he held in his hand, "Ken Harris claims he found a woman in his bathroom, dead. A couple of uniforms have already been sent by dispatch to secure the site and take preliminary statements. Detective, you and the Sergeant are it, get moving. Cravers, you take the lead."

WHAT! Flashed across Karen's brain. She was the senior, experienced, ranking officer. Was this some sort of macho slap for running late this morning?

"I'll contact the forensics team upstairs and the on-call Medical Examiner, I think it's Doc Amile who drew the short straw today," Lieutenant Melnyk continued. "They'll meet you there. Let me know if you need anything."

Russ sighed, "Well so much for a quiet Sunday." Then feeling the flow of power that had just been gifted to him, turned to Karen "Sarg, can you call for a pool car from the garage to meet us downstairs?"

It's already started. She made her mind up, she would need to have a few prime words with 'The Lieutenant'.

As Sergeant Langdon and Detective Cravers entered the elevator for their downward journey to retrieve their pool police car, Lieutenant Melnyk sprinted upwards on the side staircase to the third floor, always trying whenever possible to take the stairs, good to get the heart beating.

The Police Services Forensics Division lived in the third floor 'Hot House'. The 'Hot House' was a self-contained section complete with a separate air ventilation and heating unit. The resultant stuffy, overheated workspace was a vain attempt to keep the smells and irritants, emanating from the lab, due to their excessive use of chemicals and solvents, from gaining access into the air systems throughout the main part of the building.

During the normal Monday to Friday work week, there would be a team of two lab technicians, three lab assistants and a secretary, headed up by the lead Dr. Cornell.

This being Sunday, there was only one lab tech and one assistant manning the fort. Weekends were usually used as a time for doing mundane tasks such as cleaning, restocking of supplies and sometimes, if all stayed quiet, some projects brought in from home.

"We've got a body on the go" Melnyk called out as he streamed through the section door. "I need an onsite team."

One of the assistants, Tom couldn't quite remember his name, poked his head out from around the corner. "Hi Lieutenant, there's only two of us in today, we'll have to put calls out to bring people in. Should take an hour, maybe an hour and a half at most. Have you notified the M.E.s' office?"

"Not yet, I'm calling them next."

The crime site rules were very clear, chiseled in stone, 'No One, and that means No One, was to enter the crime scene until the attending M.E. gave the all clear.' Unless the Medical Examiners' Office could keep, and be able to prove that they had kept, clear custody of the crime scene, all evidence emanating from the crime scene would be deemed as spoiled and inadmissible in any resulting court case.

"Do what you have to, there's personnel already on site, and my two homicides are on route. Tell your people to get moving, everyone will be standing around waiting for them."

"Can you jot down the details on the call-in sheet over there on the desk for me?"

Tom found the form, scribbled on it, "There" he said. One more call to make, the M.E. had to be notified. Back at his desk, Tom put the call through.

Perched on the top floor of St. Catharine's Mercy Hospital, the Jackson County Medical Examiners' Office phone rang. From its humble beginnings in the garden wooden tool shed owned by the Order of Sisters of St. Catharine's near the end of the Civil War, the hospital had grown. Purchased by the MacArthy Group of Services, in the 1960's, when young maidens no longer wanted to give up dreams of fancy for the isolated discipline of nunnery service, all traces of the founding Sisters were now forgotten. Charity overridden; profit was now in control.

Assistant M.E., Dr. Anna Amile had been busy reading the latest article she had found in the monthly publication of the Examiners' Journal on 'Bone Decay as a Result of Open-Air Exposure.' An interesting article, she thought. As one of the two Assistant M.E.'s responsible for Jackson County, she felt it was part of her duties to stay abreast of all the latest information in the vast world of death.

Buzz…Buzz

Putting down her reading, "Examiners' Office, Dr. Amile speaking."

"Hello Dr. Amile, this is Lieutenant Tom Melnyk from the Homicide Squad, I heard that you were the M.E. on duty this weekend."

"Yes, my good fortune by being the Junior Assistant. How can I help you, Lieutenant?"

"At 1:30PM today, 911 received a call reporting the finding of a supposed female body. 911 immediately dispatched a team of officers to the site. My two, Sergeant Karen Langdon and Detective Russell Cravers are on route and should be arriving any time now. I have informed Forensics and they are calling their field investigative unit in from home which should be on site in approximately an hour and a half."

"I'll be there as soon as I can. I can call for the pickup team and wagon once I get there and am able to see what we've got. Hold on till I get something to write with," Dr. Amile said. "Ok, I'm ready, give me the address."

Lieutenant Melnyk recited the address and Dr Amile read it back to confirm she had it correct. Collecting her coat and her service bag, she headed out to the private elevator reserved for the discrete movement of bodies, or as she preferred to call them 'Clients'. Two wide when business was booming.

2:15PM

Roxworth Towers, Apartment 10B

By the time Detective Cravers and Sergeant Langdon pulled up in front of the Roxworth Towers, there were already three black and whites blocking the street. With their tires squealing, sirens blaring and their lights flashing their arrival was a clear statement to all that mischief was afoot. Their presence, with their red and white flashing lights, cast a pulsating pink glow over the street, bathing the small group of passersby that were starting to gather. Some out for a bit of air, a few held small dogs on sparkly leashes, prancing beside their masters, looking for just the right spot to deposit their afternoon business. Mingling on the other side of the street, they anxiously stood watching the show unfold. Whispering, pointing, this was an upscale, refined neighborhood and rarely were they privy to this kind of excitement.

Approaching the door, Cravers snapped his badge out of his pocket and waved it in the general direction of the two uniforms standing on either side of the large glass entrance doors. "Cravers and Langdon, Homicide, where is everyone?" asked Russ.

"Upstairs on the tenth-floor sir" came the reply from the short uniform standing on the left as he reached back to hold open the glass door for the two from Homicide to enter.

"Don't let anyone in or out unless you hear from me" Russ barked as he entered. Karen followed without saying a word. Afterall, this was Detective Russell Craver's case, at least for the moment until she had the opportunity to talk with the lieutenant. For now, she was just along for the ride.

Inside the building lobby, the doorman stood at his post behind a small upright counter. Behind him built into the wall were a series of pigeon hole boxes, each one distinctly numbered for the building's fifty-six apartments. The Roxworth Towers consisted of ten floors. The first nine floors of six apartments each, were topped off by the executive tenth floor holding two luxury suites. Some of the boxes still held various pieces of tenant mail left over from Saturdays' mail delivery that hadn't yet been picked up. Others held small yellow notes taken by 'Vincent' the doorman waiting to be claimed as tenants came and went through the lobby.

Vincent Casperian posed a striking figure. Standing six-two easily, shoulders held back, trim gray mustache dangling down above his thick upper lip, resplendent in his smartly pressed gold with black trim uniform jacket. Not easy to miss, but for now, Russ neither talked to him nor even acknowledge him, striding straight ahead towards the elevators. Another uniform stood at the sliding doors of the two tenant elevators. "Tenth floor sir" he chimed.

"I know, thank you" replied Russ. Still Karen just followed behind.

Getting out on the tenth floor, Russ and Karen were confronted by the fourth uniform on site, Officer Davis. Again, Russ reached into his pocket and flashed his badge.

“Right in here sir.”

“Is anyone else on scene yet?”

“Only my Sergeant, Sergeant Killens sir, he’s inside with a Mr. Ken Harris.”

“Let me know the minute the M.E. and forensics arrive.”

Out of the corner of her eye, Sergeant Langdon noticed a slight movement as the door to Apartment 10A cracked open. Soft brown watery eyes peaked out, drawn by the unusual commotion.

“What’s going on?” a high-pitched voice asked from behind the heavy walnut custom door.

“Excuse me,” replied Karen, “I’m sorry if we have disturbed you. My name is Sergeant Karen Langdon, and this is Detective Russell Cravers from the Police Force.” Karen was careful to leave out the Homicide, no point needlessly alarming anyone yet, there would be plenty of time for alarm, shock, disbelief later. “And you are?”

“Eleanor, Mrs. Eleanor Upton.”

“Okay, Mrs. Upton, if I can ask you to please stay inside your apartment. I’m sure one of our officers will talk with you shortly, if that's alright.”

The door closed as quietly as it had opened. Eleanor Upton couldn’t wait for her husband to come home. She didn’t like to be alone when Lord knows what was going on in that dandy’s apartment across from hers’. She had known there would be trouble with him from the moment she had laid her eyes on him. Her husband Fredrick had to believe her now.

Officers Cravers and Langdon stepped inside the apartment and stopped just inside the doorway. They took a moment to survey the inside that was laid out in front of them. An exceptionally large apartment, floors covered with a rich pile carpet. Upscale designer tables and lamps appropriately spaced around the living room area. To the one side there appeared to be two doorways. A doorway to a bedroom, which held the infamous bathroom ensuite with its' special guest, a corpse on the floor, and a doorway to a combination office/den area. On the other side was a dining table, complete with six chairs, a side table and a small glassed in china closet, holding a few pieces of what looked like expensive dishware. Beyond the dining area, hidden from doorway view, they knew there had to be a kitchen area. First impression, expensive. Second impression, way beyond their pay grade.

On the couch, in the middle of the room, sat a man whom they assumed to be this Mr. Ken Harris. Beside him stood uniformed Sergeant Killens, notebook in hand.

"Afternoon Sergeant Killens" Karen said. She had known Sergeant Killens over the years from past investigations.

"Afternoon Sergeant." With that greeting, Sergeant Killens recognized that control was now formally in the hands of Homicide.

"Sergeant Killens," Russ said, "could we step outside to the hallway to talk for a moment? Officer Davis can step in and keep Mr. Harris company." Now that Homicide was in charge; Russ would make sure that Mr. Harris was never left on his own.

In the hallway, in a muffled voice, Sergeant Killens began his report. Referring to his notebook,

"We arrived at the building at approximately 1:48PM with three cars. I stationed two men at the front entrance and one man at the elevators to secure the entrance way. Officer Davis and myself proceeded directly to this apartment. Upon knocking, Mr. Harris granted us entrance to the apartment. After introducing ourselves to Mr. Harris, who is the only occupant in the apartment, I stationed Officer Davis at the front door to the apartment. When asked, Mr. Harris freely directed me to the ensuite bathroom connected to the only bedroom of the apartment. In the bathroom, on the floor, I observed a female body with a large amount of blood."

Sergeant Langdon asked, "Sergeant, did you or anyone you see enter the bathroom?" A crucial point.

Sergeant Killens stated firmly "At no time did I, or Officer Davis enter the bathroom. Nor was Mr. Harris allowed to enter the bathroom."

"Perhaps, Sergeant, while we are waiting for the M.E. and Forensics to arrive on site, you could organize a canvassing of all the apartments in the building. Find out if anyone saw or heard anything unusual last night" Russ said, trying to gain back control of the conversation.

Russ and Karen reentered the apartment. "Davis, you can resume your post at the door."

"Mr. Harris, Mr. Ken Harris?" Russ had begun to write in his notebook. First the date, then the names of anyone in attendance.

"Yes"

"My name is Detective Russell Cravers from Homicide. I'd like to ask you a few questions."

"My lawyer told me not to answer any questions until he arrived."

This mans' already got a lawyer active, maybe he's not so dumb after all thought Russ. "That's alright we can wait a few minutes for him to arrive."

"Maybe while we're waiting" Karen said, "we could get a few incidentals out of the way just to make sure we have things straight?" Being more experienced it was her turn in the wrestling match for control. She knew you wanted to get the suspect talking. "Your name is Ken, is that short for Kenneth?" knowing full well it was.

"Yes."

Get him talking about anything, just get him talking. "And this is apartment 10A?" Karen was pulling the old used car salesman trick. When trying to get a hesitant customer to sign on the dotted line, drop your pen conventionally at the customers' feet. Let him pick it up and 'Voila', the sucker now had the pen in his hand ready to sign.

"No. This is 10B, 10A is across the hall."

Keep talking. "Oh, I'm sorry" The pen was now in the hand. "Do you happen to know who lives there?"

"Some old busybody and her husband, I think their named Upton."

Great, now he's starting to sign. Damn, interrupted.

"I just got word there's a lawyer downstairs demanding to be let in. A Jonathan Cohan" said Davis with his head in the door.

"Is that your lawyer?" Russ asked.

"Yes."

"Okay, let him up."

With a few more minutes Karen knew she would have had Ken singing like a canary.

"My name's Jonathan Cohan, from the law firm Peters, Peters & Cohan, and I'm here to look after Mr. Harris's interests. Before I can allow anyone to speak with Mr. Harris, I'll need a moment in private to confer with my client." Glancing around the open space, "Maybe we can step into the kitchen?"

Not knowing what may be in the kitchen, Karen jumped in. "Let me have a quick look first, if that's okay with you?" Without a warrant, if there was any piece of evidence to be discovered in the kitchen, Karen knew she wanted to be in there with permission.

"Okay, go ahead, you and Mr. Harris can use the kitchen, we'll wait out here."

"Sergeant," Sergeant Killens called from the apartment door. "Can I speak with you for a moment?" In the hallway he continued," it's approaching three o'clock shift change and my men and I will be replaced by Sergeant Jenkins any moment. He's bringing more men on site to take over the canvasing."

"Thank you, Sergeant, you and your men have been a tremendous help today. When you see Sergeant Jenkins, have him come find me, I have a few more things for him to do."

"Yes, thank you Sergeant Killens, when you return back to the station, make sure to submit your report," Russ trying to show he was the one in control. Sergeant Killens was no rookie; he knew exactly what he had to do and kind of resented the needless order.

Karen heard the rattle of the elevator door opening. “Sergeant Langdon?”

“Afternoon Sergeant Jenkins.”

“At the shift change debriefing your lieutenant said you could use some help so here we are.”

“Glad to have you join us. I have a number of things that I would like you to get your men busy on.”

Jenkins pulled out his notepad and started to write as Karen rattled off her list.

- Continue with the apartment block canvasing that the day crew had started.

- Canvas the surrounding outside area for anyone who might have seen or heard anything.

- Interview the front door man and find out who was working last night. Send a car over to his place and get a statement.

- See if you can find if there are any cameras outside in the neighborhood on any of the surrounding buildings.

Jenkins wrote feverishly trying to keep up with the sergeant.

- Find the building superintendent and persuade him to come downtown first thing in the morning. Arrange for a car to pick him up.

- Get the forensics boys to do a search of any garbage containers in the area when they arrive.

“Any questions”

“No, I'm good.”

Shortly more and more Black and Whites had begun to arrive, randomly abandoned willy-nilly fashion in front of the entrance. Lights left flashing, a small army of uniforms brought on by Sergeant Jenkins for the afternoon canvas. Door to door, floor by floor.

“No, we didn’t hear anything.”

“We slept soundly last night.”

“Why, what’s happened?”

Take their names, record their statements, door to door, floor by floor. For those that weren't home or deciding not to get involved in whatever the hell was going on outside and didn't answer, leave a card. ‘Please call the Police Department in regards to an urgent matter at your earliest convenience. Thank You.’ Ten floors, fifty-five apartments, all accounted for. Thirty-eight statements taken, written down, all amounting to nothing. Seventeen left requiring follow up.

As the afternoon wore on, the small afternoon group of gawkers had grown to a sizable crowd corralled in by yellow tape. ‘What’s going on?’ ‘Why are all the police over there in the towers?’ Speculation was passed around, ear to ear. ‘There’s been a robbery up there.’ ‘Some man killed his wife and her lover.’ ‘There’s a shooter running wild around the halls, the poor people are locked in their apartments.’ ‘It’s horrible, I heard one of the policemen talking, he said there was blood everywhere.’ No one realized this was all for one lone, naked girl, laying on the floor, covered in blood, in Ken Harris’s bathroom.

Reporters arrived and began circulating among the crowd. “Can I have your name please?” “Can you tell our readers what you have seen?” Plying their trade, trying to gather color to act as filler material for when they finally learned the truth from a reliable police spokesperson. “Look, over there, the TV van is setting up.” Microphones and cameras began to be positioned. Flood lights were turned on. A dark suited man with a bright tie inside the van was busy checking his hair and make-up. He stopped to check his zipper before he stepped outside. “Look, look, coming out of the van, isn’t that Rick Hanna. You know, the guy that does the onsite reporting for the news, Channel 12 every night” “He’s a lot shorter than I thought” “Do you think I can get his autograph?” The crowd's fickle attention had now moved from the apartment entrance way to the far more interesting live TV setup happening right before their eyes.

Rick Hanna was the first to see the car pull up, trying to get as close to the front door that the miss-mash of police cars would let it. He recognized Dr. Anna Amile, carrying her large bulky brown bag as she entered the building unhindered by the police guards, as being from the County Medical Examiner's Office. So, it was true, there was a body involved, he thought. Tired of doing the dog shows, or the farmer with the largest pumpkin interviews, he was finally going to get his proper fifteen minutes of fame on this one.

“M.E.’s on site” word was passed on upstairs to apartment 10B. Finally, we can get this show on the road thought Russ and Karen almost in unison.

Standing in the apartment doorway, “Afternoon detectives, I’m Dr. Anna Amile from the County M.E.'s Office.” Russ and Karen introduced themselves. Still standing in the doorway, “Can I ask, how many people are presently inside with you?”

Russ replied "Two, a Mr. Ken Harris, the apartment owner, and his lawyer, Mr. Jonathan Cohan."

"And how many other people have passed through?"

Karen didn't like where this was going.

"Only Officer Davis and his Sergeant from the day shift uniforms."

"Detective," voice firm and elevated, "I may be relatively new at this, but I would've thought you'd have declared this whole apartment a crime scene rather that have a band of random people parading through it. Do you realize the damage you could be doing to crime scene preservation?" Russ was taken aback by the downright tongue lashing he received.

"And Sergeant, I would have expected better from someone of your rank! What the hell were you thinking, or were you not thinking at all?" In the kitchen, lawyer Cohan had heard the raised voiced scolding that was going on. He instantly recognized the gift he had just been given. This bit of tasty information could just prove to be of value should Ken have to go to trial. Very nice he thought.

"Ok, I want you to clear this crime scene. Get everyone outside this apartment right now."

"The lawyer's in the kitchen conferring with his client," Russ tried to say in his defense.

"I don't care what anyone's doing. Out. Now!"

In the hallway Karen decided enough. She was taking over the lead and the hell with what the lieutenant wanted. "Officer, get two uniforms to escort Mr. Harris back to the station. Put him in one of the interview rooms, stay with him, and make sure he's comfortable until we can get to him." Then as an afterthought she added, "And get him something to eat. Tell Sergeant Jenkins to come see me right away."

"Does this mean you are charging my client?"

"Not at this time Mr. Cohan. I am merely asking Mr. Harris to submit himself for some questioning in a more suitable location. I think it'd be in Mr. Harris's best interest to volunteer, don't you?"

"Ken, I think you should go with the officers and I'll meet you later at the station. Nothing to worry about."

Nothing to worry about. You're not the one being led out of his home, between two police officers, in front of everyone as some kind of criminal. "Call my uncle and let him know what's happening" Ken called back over his shoulder as he was being led away.

"I'm going to call him now."

"You wanted to see me, Sergeant?"

Out of earshot from Cohan, "Sergeant, tell your officers with Harris to make a slight detour over to St. Catharine's. Have them take a blood sample and a swab from Harris. Make sure they get one of the permission forms filled out first and that Harris signs it. Understood?"

"Yes, Sergeant." Jenkins knew exactly what was happening. Get the tests, ok'ed by the suspect without the lawyer knowing and being able to stop it.

Outside the building, Ken, trying unsuccessfully to cover his face, was paraded in front of the all-seeing tv cameras and the crowd of onlookers. Deposited into the back seat of one of the cruisers, he was on his way.

4:00PM

Spirling World Supply

"Simon here."

"Mr. Spirling, Jonathan Cohan."

"It's four o'clock in the afternoon and you finally decided to call me. What the hell has been going on? I've been waiting all afternoon."

I attest to that thought Betty, as she listened from her office, eager to finally be able to go home.

"I would have thought that I deserved some sort of call."

"I'm sorry Mr. Spirling, but it has been rather hectic here."

"Never mind that, what's going on, how's my nephew?"

"Right now, your nephew is on his way to the Police Station. He's being detained for questioning."

"Have you talked to him, what does he say?"

"I'm sorry Mr. Spirling, but since Ken is my client, what he tells me is privileged information."

"What? I'm the one that's Goddamn well paying you."

"That may be, but what I can tell you is Ken is in real serious trouble. I strongly suggest we act quickly to bring a seasoned criminal lawyer on board. The sooner the better" he urged. "As you well know, our firm of Peters, Peters & Cohan are business lawyers and this is far outside any of our expertise."

The firm was indeed a business focused law group. Founded by old man Peters, joined by his son Arnold and then Jonathan. They specialized in International Trade, had a house full of notarized translators speaking all the major trading languages. Their work was office work, nine to five work, two-hour martini lunch work. Business was good and the fees they charged provided an incredibly good lifestyle for all three partners.

"My plan is to meet with my partners to see how we should move forward, or even if we should move forward at all. We may well decide to turn this matter over completely to an established criminal firm. I'll have to see what my partners want to do. But right now, I need to get to the police station to try to keep Ken from talking until we can get the right people involved."

"Tell your partners I want to see them. If I'm the one that's going to be footing the bill, I damn well better have a say in any decisions being made."

"I'll call you in the morning."

Simon sat back in his stuffed chair; head braced in his hands. His nephew, an executive in his company, had managed to get himself into a position where he might very well bankrupt the company. If Simon had his way, he'd cut Ken loose. Let him fend for himself, but he knew what his wife Molly would say 'Company be damned, family came first'. There's no way she would let Simon do that to her little Ken. Simon knew he was going to have to keep his hand in this to the end. Try to limit the damage before it gets too severe. Ken, what have you done to me?

“Betty.”

Betty couldn’t figure out why Simon had gone through all the trouble of having an intercom system installed when all he ever did was yell for her. “Yes, Mr. Spirling.”

“Get hold of Jeff Hughes and tell him I need to see him.”

“It’s Sunday, Jeff's at home. It’s his day off?”

Simon’s mood wasn’t one to be toyed with right now. “He has a day off if I say he has a day off. Phone him at home and tell him to get in here. Why can’t people just do what they’re told instead of giving excuses?”

“Sorry sir.” Once more and he’ll be looking for someone else to yell at because I’ll be so out of here thought Betty.

“I’m sorry to call you again on your day off Jeff, but you know how he is. He demanded I call and tell you he wants to see you right away.”

Wants to see me? I’m not ready to see him yet, thought Jeff. “Any idea what he wants?”

“He blew his top earlier this morning when I had to get the lawyers number from you, and now he’s wound up again after just getting off the phone with that lawyer Cohan. Whatever's going on must be really serious. Sounds to me like Ken’s done something that’s got the lawyers jumping.”

“Tell him I’ll be there as soon as I can.” I’ve got to find out what this is all about.

*****

"You wanted to see me?" Jeff chimed as he entered Simon's office.

"Come in, come in, close the door behind you and sit down." As Jeff went to sit down, Simon stood up. He wasn't aware he had started to pace, back and forth, back and forth. "I'm sorry I had to call you in on your day off, but I have something important I need for you to do. You'll have to keep what I'm about to tell you as a secret. Can you do that?"

"Sir, I'm sure you know by now that you can trust me."

"It pains me to have to say this, but Ken has gotten himself into a real severe problem."

Jeff tried to keep his face from showing the confusion he was experiencing. What trouble was Ken in? I haven't even had time to send the pictures. There's no way the ole man could know anything yet. Jeff had been waiting for just the right moment to anonymously send the old man and his wife Molly, the pictures he had taken of Ken last night. Laying on his bed, drunk as a skunk with two naked women crawling all over him. When Molly saw those pictures, she wouldn't be so protective of her dear sweet boy. Then the old man would be ripe for Jeff to make his move.

"He's somehow managed to get himself involved in murder; God help us. He found a dead girl in his bathroom this morning and all he can say is that he doesn't remember anything. Can you believe that? He doesn't remember anything."

The bolt of lightning that shot through Jeff almost made him pass out right at Simon's feet. Dead girl, dead girl, what's he talking about? He only had taken pictures, harmless pictures, a little bit of fun that's all.

He knew nothing about a dead girl. Was the old man finally going senile? This is crazy.

"I don't understand, what do you mean there was a dead girl in his bathroom?"

"Exactly what I said"

"Last night? Are you sure?"

"Jeff pull yourself together! Anyone would think you had a hand in this."

A hand in this, my god. I orchestrated the whole night. How in the world could there have been a dead girl? Step by step Jeff's head ran through the evening, and at every step he had so carefully planned there was no dead girl.

"I need you quietly to have a look at our financials. This business with Ken is going to put a heavy drain on our companies' resources and it has me worried. So far, I've been able to withstand the damage Ken has caused, but this might just be too much. I don't want to scare any of our employees, but I need to know. How much of a hit can our bottom line take before they are all unemployed? Work all night if you have to. I need this by the morning. This might just be the end of everything."

And the end of me thought Jeff. This was never supposed to happen. He worked so hard to put everything in place to get Ken booted out of the company so he could be the top dog. Then when the time came for Simon to retire, the company would be his. Damn that Ken, he's screwed up everything again.

Roxworth Towers, Apartment 10B

In the hallway, outside of the now declared crime scene. "Alright detectives let's see if we can get this back on the proper track," Dr. Amile said as she reached into her bag and pulled out her crime scene protection gear. Bundles containing a gauze hair net, white paper coveralls, gloves and a pair of blue paper booties. "Go ahead. Get suited up." Karen and Russ took a set each from the bag and started to get dressed. Karen slipped her gauze hair net over her short 'bob' styled haircut. She had learned early in her career, from her street patrol duties, after a drunk grabbed hold of her hair and nearly ripped it right out of her scalp, definitely short hair and no dangly jewelry.

At the door to the bathroom, Dr. Amile stopped. "Christ, how long has this poor creature been laying here? The blood on the floor has all congealed, and I can see from here the lividity present in the buttocks, back of the legs and shoulders." The girl's backside showed a deepening purple hue from her life-giving blood, no longer circulating through her body, now pooling in her lower extremities.

Karen snapped back, "We received the call around 1:30 and since that time, we have been waiting for you!"

Stepping in, Amile lifted the girl's right arm. Stiff as a board. "Rigor mortis has fully set in. This girl's been lying here for more than a good twelve to eighteen hours, far more than the time waiting for me." Looking at the pool of blood, "See here, these footprints on top of the congealed blood, someone's been in here after the girl was killed. Detective, reach into the side pocket of my bag there and hand me one of the toe tags." On the bright yellow tag with dangling string Amile wrote 'Jane Doe #6, November 10, Roxworth Towers. Then signed it. "Sign the back of the tag as a witness," handing the tag over to Karen.

Detective Russ jotted the new name into his notebook. After Karen tied the tag to the left big toe of the body, the dead woman was now officially christened Jane Doe #6.

Three white suited shapes carrying an assortment of equipment appeared at the door. Two men and one woman. “Afternoon everyone,” the white suited man at the front offered. “If you two detectives wouldn’t mind stepping out and giving us some room, we can get to work.” The forensics team knew what needed to be done and wasted no time.

Dr. Amile chimed, “Afternoon John” as she stepped back out of the way but stayed in the bathroom. “Get some close ups of those footprints” directed to the white suited woman who had begun snapping pictures. Pictures were taken from every angle, overall shots and close ups. There were shots of the edge of the splattered white toilet that Jane's head had smashed against. A close up of the yellow Jane Doe #6 tag clearly linked this series of photos to their unfortunate owner. Jane’s hands and feet were bagged. Scrapings of the congealed blood were taken from various spots of the mess. Measurements of the overall size of the bathroom were taken. Distances of the objects in the room to the girl were taken and recorded.

“Mind if we flip her over?”

“No go ahead” Dr Amile responded, “I’ve seen all I need to for the moment.”

Over at the side Dr Amile was quietly speaking into her handheld recorder. She recorded first the date, location, people in attendance, then her observations. “Young female, toe tagged as Jane Doe #6, naked, in her late twenties, lying on her back.

Lividity has set in throughout her back area. Rigor mortis fully engaged. From the state of the body and surrounding area, estimated time of death would be somewhere between one to three on the morning of Sunday November 10th." Then more pictures of the back side were taken. No modesty, no discretion offered, pictures were taken for the entire world to see. Dusting for prints from the door, the toilet, the facets of the sink and the shower were taken. Swabs of the lining of the toilet, sink, shower taken and deposited into their labeled glass tubes.

"Okay, I think we got everything, you can take her now, we'll start on the rest of the apartment."

Dr. Amile put the call in for the pickup truck. "They'll be here in ten minutes."

In the apartment the process began all over again. Dirty clothes taken from the clothes hamper at the end of the bed were bagged. The bed was stripped. The sheets and pillowcases were bagged.

"Doc, have you seen these brown footprints on the carpet?"

"Yes, I noticed them, get good shots of the prints and also where they start and end."

From the kitchen came the cry, "Detectives, you might want to see this." Karen and Russ hurried over to the voice. "There in the waste bin." Looking in, Karen could see the pair of shoes with traces of dried blood on their soles, looking back at her. She instantly knew she might as well throw the shoes out the window for all the good they'd do now. She'd been stupid enough to let the suspect and his lawyer in the kitchen alone, making the finding of the shoes worthless in court.

“Before you move them, get pictures of them there in the trash, also pictures of this whole kitchen.

Pictures were taken, in the trash, out of the trash, tops and soles of the shoes.

“Have you come across any of the girl’s clothes?”

“No, we’ve looked everywhere, and we haven’t found any.”

“Search again, look in the garbage chute and in the building basement trash, they have to be here somewhere.” Search as they might, every cupboard, closet, drawer and possible hiding place was searched and searched again. No clothes were to be found.

“Okay, detectives, I think we’re done here.” as the forensics team began gathering up their equipment and bags of evidence they had collected. “Tomorrow morning we’ll begin figuring out what we have. Unless something else comes in, pretty much everyone is available to focus on this stuff. Should take three to four days. I’m sure Dr Cornell will keep you informed.”

Detective Russ Cravers had spent most of his time wandering around the apartment, looking at this and that. Every once in a while, he’d find something that stroked his interest and he’d jot it down in his notebook. He really didn’t know what he was looking for or what he was supposed to be doing. Sure, The lieutenant had told him to take the lead, and he tried for the first little while, but he had never experienced a full-blown, blood-soaked body. His only deaths to date had been the simple drug stabbings and gang related shootings. Easy stuff, just point to a suspect and you pretty much had the guilty party. This was far more than that. This was a true mystery to him. Maybe, back at the office when he had time to study all the photos, read all the statements, digest the evidence he might be able to narrow in on someone. Besides, it was obvious that the sergeant had stepped forward and assumed control. She was issuing orders, and people were responding to her. She was calm and gave off the appearance of confidence that she knew what had to be done, and people were doing it. There really wasn't much for Russ to do.

*****

The plain black van with the simple white letters 'Jackson County Medical Examiner' on its side panel pulled up to the front of the building. Two casually dressed men got out, opened the back and pulled out a gurney. They wheeled it through the front entrance way and disappeared into the building.

"Look sharp guys," Rick Hanna called up to the two camera men perched on top of the tv van. "They'll be bringing out the body soon. I want a long shot as they come out from the door and lift it down the steps. Then zoom in as they put it into the van. Once they close up the van, fade over to me and I'll add some voice tracks."

Upstairs the gurney wheels rolled into the apartment, through the thick carpet leaving railway tracks behind. Jane Doe #6 left without a whimper. Off to the morgue for her next big adventure.

"You all done Doc?" Karen asked.

"Yes, I'll do the autopsy tomorrow around one. I assume one of you will be there?" Amile asked.

"Yes, of course, someone will be there. We'll see what Lieutenant Melnyk wants to do. We'll let you know."

“Russ, turn the lights all off and I’ll affix the seal on the door” Karen directed.

And just like that, the apartment was just as it was. Except now, there was a bloody bathroom waiting to be cleaned and its special guest had moved on.

Chapter 6

Last Week, Wednesday
Morning
365 Maple Row, Eastgate, the suburbs

Matt pulled his ringing phone from his hip pocket. "Eastgate Family Construction, Matt speaking."

"Mr. Matt Langdon?"

"Yes, how can I help you?"

"Mr. Langdon, it's not how you can help me, but rather how I can be of help to you."

"Excuse me, who are you exactly?"

"My name is Jeff Hughes, you don't know me, but I'm sure you know the firm I work for. I am the Senior Accountant of 'Spirling World Supplies'. Does that name ring a bell?"

Matt knew the firm alright, that name rang a lot of bells rather loudly. A bunch of backstabbing, money grubbing, crooks and thieves.

"Mr. Langdon, I'm well aware of the predicament you and your company are in and I think I can be of great help to you."

Hairs on the back of Matt's neck had begun to rise. It was because of his dealings with Spirling World Supplies and that crook of a business manager, Harris, that he was in this predicament. He had fallen into this dark hole under the spell of Harris's sweet talk. Seduced with promises of being able to get enough money to keep his family business afloat and in return, all he had to do was just do as he was told. It was so very simple. Assurances of not doing anything illegal, just using the system instead of having the system using him. Assurances that it was being done all the time. Savvy business people who knew what they were doing, knew the tricks of the trade, were constantly maneuvering the system. A little massage here, a little sleight of hand there, trust me, it's what makes rich people richer, Harris, had told him. And he had fallen for it.

"What do you mean you can help me? I'm on the verge of possibly losing everything because of your company. My business, my home, and maybe even my wife. Why would you help me?"

"Let's just say it would be to our mutual advantage. You scratch my back and I'll scratch yours. I'm in a position where we can both benefit. Are you interested? I'm throwing you a life line, if you're smart, you'll grab hold."

Matt heard this all before. The same sounding line that Harris had fed him. He knew nothing good would come from this, but he was going down for the third time and running out of air. Nothing to lose, up tight against the wall. Damn it.

"I don't want to talk over the phone. Meet with me, you won't regret it."

"I might be interested. All right. Where?

"Make it Greg's Grill around two."

Matt Langdon was average and had been right from the moment of birth. All through school he never really excelled in anything. He studied hard, tried hard, but he always came out the same, always average. In all the sports he had played growing up, baseball, football, he was always just one of the team, never one of the stars. There were no girls flocking to him trying to catch his eye. He wasn't the one they were after. His good looks didn't help him either. He just came across as the run of the mill guy standing over there. His mother and father loved him and gave him a solid middle-class upbringing. At night, his mother used to read the story of the ugly duckling and its transformation into the beautiful swan as she tucked him into bed. Matt wanted his transformation, but it never came. He didn't know the why or the what of the problem he had.

Maybe the way he walked or talked or thought kept him in the middle zone. He gave up trying long ago and just accepted it. He was average and there was nothing he could do about it; he was always going to be average. Matt didn't know that his real problem lay with nature. A fate right from his moment of birth had made him fall victim to natures' 'Law of Duplicity.' The law of nature that decreed a copy of a copy of a copy no longer carried the sharp clear lines of the original. It no longer showed the bright bold colors of the original. No longer stood out proud, on its own. Matt, the only son of an only son, was born into a world of blurred lines, faded colors, of being lost in the crowd. That was his fate.

His grandfather started the family business as a Master Craftsman long before Matt was born. The business thrived, sharp clear lines, bold colors, proud.

As time passed, so did the company pass to Matts' father. A craftsman, different from the grandfather, the company moved along, hiccupped, burped, but still prospered. Time continued till Matt the average arrived to take his rightful place in succession. Eastgate Family Construction, no longer the proud, sharp lined, bold colored, company of his grandfather had evolved into a world of budget renovations, of corner cutting, of using the cheapest materials Matt could find to try to stay afloat.

2:00PM,

Greg's Grill

A lot had changed at the restaurant where Matt had first met Karen so many years ago. The tiled black and white checkered floor had long since worn through and been replaced by some sort of fake plastic wood grained planking that dented whenever a cup or plate dropped onto its surface. The booth where he sat when Karen served him was now gone, and in its place sets of high bar stools wrapped around small wooden tables providing barely enough room for coffee cups shared between friends. Instead of the record playing jukebox placed up against the far wall, soft mellow music filled the air. Piped into the background, just loud enough to be heard without being too loud for cozy lovers whispering secrets to each other. The restaurant had changed and so had Matt. Ken Harris had found him, seduced him, exploited him, and when he was all used up, threw him away. Now Matt waited in vain hope for the lifeline Jeff Hughes said he was throwing his way. Matt didn't know how, but he needed that lifeline badly. Without it he risked losing it all.

When Jeff arrived, he was upbeat, humming to himself, ready to put the first step of his plan in place. He had thought it all through, dozens of times over the last couple of days. No more thinking or wishing about it, confident it was time to start putting it into action.

“Trust me when I tell you I know all about the predicament you have gotten yourself into. I’ve been watching it all happen, as it played out, waiting for just this moment. And you're not the only one that Ken Harris has used for his own gain. There are many just like you, but you, my friend, with my help and guidance, have the unique ability to strike back and free yourself.”

“What do you mean, you’ve been watching it all happen? If you knew that Harris was piece by piece destroying me, my company and my life, why didn’t you do something about it? Why did you just stand by and let it all happen?”

“It’s far too complicated to get into now.” Jeff was the accountant, Ken was the nephew, he had to bide his time, gather up all the information he could, plant many seeds of disappointment with the boss, Mr. Spirling, before deciding the time was ripe to make his move. “What you need to be grateful for, is that I’m here now. Remember you’re not so lily white either. You must have known Ken was putting in fake, grossly inflated invoices for the work you were doing. And when you were signing for the delivery of what supposedly should have been run of the mill materials, clearly you could see that it was in fact top of the line custom marble shipped special, direct from Italy. So don’t play holier than thou with me. You were happy until Ken was caught and he saved himself by throwing you under the bus.”

Matt couldn't deny what Jeff said had a ring of truth in it. At the time his company was struggling from no work, no money coming in, having to live on what his wife Karen brought home was demoralizing. He felt finally his chance to be the man of his family had arrived. He made good money doing the renovations to the Harris apartment. It was more money than he had been able to put into his bank account for a long, long time. Enough money to buy Karen the new SUV that she wanted. And when he gave it to her as a surprise gift, her happiness justified all the under the table dealings. That was until the bottom fell out with the arrival of the special delivery letter from the lawyers Peters, Peters and Cohan. On official letter head, Fraud, Racketeering. All monies to be fully repaid or we will proceed with the laying of formal charges. Matt couldn't tell Karen she had to give back her gift because he was a crook, especially since she took her job as a Police Sergeant seriously. He knew she wouldn't react well.

"You still know the key code for the loading doors at Kens place, don't you?"

"Yes, 3758. Why?"

"Excellent," for the last and most important part of the master plan, Jeff needed that number. It wasn't necessary for Matt to know the full extent of the plan, only to do what he was told. Then everything would fit together like a glove. Jeff started humming again. This was going to be good. Ken Harris was going to get his, and when he did, he's not going to like it one bit.

"Ken's birthday is coming up this Saturday, and you and I are going to give him a birthday present that he's never going to forget. This is what I want you to do..."

Chapter 7

Sunday, November 10th
5:30PM
Police Services,
Third Floor.

Ken Harris sat at the table by himself, in Interview Room #2, on a hard molded green plastic chair. His backside was sore. He couldn't get comfortable no matter how much he wiggled and squirmed. Probably done on purpose, he thought to himself. Wouldn't do to have the guests getting too comfortable, would it? And he still thought of himself as a guest. This was all just a terrible misunderstanding. He had done nothing wrong. If he explained everything calmly, didn't lose his head, step by step, they would see that girl, that blood covered girl had nothing to do with him. He didn't know who she was or why she was naked on his bathroom floor. He'd never even seen her before and she certainly, wasn't the kind of woman that he'd be seen with. Surely, they would be able to tell that he was sophisticated and had a refined taste in women. Not in the kind of woman that goes around getting killed on your bathroom floor. That was for certain. He really wished he could remember.

He was sure he was being watched, but he couldn't tell by who. In each of the two opposite corners of the room, cameras were fastened to the wall. Their small red blinking lights were flashing out to him 'We have our eye on you.' They had their nerve keeping him waiting like this. Why, if someone didn't come into this room in the next couple of minutes, he was getting up and leaving. He was tired and he was going home. If anyone wanted to talk with him, they could make an appointment at his office, and he'd see if he could fit them in. That would serve them right.

"Mr. Harris, at last I finally found you." lawyer Cohan said as he entered the room. The red blinking camera eyes went dark. "I've been walking all over this maze looking for you. How are you doing? Have they been treating you alright?"

"I'm tired and I want to go home."

"Mr. Harris," Cohan said as he sat down beside his client, trying to speak in his most comforting voice. "Ken, you must brace yourself. We are in some very serious trouble here. We might not be going home just yet."

"What do you mean WE?" Ken screamed. "You're going to leave here, go home to your wife, have a warm cooked meal, and I'm stuck here. All I've had to eat all day has been a cold turkey sandwich and a small salad topped off by two cookies in a plastic bag that they finally gave me from the hospital cafeteria. There's no 'WE' in this."

"What do you mean, hospital cafeteria?" Lawyer Cohan wasn't expecting to hear those words, 'Hospital Cafeteria'.

"I was taken there and had to wait for over an hour to give some blood and a mouth swab that they wanted taken. Then I've been left waiting in here for God knows how long."

"Calm down Mr. Harris."

"Calm down, calm down. Easy for you to say. You're not the one sitting here with some stupid girl hanging over his head. I never asked for her to die in my bathroom."

Even though Cohan was a business lawyer, he recognized that the police were attempting to pull a fast one on him. "Before they took these samples from you at the hospital, did you give them permission or sign anything?"

"I signed some form a nurse put in front of me, I have no idea what it was."

5:30PM

Police Services, Second Floor.

"Give me a minute Sarg, I've gotta phone home and let the misses know not to hold supper. She gets mad when the kids aren't fed on time."

"Yeah, go ahead," Karen shrugged. "I'll get started sorting out all these interview statements left by Sergeant Killens. It'd be so much simpler if they gave the uniforms some workstations so they could put these right into the computer instead of us having to do it." With the stack of gray interview forms in front of her, Karen wasn't too concerned about phoning Matt. Since there were just the two of them, they usually only ate a sit-down meal together on their days off. Matt was quite capable of fending for himself.

"Hi dear, it's me." Russ phoned from his cubicle. "Just wanted to tell you not to wait supper for me. Go ahead and feed the kids. This looks like it could be a long one."

"I've already fed the kids. You know dinner is at five. I only made spaghetti tonight, I'm afraid."

"Katie's favorite. Hey, did you get a chance to watch the evening news? I'm on it. I got interviewed by Rick Hanna this evening." Russ enjoying his 15 minutes of fame.

"Do you think with these three monsters running around, picking up after them all day and making dinner that I have any time to be sitting eating chocolates in front of the tv?"

"I'm sorry, but this is my first big murder case and I've been given the lead," Russ said. "Don't worry about me, I'll just pick up something here. We're going to be awhile more. Gotta go, the lieutenant's coming. Luv ya."

You're damn right you had better pick something up after the day I've had, thought Mary as she hung up the kitchen phone. And you better not wake me or the kids up tonight either.

"You're back. In five minutes let's get together in the room and you can fill me in where we are."

"Whoa, Lieutenant, before we get started, I want to speak with you in your office" Karen called out.

"Okay, come on."

Russ had a feeling he knew the lieutenant was going to get an earful about his performance today. He could tell the sergeant wasn't impressed.

"Close the door."

Karen started in right away, "What the hell were you thinking telling him to take the lead?" cocking her head in the direction of Russ. "If you have a problem with me being late this morning, then man up and tell me to my face instead of this crap. I'm the senior officer, I'm the most experienced officer. I think I deserve the respect, or if not the respect, at least the common courtesy my rank entitles me to." Melnyk sat and said nothing knowing it far better to let his sergeant unload and get this all out, off her chest. "Today he was nothing but a screw up. I took a beating from the M.E. because, by following his lead we contaminated the crime scene. God help us if that lawyer of his gets word of that. I had to step in and take control to get the uniforms moving. Then to top it all off, the moron was giving tv interviews instead of keeping his mouth shut."

"Are you done Sergeant?"

"You know it's not right!"

"First let's get the record straight. You're not being punished because of being a little late this morning. And," Melnyk paused, "if I did have a problem with you, trust me, I'm more than man enough to tell you to your face. What I can tell you directly to your face is that I'm disappointed in you."

"Disappointed in me?" the phrase caused Karen to step back.

"You are the senior ranking officer, and as such, I would have expected you to act as the ranking officer. You think I told Russ to take the lead to belittle you? Give your head a shake. Open your eyes sergeant. Why do you think Detective Cravers has been paired up with you as your partner? Did you think that was by accident? Do you think straws were drawn and you got the short end of the stick? Russell was paired with you to learn from you. Yes, to learn from you. Who has more experience in the department than you? Who better to learn from than you? He's green, wet behind the ears. You, better than anybody, should know how short staffed we are. He needs to be on a steep learning curve so that he can start carrying his weight. Right now, of course he's of no use to anyone. Sergeant, it looks to me that you first need to put your ego in your back pocket and realize the difference in someone being in the lead and someone being in charge. Let me be perfectly clear, you are in charge. If the crime scene was contaminated, why did you let that happen? Teach him the right procedures. If the uniforms needed a kick to get moving, teach him. As a sergeant you don't have the luxury of time to be doing a detective's job. Use your rank, your experience and your brain to teach, to control and most important of all to be thinking two steps ahead for what needs to be done next. Then point the detective in that direction." Silence. Obviously, Sergeant Langdon had a lot to think about. "Okay, let's get out to the room and both teach the detective how to move forward."

The room wasn't in fact a room at all. It was a movable space. Consisting of a series of portable wall partitions that could be easily moved to allow the space to be shrunk or expanded depending on the number of people gathering. At the front of the space there was a small table with a laptop, an overhead projector and a large viewing screen. A white board along with a large bulletin board were fastened onto two of the partitions stationed at the front. For now, the room was compact, filled with the afternoon shift Lieutenant Truken, Lieutenant Melnyk, Sergeant Langdon and a nervous Detective Cravers.

"Okay Detective, get up there and tell us where we are at so far," Melnyk sat down beside Karen. Russ looked quickly at the lieutenant then at the sergeant, not sure if he was the one to be speaking. His sergeant gave the slightest of nods, assuring him. Lieutenant Melnyk showed no indication that he had noticed the nod, kept a straight face but smiled inside. Maybe everyone was beginning to learn.

Russ, with his notebook in hand began his report. Constantly referring to his notes, he tried to keep all the events in chronological order from the arrival at the scene through to the exit. At key points, Melnyk would stop him and ask questions to better flush out the information. "Detective, sketch up on the board the layout of the apartment." Russ took a marker and sketched the apartment from his memory. "And, when you arrived at the apartment, tell me who exactly was inside."

Russ checked his notes, "Outside at the apartment door was Officer Davis. Inside there was Sergeant Killens, lead of the uniforms on site."

Melnyk interrupted, "And where exactly was this Ken Harris"

"He was sitting on the couch here," as he marked an X on the board, "beside Sergeant Killens."

Melnyk thought for a moment, "Okay, now where was the body?"

Again, Russ marked an X in the bathroom on the board.

"And how did you verify that from the moment the body was first discovered by Mr. Harris until the time you and the sergeant arrived that no one had entered the bathroom?"

"We put the question to Sergeant Killens, and he reported that at no time did he, Officer Davis or Mr. Harris enter the bathroom." Russ read from his notes.

Sergeant Langdon piped in, "There were what appeared to be a dried set of footprints, embedded in the carpet, exiting from the bathroom leading to the living room. Forensics took a number of detailed photos showing footprints on top of the congealed blood on the bathroom floor. Clearly indicating someone had entered the bathroom sometime after the death. A pair of blood-stained shoes were also found by the forensics team in the kitchen garbage can."

"Can we link these shoes to Mr. Harris for certain? When you first saw Mr. Harris on the couch, did you notice if he was wearing anything on his feet, or was he barefooted?" Melnyk asked. Russ flipped through his notepad,

"I don't have anything written down, but I'm sure they belonged to Mr. Harris." Karen winced. A fair size hole that would have any half decent lawyer rip you apart on the stand. Karen knew that phrases like 'I assumed' or 'they had to be' were like waving a red flag in front of a bull. Only what was written in your notebook at the time would stand.

"What's the M.E. saying about the time of death?"

Russ read "Dr. Amile gave a preliminary estimate of between one to three in the morning. She said she would verify that time when she does the autopsy tomorrow afternoon, starting at one."

"Didn't 911 get the call around 1:30 in the afternoon? Why the big-time difference? What did Harris say?" Melnyk asked.

“Due to some discussion at the time with the M.E. we haven’t yet fully questioned Mr. Harris.” Russ replied. It was a little more than discussion, more like a whipping thought Karen.

“Do we have a cause of death?”

“Preliminarily, it looks like from striking the back of her head on the edge of the toilet bowl.”

“Have we identified the victim? Do we have a name?”

“Not yet, with the amount of blood on the scene, forensics was unable to get a good picture that we would be able to use.” answered Russ.

Karen added, “For now, the M.E. has her tagged as Jane Doe #6.”

“Okay, maybe we’ll get a hit when the M.E. takes fingerprints and a dental impression tomorrow. Plus,” the Lieutenant continued, “at the morning departmental briefing I’ll see if I can get a couple of detectives from the pool. We can use them to start to go through the missing persons database. In the meantime, Detective, leave word for the downstairs Day Watch Commander to be on the lookout over the next couple of days for anyone coming in reporting someone missing. Where is Mr. Harris now?”

“He’s sitting in interview room #2 upstairs cooling his heels. I believe his lawyer,” Russ checked his notes, “a Jonathan Cohan, is with him.”

“I haven’t heard of him.”

“He’s the family business lawyer.”

Karen added, "I took advantage of the lawyer and had Mr. Harris taken on a slight detour to St. Catharine's on his way to the station for a blood sample and DNA swab. Don't worry, I had them make sure Harris signed a volunteer release form."

"Does the lawyer know?"

"No" smirked Karen, quite proud of herself.

"Detective, what's your plans for Mr. Harris?"

Russ, looking a little puzzled, "I believe that when the Sergeant and I are done here we will go upstairs and begin questioning him."

Lieutenant Melnyk thought for a minute. "We can hold him for seventy-two hours before we have to officially charge him. I have a better idea. You and the Sergeant go home and get a good night's sleep. It's going to be a busy day tomorrow. Let's have him spend the night in one of our cells, it just might make him a little more receptive to questions." Turning to Karen "Sergeant, you go upstairs and break the news to him and get him settled. Short and sweet. When they book him in, get a hold of his phone."

"We never saw a phone." Russ stated as he thumbed through his notes.

"A guy like that has got to have a phone. You're telling me that neither of you two nor forensics found a phone?"

"No sir."

"Sergeant, first thing in the morning get Carol working on securing a search warrant for that phone." Looking at the apartment sketch on the white board, "and I'd suggest you start with that couch that Harris was sitting on."

"There're also the dead girl's clothes. They're missing." Karen added to the bad news.

"How can there be no phone and how can there be no clothes?"

"We searched the apartment twice and came up with nothing." Karen replied defensively.

"I don't care if you have to rip the place apart, they must be there. Find them!"

"Detective, you and I will attend the autopsy," Melnyk directed to Russ. Then added "And eat a lite breakfast." Russ had only ever attended one autopsy, a street stabbing and at that he was violently ill. He became the butt of jokes from just about everybody as word spread around the station.

It was not really an experience he was eager to repeat. "Lieutenant, wouldn't it be better if the Sergeant attended with you, and I stayed here and worked on pulling the reports together?"

Melnyk looked directly into his detective's eyes, "You and me, Detective."

6:00PM

365 Maple Row, Eastgate, the suburbs

Matt Langdon enjoyed the earthy taste in his mouth from the cold beer trickling down the back of his throat. A couple of empty brown bottle soldiers held their positions, standing at attention, having been left in various corners of the house. Being Sunday, he had a slouch day, doing a lot of nothing. Just wandering around the house, puttering a little here and there. Stretched out on his couch in front of the tv, he was starting to feel the beginning pangs of hunger as he waited for his wife Karen to come home. If it looked like she was going to be late, he felt he might as well order a pizza. Beer and pizza were the perfect man food for a lazy Sunday.

"We take you now to our Richard Hanna, reporting from Roxworth Towers. What have you got Rick?" "Good evening, John. I'm standing in front of the Roxworth Tower Apartments where it appears a homicide has been committed." The tv screen shifted to the tape of a man, with hands in front of his face, being escorted to the back seat of a police cruiser. Then the white plastic body bag exited the front doorway and was lifted into the back of a black van, filled the screen. Matt bolted upright. He recognized Ken Harris, and a body. There was no body!

"I have here with me, Detective Russell Cravers, from the Police. Detective Cravers, could you tell our viewers what has occurred here at the Roxworth Towers?"

Russ cleared his throat and attempted to talk in his most professional voice, "At approximately 1:30 this afternoon 911 received a call indicating a deceased female had been discovered in one of the apartments. Upon investigation it has been determined that the deceased female's death has been deemed as suspicious by the Jackson County Medical Examiner's Office. Our investigation is in the preliminary stages at the moment. At a later date, Police Public Affairs will be issuing a formal statement. That's all I can say at this time."

Matt Langdon, leaned in as close to the tv as he could, listened intently to everything that was being said. He listened for the clues in the words that weren't being said.

"Detective Cravers, can you tell us the name of the deceased?"

Russ knew that Jane Doe #6 probably wasn't the right name to give. "Not at this time. As I said, a formal statement will be issued." Sergeant Langdon stayed in the background trying to show no emotion. Trying to hide the anger boiling inside of her. Why couldn't the idiot just say 'We have no comment. A formal statement will be issued at the appropriate time.' Karen knew front line detectives never talked to the press. More often than not it always came back to bite you in the ass.

Falling back into the couch Matt grimaced, this wasn't good. No, not good at all.

*****

Russ's bright headlights were giving off the only light in the neighborhood, shining forward as his car approached the house. He's going to have to add the repair of the porch lights on his to-do list when he next has some free time. Right now, he wasn't sure when that would be. None of his handyman skills or tools would be of any use to him, Jane Doe #6 was going to be his full-time focus for the foreseeable future.

Feeling his way up the porch, hunting to finally find his key, he slipped inside as quiet as he could. *Creak, creak, squeak,* he climbed the wooden staircase. His socken feet failed to quiet the stairs. Each one called out from his weight as he crept upwards. He heard the soft breathing of his kids. Russ wanted to be in bed, to sleep, if he could. He wasn't looking forward to tomorrow and hoped just coffee and dry toast would work.

*****

Karen's house was different. Her headlight's bounced off the side windows competing with the light still on inside. Matt must still be up. She was used to having to nudge him over to his side of the bed, while he never missed a beat of his nightly snoring song. Her hope was that her tiredness would drown out the chorus and bring her to deep peaceful sleep.

Propped up in the corner of the couch, Matt didn't hear Karen when she entered the den. His mind was busy somewhere else clouded in deep thought. "How come you're still up? Matt, snap out of it. Are you okay?"

"Yeah, yeah, I was just thinking." Turmoil turned over and over again in his brain. "I saw you on the news tonight."

"That dumbass Russ." Karen snapped.

Maybe the best thing was for him to stay silent and let her talk instead of trying to subtly probe. He had to be careful. She was a good detective, and she was stubborn.

"Well, if you're okay, I'm exhausted and going to bed. Turn the lights out when you come up." Turning she was gone. He'll have to wait and see. Let it play out.

Chapter 8

Saturday November 9th
8:30AM
Roxworth Towers,

The apartment intercom chimed, '*Ring*'....

"Yes"

"It's 8:30 baby, I'm here downstairs in the lobby. Let me up."

"No, just wait there, I'll be right down."

In the lobby, Vivian, dressed to the nines, waited. Her pastel-colored dress, printed with bold flowers, that she had picked out of her wardrobe especially for this morning complemented by her yellow stub heels, and dangling gold bracelet gave a bright summery look. Only problem being, she was one season too late. It was November, when everyone in fashion knew to be wearing warm browns and tans.

She recognized Ken as an extremely good catch who had taken a lot of time and maneuvering to latch on to. He was sophisticated, good looking, had good taste and lots of money. Vivian struggled most of her life, on her own. In Ken she felt she had found her mister right, and her life could finally change for the better.

Vivian had dropped out of school. It was easier than being whispered about everywhere around the school she went. Not part of the 'in crowd', always dressed in hand me downs and thrift store finds. Being awkwardly out of step with the trends and fashions of her peers made her stand out. She couldn't take being 'THAT' girl, every time a whispered finger pointed her way.

At home it was grueling. The stress that dad created, being constantly out of work, constantly drunk. Of mom having to act as peacemaker with the irate neighbors, basically made life hell for her. Every night, right after spending all day on her feet, working at the local grocery store as a cashier, putting up with the odd little "accidental" butt taps from the customers, Vivian had to deal with her father. Off to night school. Her mother insisted she go. Insisted Vivian's only way out to a future was through her brain, not her smile or her body. Of course, now, Vivian knew that mom was right, but back then she only knew exhaustion.

Long hours cramped over books. She slowly completed, one by one, all her course requirements to earn her graduation diploma from high school. She was denied the young girl's joy of picking out a fresh new prom dress. Denied the thrill of the all-night graduation dance in the cutesie decorated high school gymnasium. Denied being able to attend the ceremony to receive her diploma in front of her family and friends. She got her diploma, unceremoniously, delivered in a plain brown paper envelope by the postman. In spite of this, she was proud of herself. She had pulled it off. It was never easy, but she had pulled it off.

Then the real work began. Dad had died. Good riddance. While still working evenings and weekends at the grocery store, Vivian enrolled herself in the local community college. Jackson County Community College, 'The Place where Futures Begin for Those That Want It'. She bought herself a small, little used, red Ford Escort. She had to. Mom didn't drive. Dad would never let her. He was the man of the house, only he was allowed to drive. Vivian loved the freedom that being able to drive her own car gave her. Granted it was only back and forth to her college classes and to the supermarket for the weekly shopping. But it was hers', not counting the regular monthly payments, and the cost of gas. With her shiny new degree, she lucked into the job of 'Business Assistant' at one of the smaller Engineering Firms in the city.

Ken, stepped from the elevator and soaked in a long look at Vivian. She definitely was good eye candy. Tall and slim, he liked that. Looked good on his arm, he liked that. Eagerly shared her favors with him, he certainly liked that. But she was clingy, possessive, and he didn't like that.

"Happy Birthday" Vivian called, as she ran across the lobby and planted a deep throated probing kiss on him. Ken wasn't comfortable with overly displays of affection in public. It wasn't the sophisticated image he worked on projecting. And there behind the desk was Vincent watching them. Behind closed doors, Ken wanted all he could get. His appetite was ferocious, but in public, restraint was the word.

"I booked us a private booth over at Elmo's so we can start your birthday off right." With a twinkle, "then we'll see where we go from there. We're gonna have such a good time." Her language slipped every once in a while, betraying her.

"Call us a cab." Ken directed towards Vincent. Holding the taxi door open, Vivian shimmied in, showing a nice piece of leg that Vincent was happy to see. Ken climbed in beside Vivian, closed the door, clasped her hand and the taxi was off, leaving Vincent alone on the sidewalk, his hand discreetly open at his side. No tip. Cheap, thought Vincent. Vincent had made it his business to know people, and this pair, a floozy and a cheapskate, both wannabe's, didn't fool him, not by a long shot.

Elmo's Restaurant

Elmo's was a small upscale restaurant located on the east side of the city. Trendy and expensive. The type of place the right kind of people frequented. Those that could afford it and those who wanted to be seen to be able to afford it. It opened early in the morning for patrons who wanted to start their day off on a good foot, and for those still on their feet ending their night before. This was costing Vivian, but she knew her investment would be worth it. She enjoyed sharing the little bit she had with Ken, trying to make him happy.

"Good morning sir" the cute red headed waitress said directly to Ken, ignoring the look that Vivian was giving her.

"It's your birthday baby, I'll order for us" Vivian said, not looking at Ken at all, but continued her glare at the waitress. Not waiting for Ken to respond, "We'll start off with two sparkling Mimosas, followed by Eggs Benedict covered with lots of that wonderful cream sauce and topped with a sprig of thyme for flavor." She had seen it in a magazine and wanted to order it special.

"Very well, and Happy Birthday sir."

Well, she can kiss any hope of a tip goodbye thought Vivian. She wasn't paying some tart to be flirting with her man.

The Mimosas arrived in tall, fluted glasses. Sun bright orange juice combined with crisp sparkling champagne. Being chilled to just the right temperature caused delicate crystals of ice to form on the sides of the shining glasses. "To us, baby. Happy Birthday." Vivian toasted with her glass raised.

"Thank you."

When they arrived, the 'Eggs Benedict' were cooked to perfection. A poached egg with soft yolk, a thin slice of honey baked ham sitting on a warm toasted English muffin covered with the pale-yellow creamed Hollandaise sauce which made the dish so special. On the top was the small sprig of thyme but as an added bonus, a teaspoon size dollop of salted black caviar lay perched on the gold rim of the plate. Ken ate slowly, savoring the luxurious taste of the food in front of him, always 'Eat with class, never with vigor'.

Looking around him, Ken could see the restaurant this morning was host to just a small group of the right kind of people, dressed in the elegant casual attire only truly refined people of quality could pull off. Even Vivian seemed to fit in this morning, and the breakfast was wonderful.

"Could I interest the gentleman with a coffee? Our barista is a wizard with an extensive assortment of specialty coffees" the smiling waitress asked.

This time Ken jumped in front of Vivian. "Yes, I'd like a skim milk latte please"

"And for the lady?" the waitress asked Ken, still refusing to address Vivian.

“She’ll have the same.” No choice, Ken had chosen. Sipping his latte, Ken was proud of himself. Here he was, enjoying what had turned out to be a fabulous meal, among the right kind of people, with a good-looking piece of woman, albeit a little overdressed. Nevertheless, life was good. For Ken, life was really good.

Buzz...Buzz...Buzz

“Excuse me” as he put the phone to his ear. “Ken here.”

“Hi, it’s Jeff. I wanted to know if we were on for tonight. You said you’d call me back and let me know.”

“I don’t know, I—”

Jeff cut him off mid-sentence. “I phoned around to some people I hang out with and apparently tonight is going to be hot. A lot of really special people are going to be there, people you really want to meet. I scored a pair of VIP passes to get us into the Club’s private party room. It’s going to be a blast.”

Boy, Jeff was piling it on pretty thick. “All right, maybe for just a little while.”

“I’ll fly by your place and pick you up around nine. You won’t regret it.”

Ken was already regretting it. He didn’t like owing Jeff, being indebted to him. That’s not how their relationship was supposed to work. Jeff was supposed to owe him, that’s how you kept the upper hand.

Vivian asked, “Who was that?” A little put off that her moment was intruded upon.

“Just one of the people I work with. It appears he’s gone and set up an evening at a club with some people from work to celebrate my birthday.”

“Baby, I thought you and I could celebrate your birthday, just the two of us.”

“Listen” lying through his teeth “it’s a work thing and you don’t fool around with work. I have to go. We can go out another time. I’ll make it up to you. I promise.” Another lie.

Vivian wasn’t thrilled to have Ken going out to a club without her. She had too much invested to risk him picking up one of those celeb party girls she read so much about in her magazines. She wasn’t going to lose out now, no way. Right there she decided. If he was going to go out tonight, she would make sure he remembered her with an afternoon he’d never forget. “Well, baby, I guess since we only have the afternoon, let’s go back to your place for dessert.” Whatever it takes, she thought. He’s going to get the ride of his life. He was hers and she was going to keep her ticket.

Jeff smirked to himself as he hung up from talking, or should he say handling Ken. His plan was coming together. That pompous ass was about to learn who really had the upper hand. Jeff knew that ‘Uncle Simon’ was showing all the signs of being finally pushed to the breaking point with his nephew. All Jeff’s quiet trips to the president's office with details of the irregularities happening were paying off. ‘Good work, Jeff. Let's just keep this between ourselves for now.’ ‘Yes, sir. I’m just bringing this to you because I thought you would want to know. This company means a lot to me, has always treated and rewarded me well.’ Honey would roll off his tongue. ‘I appreciate your loyalty Jeff, if only that nephew of mine would shape up. I’ll remember this.’ ‘Thank you, sir, I try my best.’

Ken might have thought he was the master of the silver tongue, but he had nothing compared to the slime that Jeff could spill out when it was to his advantage.

Jeff remembered the dealing from last summer that Ken thought Jeff had tucked away that had conveniently been allowed to surface in the quarterly audit of the company books. It was all too much for Uncle Simon to bear. Unfortunately, Ken was able to dodge the bullet and have the blame fall right onto some dumb gullible contractor. Custom hand cut marble, was shipped in specially from Italy, and just happened to end up being misplaced somewhere in the company warehouse. Weeks of fake invoices were issued to pay for the supposed critically required improvements to the factory shipping floor. In reality, the invoices were for installing the marble floor that had taken place in apartment 10B. To Simon, it amounted to downright fraud, and the lawyers Peters, Peters & Cohan would deal with it. Ken quickly passed a few prime gifts to the younger Peters and surprisingly the internal investigation somehow proved that Ken was an innocent victim of an overly aggressive contractor. Eastgate Family Construction was set up to take the fall. But not this time, Jeff was bringing out the hammer, out with the old, in with the new. Good things were coming Jeff's way.

"Is everything set?" Jeff phoned Bernie, the manager of Club Envy. "I'm picking him up at 9, so we should be there around 9:15."

"Yes, everything's in place like you wanted, but this now makes us even." Bernie owed Jeff big time. The club had been on the verge of losing its liquor license which would have closed it down. The padding of receipts from serving overpriced, watered-down drinks had been picked up by the city's licensing inspectors. Through a friend, Bernie was able to get Jeff to work his magic on the club's books, and Hocus Pocus, problem solved.

"The bouncer at the door will take you directly to the party room. The girls are lined up along with the special party treats. Remember, I had nothing to do with this if it blows up in your face."

"It won't." Jeff was almost giddy with himself.

Chapter 9

Saturday November 9th
Afternoon
Roxworth Towers, Apartment 10B

Ken, skin flushed pink, covered in sweat, withdrew and rolled off of Vivian. Lying back, staring at the ceiling, drained, he tried to catch his breath, "Whew, what's gotten into you. That was fabulous." It was an afternoon filled with surprises. Bringing Vivian back to his apartment for 'dessert' as she had so sweetly put it, usually meant that he would treat her to a quick 'wham bam thank you mam' session and send her on her way. This time fulfilling the required payment for his birthday breakfast. Boy, was he mistaken. From the minute they crossed the threshold Vivian was a woman possessed.

Having had many women be the recipient of his favor, Ken had always been in charge, always in control. He had a proven game plan scripted out, seldom varied, that regularly seemed to please. Ken followed his plan, from the opening advances, rising to the building expectations stage, following through to completion. Then, at the finale, the 'You were great' exit. It was a game plan he was quite proud of, but nothing like the Gold Medal winning performance Vivian had just unleashed on him.

He had never experienced the clothes ripping, neck biting, nail scratching hunger that this wild cat unleashed upon him. She didn't just make love with him, or have sex with him, she totally devoured him. He held on through twisting, turning acrobatics that would have made a gymnast envious. She kept driving him higher and higher till he thought he'd explode, then control down, then right back up again. His muscles ached, eyes bulged, blood pounded, demanding release. But Vivian wasn't done yet, not twenty minutes, not an hour, but more. When sweet release was finally granted, Ken swore he could see nothing but stars in front of his eyes.

Vivian was happy with the job she had done. She had given her all. There was no way Ken would be seduced now by some club groupie. With this workout she had him, hook line and sinker. But still, in the far back recess of her brain, the slim sliver of doubt lingered. 'You can never be too careful'.

Exhaustion took hold of Ken drifting him off into a deep satisfying sleep, oblivious to the world. He didn't hear the humming from the shower as cool water, rained down over her body, cleansed the afternoon away. In the shower, Vivian was dreaming. Imagining how it was going to be when she moved into 10B, the perfect love nest for her and Ken. Why, she was more confident than ever, especially after this afternoon's workout, that it was only a short time away. 10B was large enough for both of them, perched up high over the city. She'd bring her womanly charms and touches that would make Ken want to come home every night to her. Mail would arrive, addressed to Mrs. Harris. She had been practicing signing her name for some time now, Mrs. Vivian Harris. The doorman would hold open the big glass door for her, 'Good afternoon Mrs. Harris, we're so glad you're here. What a change you've made in Mr. Harris. He seems to finally be complete.'

Out of the shower, dressed ready to leave, Vivian stopped, bent down and kissed her sleeping prince on his brow. Closing the door behind her, smiling, knowing that it was just a matter of time till Ken would be carrying her across its threshold. But, in the elevator, it wouldn't leave her alone. That annoying sliver of doubt at the back of her consciousness kept calling to be let out. 'You can never be too careful.'

The bedroom was growing dark when Ken began to rouse himself. How long had he been asleep? As he looked around, it was quiet, and he was alone. Old habits were kicking in. He was glad to be spared the awkward back and forth jostling that he normally would have to go through to walk his playmate of the moment out the door. At only 36, there was a line that he wasn't ready to cross, not yet. This was his apartment, and he had no plans on sharing it with anyone. No matter how good they were in bed.

9:15PM
Club Envy

As the taxi pulled up to the front of the club, Ken couldn't help but stare out at the number of people. They were mostly young working females standing in a long line, hoping to get in. Saturday night was their one night to breakout and live, wanting to be more than a 'yes sir, no sir' workaday office robot trying to survive. Short sparkly dresses reflected the glow from the overhead streetlights. Legs turned red as they shivered trying to hold in their heat, to no avail. Why didn't they wear coats, Ken thought, betraying the difference in age between him and these party hopefuls? The young knew it was all about the look. They needed the freedom to be themselves, to express themselves, even if it meant that they all looked the same. It didn't matter, you needed to have the look to get inside. Without the look, you were turned away. To join in the party, and they all wanted to be in the party, you had to be one of them. They had to have short slinky dresses, long flowing manes of hair, extended eyelashes, pouty pink lips. The plain, the average people were left outside. These weren't the sophisticated corporate people Ken was accustomed to.

"See, I told you it was going to be great," Jeff said as he hopped out of the cab. "Come on, we've got passes, we don't need to be standing in the line." Already as he approached the door, the steady '*Boom, Boom, Boom*' pounding bass escaping from inside was causing his eardrums to vibrate. Jeff showed his pass to one of the two bouncers stationed at the door busily checking for ID. The sign bolted to the wall clearly warned, 'If under 21, DON'T even try'. Bouncers big enough that you could see they took no crap. The bouncers turned away the pretenders trying to talk their way inside by using fake IDs that some John, Peter or Joe assured them would work. "Follow me" Jeff yelled over the noise. As Ken walked inside. it was like hitting a wall. The ear-splitting music was now striking his chest like a hammer. The flashing lights, bouncing off of the walls and from all the metallic shining dresses, were strobing on-off, on-off, caused Ken to have to put his hand up to protect his eyes. As they snaked their way across the dance floor, through the mass of gyrating bodies, Ken was assaulted by the smells. The sour smell of sweat was combined with the smell of overused heavy perfume. And there was another smell lingering in the air. It was a sweet sickly smell that Ken didn't recognize but was making him want to gag.

The party room was awash with red velvet. It was everywhere, on the walls, on the ceiling, on the couches. Well-worn beaten couches were wearing the stains from countless special people who had occupied the room before them. A private bar was on the side, manned by a skinny waif of a girl, looking for all the world like she wasn't old enough to be witness to the spectacle of this room. Ken instantly felt cheap and dirty.

"Jeff, I appreciate this, but it's not really my kind of place."

"Hold on, just give it a little time." Waving over to the waif he called out, "How about getting my friend here a drink." Rustling and giggling from the door alerted Jeff, "Come on ladies, don't be shy. I'm Jeff, and this good-looking guy is our birthday boy. Say hello to the ladies, Ken."

These weren't ladies as Ken knew ladies. These young women showed more skin than the strippers from the so called 'Gentlemen's Clubs' where Ken was used to treating suppliers, getting them ready to sign contracts. Already he was starting to feel the effects of the alcohol he was drinking. Every time he took a drink from his glass the bar waif topped it back up. It was never emptying, and the music kept pounding and the lights kept flashing. "Hi ladies" Just a little while more and he could get out of here.

But these women weren't shy. On the outside, they were young. On the inside they were hardened veterans. They had earned their privileged access to the party room through many visits, partying with a host of Bernie's special friends. They knew what was expected of them to be included in Bernie's stable and eagerly complied. If they were good, and treated Bernie's friends well, Bernie would keep them supplied with cheap trinkets, endless alcohol, and party drugs. They thought that it was the perfect life, a life in a perpetual state of dazed utopia. They were totally hidden from reality.

"Go on girls, get over there and wish Ken a Happy Birthday. We gotta get this party started." The girls were climbing all over Ken. Each one gave him a long slobbering birthday kiss. One of them, using her tongue, pushed a capsule into Ken's mouth, then down deep in his throat. It was so quick and so smooth; Ken didn't even know it happened.

*****

Out on the dance floor she was looking. He had to be here somewhere. The sliver of doubt that used to live in the back of Vivian's brain had escaped. Now it occupied all of her mind and it called for her to take drastic action. She had to know, was Ken serious or was she being played again. The doubt, strong now, told her there was only one way to be sure, find him and ask him directly. After wasting so much in past losing relationships and office romances gone wrong, this one felt so right, it just had to be right.

So far today it'd been costly for Vivian, from paying for the ridiculously expensive breakfast, to the fifty bucks she had to slip to the bouncer to get through the door. Vivian wasn't one who had the required club 'look'. She was good looking, dressed very attractively in a mature way, but by being mature, she advertised that she wasn't one of them, and that she was older than the vast majority of the door crowd. The flashing lights, the blaring music, the bodies gyrating, all tried to distract her from her mission.

Determined, focused, she kept looking. She didn't know what she would do if she couldn't find him. She couldn't think like that. This moment was too important to her. She'd find him, one way or another, tonight, she had to know.

Jeff stood watching, pleased with himself. Things were going perfectly to plan. The ladies were warmed to their task, aided by the white lines of powder, laid out across the bar. The alcohol that Ken was consuming, along with the alien capsule were well on the way to defeating Kens' resistance. Jeff could tell Ken was starting to like it. He could see as Ken's face changed, morphing from unattached dislike to developing that stupid grin. The grin that displayed the tell-tale sign of surrender.

Vivian saw red. It wasn't the red of the ceiling or the red of the velvet walls. She didn't see any of that. Her red came from the blood of her body boiling up filling her eyes. Her skin was red from anger. An anger turned to rage. A rage so strong her muscles clamped; her jaw locked. She couldn't yell out. All she could see was her man being taken advantage of. Locked inside her hardened shell she couldn't move. Helpless, she could only watch as her future turned away from her. She could hear a voice, a loud screaming voice, a wild animal roaring out in pain, but she didn't know it was coming from her. Jeff looked, what the hell was she doing? She's going to ruin everything. The girls who were twisted all around Ken looked. Some burn out was on a weird trip. Ken looked with eyes unable to focus on anything. The bar waif looked and she pressed the silent alarm button.

"Get her out of here" Jeff demanded to the gorilla summoned by the alarm. "She's not supposed to be here. This is a private party."

Smashing her shell, Vivian ran across to Ken, grabbed the girl draped across Ken's lap, and threw her to the floor.

"Ken, Ken, you can't do this" Seeing Ken deep in his mindless stupor brought memories of her drunken father racing back through her brain. "What have they done to you? This isn't like you" With Ken so vulnerable, she wrapped her arms around him, smothered his face with kisses, in her way, trying to protect him.

"Vivian?" from Ken's stupor, "Vivian, what are you doing? These are my friends. We're having a party, it's my birthday."

"Baby, baby, it's me. I'm here. You're not well, I need to take you home."

This was more than Ken could take, his words slurred, his brain was shutting down. "Leave me alone. I don't need you; I don't need anyone. Get away from me."

"Baby, you don't mean it. You're not yourself."

But Ken's brain had left the party.

"Get her out of here I said, Get her out!" Jeff screamed.

Lifted, half by her arm, half by her hair, Vivian left the party. Pulled out by a gorilla with a fifty-dollar bill in his pocket.

There's nothing worse for a woman than to be tossed aside by the man she loves. The man she had built her dreams upon. She was willing to give everything she had to Ken, hold nothing back, her heart, body and soul. Vivian's heartbreak hurt deep in her chest, wracked now by sobs of despair. She had to do something; she couldn't let it end like this, not again. She couldn't sit back and let Ken throw both their futures away. Like Jeff, she started to develop a plan. First, she'd write a deeply personal note to Ken, telling him no matter how much he hurt her, she still loved him.

The note she dropped off with the doorman at Roxworth Apartments on her way back home, alone in the taxi, turned out to be vastly different from the one she originally had planned. Her heart might have been broken but it stayed warm to the dream of her and Ken. Her brain was another matter altogether. She had been hurt so many times before. Maybe the chill of the night air helped it along as it started to turn cold. She didn't deserve to be hurt; she had done nothing wrong.

It should be Ken, coming to her, trying to win her back.

Chapter 10

Saturday November 9th
Midnight
Roxworth Towers, Parking Lot

Pulling up to the side door, Matt was glad he had decided to take Karen's black SUV. It wasn't nearly as conspicuous as his boldly lettered "Eastgate Family Construction' truck would have been. It had taken a seemly long time for his wife to drift off into her customary deep sleep. Matt, in bed beside her, listened for her breathing to change. He waited to hear the brief sound of snoring progress to the long slow in and out that signaled it was safe to ease out of bed and slink out of the house. With any degree of luck, Karen wouldn't even notice he wasn't there. But he would have to be quick. Do what he had to do and get back.

He wasn't happy about having to break into Ken Harris's apartment, but he had no choice. His stupidity in believing the twisted snake Ken, had got him into this mess, facing Fraud and Theft. Now he had to hope that this stupidity with the wiry weasel Jeff, would get him out of it. Jeff had assured him the apartment would be empty and it'd be an easy matter to go in and search Kens' desk. Get the papers and get out. If he did this one simple thing for Jeff, all his problems would disappear. Matt thought, as long as his problems vanished before Karen found out, the risk was worth it. But if Break and Enter joined with Fraud and Theft, there would be no saving him. Everything would be lost, and Karen would be gone.

On the tenth floor, he had to pray the watery eyes behind the heavy door of 10A would be closed in their bed. He had seen those eyes every day during the summer when he was doing the renovation to 10B. They were always there, watching. He couldn't worry about that now, those eyes were old, probably senile. Who would possibly believe those eyes had seen anything?

Turning the apartment lights on wasn't a problem. Being up ten floors from street level no one would notice light streaming from the windows. Besides, he needed the light to search and find the original cost invoices that he had submitted before Ken had doctored them up. The invoices proved he wasn't a crook. At first sight, a twinge of jealousy struck him. Ken's office, straight from a fortune 500 magazine was the kind of office he always dreamed he would have. He could see himself, sitting tall, behind the dark mahogany wood, directing his construction empire. In reality, he had never reached beyond a cell phone, a clipboard, and the front seat of his truck.

Searching for the papers wasn't as easy as Jeff assured him it would be. Not wanting to leave any trace of being there, he took time, careful not to disturb anything. Precious time, he didn't have to waste. He still had to creep back into bed before Karen realized her bed had become cold without him. Searching everywhere, top to bottom, left him feeling empty. All this risk for nothing!

Sunday, November 10th 1:00AM
Roxworth Towers Parking Lot

"Park over at the side of the building." Jeff directed the taxi driver.

"Get him out of here before he pukes in my cab. If he does, you're going to pay to get it cleaned up." The driver had grown used to hauling Saturday night drunks' home from parties when they could barely walk or talk. It was nothing new to him. The girls were another matter. Half dressed in party clothes they giggled and laughed the whole trip. He didn't know what was going on and he didn't want to know. He just wanted this drunk out of his cab so he could get back to hunting down another one. Pulling up at the side of the building so that its' lights shone on the door, showing the keypad, Jeff climbed out. He grabbed Ken by one arm, and tugged, as he tried to break him free from the cramped quarters of the back seat. "Push him, harder" he grunted to the girls. Ken was slowly dragged out and deposited face down on the parking lot pavement. "Wait until I get the door open." Entering 3758 into the keypad, he heard the solid '*Click*' of the door lock releasing. Darkness covered them as the taxi, wasting no time, turned and sped away. "Okay, give me a hand carrying him.'"

"God, he weighs a ton" as the bigger of the two girls slung Ken's arm around her shoulder. Her companion, completely useless in the struggle, continued to giggle. All she knew, in her dazed brain, she had left one party at the club to go to an even better one.

"Be quiet, we don't want to wake the whole building." Matt had told him that the camera was broken by the side door, so he just had to be careful not to draw any unwanted attention from the sleeping tenants.

At the tenth floor, the elevator doors opened fully and the door for apartment 10A opened only a silent crack. A crack barely large enough to see Ken Harris dragged down the hall by a parade of partiers. Jeff never saw Eleanor, but she certainly had seen him.

Inside the apartment, Ken was hauled across the prized carpet. Jeff knew, by the time this night was over, everything that Ken had cherished, including this apartment would be his.

Matt stopped, frozen in place. He heard the sound of the apartment door as it opened. He had taken too long doing his search, and now, people had returned, and he was trapped in the office.

"Throw him on the bed." Jeff directed. Thud, Ken dropped. Stretched out across his bed he had arrived home.

Matt could hear the giggling and laughter that came from the bedroom as music started blasting.

"Whe, whe, where am I?" the mound on the bed slurred.

"You're home, old buddy"

"That you Jeff. Who are the girls?"

"Some special friends of yours, they're here for your birthday present. Just lay back and relax. I'll take care of everything." With that, Ken returned to oblivion, beyond all worldly cares.

"Okay girls, climb up there and make nice with our friend. I need a couple of really good pics; then we can get out of here."

Taking the chance, Matt crept to the bedroom door. The nervous tension he had been feeling began to ease off. There, before him, Jeff stood at the end of the bed and was madly snapping pictures as two naked women posed around a drunken Ken who lay helpless in the center. Clearly, Matt felt he was witness to some sort of blackmail set up.

It wasn't much of a party for the girls, as they crawled around and posed beside the stiff in his bed. It was all rather boring.

Reaching into his pocket Matt retrieved his phone. He needed to take one silent picture from the shadows. With one picture, Lady Luck had delivered both Ken and Jeff to him. His problems were now over.

All Matt had to do now, was wait till the coast was clear, race home and climb back into his bed beside his sleeping wife.

"Okay, that's enough. Let's get out of here" Jeff said to the girls.

Jeff paused at the door in the hallway. There was only one girl. "Where's your friend?" said Jeff.

"She's not my friend, I don't know who she is. She's probably still on the bed, passed out, curled up against the stiff."

Well, thought Jeff, that'll be an added surprise bonus for when Ken wakes up in the morning. There was going to be a bonus alright, and it was going to be a real surprise to everyone.

With Jeff gone, Matt crept out, leaving the door ajar as he found it, confidant no one, even the watery eyes of 10A, had seen him. But it wasn't that easy. The switches on the building side door recorded the time he came and went. The camera from the front lobby recorded his blurred figure in the background, and the eyes of 10A weren't senile. Eleanor Upton had seen him, recognized him and remembered who he was.

Chapter 11

Monday, November 11th
8:00AM
Police Services 2nd Floor

Sergeant Langdon called out, "Carol, can you rush through the paperwork for a search warrant on Roxworth Towers, Apartment 10B? We're looking for a phone and a missing set of women's clothing. I've written everything down here."

"Already done, sergeant. Lieutenant Melnyk asked me earlier right after the shift change meeting. Also, I've gone ahead and had the wall partitions moved to make room beside you and Detective Cravers for the two pool detectives he picked up. I'm just waiting for IT to get a couple of computers hooked up for them."

"How long do you think before the warrant will be approved?"

"Shouldn't be long. It was being hand carried across the street to Judge Klainet. It's pretty straight forward, I'd say 20 to 30 minutes at the most."

"Thanks."

Carol was the ever-efficient clerical assistance assigned to homicide. She might have started out in the beginning only providing clerical services to the group, but over time her role quickly grew. She took pride knowing she was now thought of as the go to person if you needed anything done. If Carol couldn't do it, she knew who could. Either way, if you gave it to Carol, it got done.

"Morning Sergeant," the lieutenant greeted, standing by Karen's and Russ's cubicle. "What have you two got lined up for today?"

"Right now, I'm just waiting on the warrant you had Carol rush through this morning. Once I have it, I can begin the search of the apartment again for the phone and clothes. She tells me I should have it anytime now."

"Good, okay Detective lets you and I begin interviewing Mr. Harris. Call downstairs and have him brought up to one of the interview rooms. I think I saw his lawyer wandering around in the building. Make sure he's there, I don't want to start without him present." Then he added the reminder, "Don't forget, you and I have an appointment over with the M.E. this afternoon. We don't want to be late." You don't have to remind me, Russ thought. It's an appointment I'd be happy to miss. Already his stomach was on edge.

"Langdon here", Karen picked up her ringing phone.

"Sergeant, we have a couple down here at the front desk who say they have been told to see you."

A wide-eyed Mr. and Mrs. Morrison sat on a couple of dark green molded plastic chairs that were bolted to the floor and waited. Immediately in front of them, the team of senior uniformed officers, acting as receptionists, scurried about their business, not paying any attention to them. These were the uniforms that had paid their dues on the beat, handling snow, rain, cold, drunks, druggies and pimps. As a reward, they had earned the inside job, leading to their soon to be retirement exit.

Karen inquired. "What are their names? Did they tell you why they were told to see me?"

"They're a Mr. and Mrs. Morrison. They claim to be the managers of Roxworth Towers and that a police officer yesterday told them to come to the station first thing this morning to see you."

"Great. Can you have someone escort them up to the third floor? I'll meet them at the elevator."

'Morrison, Mr. and Mrs. Morrison.'

Silvi Morrison, startled by the calling of their name, jumped in her seat. They were being summoned by the scratchy speaker fastened on the wall above their heads. 'Proceed through inspection and an officer will escort you to Homicide.' Now it was her husband's turn as he flinched at the word homicide. After Silvi and her husband passed through the bulky metal detector and had her purse and bag screened, the Morrisons were led inside the secure locked doors. It didn't matter that the lights were on, their eyes were big enough they could have seen their way in the dark.

"Good morning, Mr. and Mrs. Morrison, isn't it?" Karen greeted the pair, hand extended as they walked off the elevator. The gray-haired man was short, with his stomach hiding his belt. Karen could feel the roughness of his hand, it reminded her of Matt's hands, and she knew instantly, this man was a worker.

“Yes, I’m Bert and this is my wife Silvi,” the man answered. “Silvia” the wife corrected her husband. Purple tinted hair, fresh from the hairdresser, and the black handbag clutched tightly in her hand, secured this woman as Bert’s wife.

“Well thank you both for taking the time out of your busy morning to come down here to the station. I’m Sergeant Karen Langdon.”

“There was a very nice policeman at our door first thing this morning. He offered to drive us here.” She added, “Bert doesn't like driving downtown unless he has to.”

“Perhaps we could make ourselves comfortable in here, where we can talk without being interrupted” Karen said, using her arm to gently steer Silvi towards Interview Room #3.

“Can I get you a coffee or anything?”

“No thank you, we ate this morning before we came. We try to limit ourselves to one coffee a day. Too much caffeine isn’t good for Bert’s nerves.”

It looked like Silvi would be the talker Karen thought to herself. She could see Bert had noticed the cameras in the corners blinking. “Don’t mind them.” She wanted to keep the pair relaxed so that they talked freely. “They’re just there so that I don’t have to keep writing everything down.” Karen looked at Silivi, “So much easier” she said with an added chuckle “I don’t have the memory I used to have.”

“Amen to that” agreed Bert Morrison.

“As you have probably heard, yesterday there was unfortunately a young woman found dead in apartment 10B”

"Yeah, Ken Harris's Apartment." Bert stated matter of fact.

"Sergeant, this has never happened before. We've managed Roxworth for nearly twenty years and have never ever had anything like this happen. You can check." Silvi said, getting on the defense. She had heard tales of innocent people going to the police and never being seen again.

"No, no, I'm not accusing you of anything. In fact, I was there in your building yesterday and I've got to say how impressed I was. It looked clean and in really good shape."

"Thank you. Bert and I try. It's not always easy, but we try."

"Damn right we do, it's a lot of hard work" Bert said, puffing his chest out.

"I'm sure it is." Appetizers done, now let's get on to the meat. "Mr. Morrison, can you tell me about any kind of security systems there are at the Towers? We just want to be sure we don't overlook anything."

"We have our two front doormen of course. One's there during the day and the other in the afternoon till midnight. At night the door is locked and the tenants use the number keypad to get in. The rest is pretty standard stuff, I guess. There's a camera in the front lobby monitoring who comes and goes. There's also a camera at the back side loading door that's usually used by the movers, but it's not working right now. I haven't had time to getting around to having it fixed. The loading door is opened by a numbered keypad, similar to the front door. Each apartment is given their own code, so we know who opens either door. And I almost forgot. Recently we had switches added to both the front doors and the loading door along with the elevators. They tell us if any door is left open and the time it was opened."

Good, Karen thought, "And are there any cameras inside the elevators or on any of the building floors?"

"No, only the ones I've told you."

Hmm. So, we have no way of knowing once someone gets into the elevator whether or not they get off on the 10th floor. That would have been too easy Karen thought.

"Can you tell me how long the loading area camera has been broken?"

Sheepishly Bert replied "For a couple of months." Then in his defense he added, "It happened when that Harris was having some contractor going in and out continually, doing renovations to his apartment. It was a damn nuisance."

Interesting, "And can I ask, where is all this security information kept?"

"When the system was bought a couple of years ago, the building owners had a small computer panel installed in our apartment. Apartment 1A" Silvi added.

"Do you think I could get a copy of the information from this past weekend? It would be extremely helpful."

Bert felt a little uneasy with the request, no one had ever asked for this before, and he sure as hell didn't know how to get any information out of the box on his wall. What would the building owners say? "I don't know, I might have to ask the building owners."

"Oh Bert, of course she can have it if it's going to help her and that poor girl."

Stopping at Carol's workstation on the way back to her desk, Karen asked Carol, "Can you send an IT tech along with a uniform over to Roxworth, Apartment 1A, and get a dump of the building security system along with the camera footage from this past weekend? Tell them to make sure they get a release form signed by the wife, Silvi Morrison, not her husband."

"No problem, I think they're all done hooking up those two computers I had them doing."

8:00AM
Offices of Peters, Peters & Cohan

Annoyed, in his office, Alister Peters, the Old Man of the firm along with his son Arnold sat waiting for Jonathan to arrive. Alister Peters wasn't used to being kept waiting. It wasn't professional, and the firm he started so many years ago had the reputation of being very professional. Dressed in his standard dark blue pinstripe suit, starched white shirt, solid tie and shiny black leather shoes, he kept looking at his watch. The daily partner meeting was held every workday, starting at eight o'clock sharp, and Jonathan knew it.

"Mr. Peters." His desk intercom paged, "Sorry to interrupt you, Mr. Cohan has phoned and says he won't be able to attend your meeting this morning but asks if he could see you this evening on a particularly important matter for the firm."

"Dad, I've plans for this evening," Arnold really didn't have any plans for the evening at all, he just didn't want to spend any more time in the office than he had to. It was bad enough his father made him come to the office every morning early to attend these stupid meetings. Day after day there was a meeting, and at every meeting the same items were discussed. Contract this and contract that. Most of the time he had to fight to stay awake. And now, to have to stay late till Jonathan finally decided to grace them with his presence, stretched him too far.

"You and that wife of yours may think you have plans for the evening, but I think we owe it to Jonathan to be here to see what this very important matter might be. It had better be very important."

Well, this might be worth staying late if dad is going to get into it with Jonathan, thought Arnold. A chance to see the Golden Boy being knocked down a notch or two could be really entertaining.

Police Services
Upstairs in Interview Room # 2

The lieutenant started... "My name is Lieutenant Thomas Melnyk, and with me is Detective Russell Cravers from the Homicide Division." He glanced at the blinking cameras, "For the record, please state your name and your address."

Ken, looking a little bewildered glanced at his lawyer for approval, uneasy with the formal tone that the lieutenant was taking. "Kenneth Harris, Roxworth Towers, Apartment 10B."

"I'm Jonathon Cohan, from the legal firm of Peters, Peters & Cohan."

"Mr. Harris," the lieutenant continued the formal declarations necessary to begin the interview, "Do you acknowledge Mr. Cohan as your legal counsel?"

"Yes"

"Mr. Harris, I want to inform you that everything we say is being recorded. Do you understand?"

"Yes"

"Mr. Harris, since we view you as our prime person of interest in the recent death that has occurred in your apartment early Sunday morning, I'm going to ask Detective Cravers to read you your legal rights. I want to be clear; you are not being charged at this time, rather you are being detained as a significant person of interest." The lieutenant knew that he wasn't required to read Ken his rights for an interview, but he thought of this as a 'Slam Dunk' case, and wanted to make sure he plugged every possible hole that Cohan might be able to raise later. Russ pulled a plasticized card from his shirt pocket and mechanically proceeded to read the contents out loud.

"Mr. Harris, do you understand your rights as read by Detective Cravers?"

Again, Ken looked to his lawyer for approval, "Yes."

Cohan finally decided that he should speak up and say something. "I want to say, for the record, and with my client's approval, that we are fully cooperating with the police in their investigation and want nothing more than to have the true perpetrator of this crime brought to justice."

I plan to, thought Melnyk, and I'm looking right at him.

"Mr. Harris, I want to give you the opportunity to tell us your version of events leading up to the discovery, by you, of the female body in your bathroom. Please don't leave anything out. No matter how trivial it may seem to you."

"Okay Ken," Cohan turned in his chair and talked directly to Ken, trying to use his most comforting voice. "I know that this is difficult, but I want you to take your time. Don't be nervous and tell them everything exactly as you told me. Do you think you can do that, Ken?"

Sitting back in his chair, Melnyk waited, giving Ken time to get it all out. Then he planned to come back in and pick it apart, piece by piece. Russell took his lead from his lieutenant and sat back and waited. This case might wrap up sooner than expected thought Melnyk.

"Where do you want me to begin?" said Ken with trepidation.

"Ken, tell them right from the start, remember, exactly as you told me."

If only he could remember, that was the problem. The easy part would be telling them what he did remember, that was pretty straight forward. The hard part would be convincing them of the parts they were looking for that he didn't remember. It wasn't his fault; he simply couldn't remember. He had to make them understand, he didn't know the girl and he had no idea why she was dead in his bathroom. How could they possibly believe that he could kill her? It simply didn't make sense to him. Sure, he's done a lot of things that have skirted the line. He has wheeled and dealed, often stretching the truth to his advantage. That was business, a game he played, that wasn't really him. He knew he made a lot of enemies out there. That was fair. Trying to better himself, he just played the game better than they did. Anyone of them might have done this, just to get even with him.

The lieutenant waited. He had seen it many times before. The look they all got when they realized they were caught. The trap was snapping shut.

Taking a deep breath, Ken began to tell his story. He had been through it so many times already, in his head and with his lawyer, that he really didn't need to do a lot of thinking. He opened his mouth, and the story came pouring out. Step by step, he walked through the events of the weekend. He spoke of the birthday breakfast at Elmos', the call from Jeff. He smiled as he remembered the afternoon dessert in bed with Vivian. He had a vague recollection of the birthday party arranged by Jeff at Club Envy that was spoiled by the crazed attack by Vivian. Finally, there was the ride home in the back of a crowded taxi and of being dragged across his carpet and thrown onto his bed.

As Ken rambled on, Russ had his pencil busily making notes for himself. Elmos', Vivian? Jeff? Club Envy. He created a list of items that would need to be followed up on. Listening to the story, Russ tried to figure out if his 'Gut' had any opinion. He might have started to feel a little sorry for Ken, had it not been for the thought of the girl, covered in blood, lying on the bathroom floor.

Ken couldn't be stopped. His mouth kept moving, he was on a roll. He spoke of waking up alone, going to the bathroom and finding the girl on the floor. The first call he had made was to his uncle, then to 911. He told them of being taken to the hospital, and while he was at it, in pure exhaustion, he told them of being given a terrible turkey sandwich.

At this last point Cohan piped in, "Lieutenant, I believe my client needs a break. We have been at it for some time now." He looked at his watch, "Since it's approaching lunch, can I suggest we stop here?"

"All right, we'll continue later this afternoon, say around five, if that's good for you?" The Lieutenant and Detective had an important date approaching for which he didn't want to be late for, no matter how much his Detective wanted to miss it.

Afternoon
Roxworth Towers, Apartment 10B

"Sergeant, we've already been through this place yesterday, twice as a matter of fact," the technician retorted.

"Melnyk wants it done again, right from the beginning." Karen directed back to the forensics tech she brought with her. "We're looking for the phone, the lieutenant is convinced that it has to be here somewhere."

"Alright, but if we didn't find it before, don't be surprised if we don't find it now."

The search began again. This time more slowly than before, making sure every nook and cranny was being checked. Hands reached in, felt every corner, probed every opening. Drawers were pulled out; cabinets opened. Check, check, double check, and there was still no phone.

“This guy's sure got a lot of good-looking clothes, and they appear to be all upscale brand names. I haven't come across one knock off from China.” In the bedroom closet the row of suits, each one contained in its own individual zippered dust jacket, were checked. At the bottom of the closet a dozen shoes, black, brown, tan all polished clean from any sign of scuff markers, sat meticulously organized waiting to be used. “One of these shoes alone would likely chew up my whole pay for a week. God, I don’t know how these people do it.” Each shoe was lifted out and its insides checked.

“I know” Karen replied, “Keep looking.” She herself now turned her efforts towards the couch. The infamous couch that the lieutenant felt would more than likely give up the hidden treasure. First one by one, each pillow was removed, felt then tossed on the carpet. Next the cushions, one by one were tossed to their new home beside the pillows. Matt, her husband, thought of them as her ‘man hands’ couldn’t squeeze down the now exposed side crevices. “Can you come here for a moment? See if you can reach down here, I can’t get my hand in.”

“Sure, here let me try.” It was tight, but down the tech’s hand went. “I can feel stuff down here.”

“Can you bring it up?” Karen questioned. A quarter, three pennies then a dime surfaced.

“Thirty-eight cents, I’d expect to find at least a couple of bucks.”

“Try this other side.”

“Owh” as the tech snapped his hand out with the end of an earring stuck into his middle finger. “That hurt.”

"Oh, come on, you're a big boy." Karen chuckled. "Try again."

Hesitantly the hand slipped back down. "Wait, I think I can feel it. It's wedged in, hard to get a grasp on." Fingers maneuvering, the tech's hand slowly withdrew. "Is this what you've been looking for?" as he triumphantly waved the sleek phone in the sergeant's face.

"Good job, bag it so we can get out of here." Have to give Melnyk credit, he said it'd be in the couch Karen thought, but she wasn't going to tell him. She hadn't yet fully forgiven him for the 'Russ is the leader' incident.

Afternoon
St Catherine's Hospital, Top Floor

In her office Dr. Amile checked her watch, almost one o'clock. Time to prepare. She knew the tech assistants had completed all the preliminary tasks spelled out in exacting detail on their standardized check sheet. Now the 'client' waited, resting quietly in the middle of the sterile room, covered with the factory supplied white sheet. Under normal circumstances this sheet would have provided Jane some comfort and warmth from the cold stainless table beneath her. A comfort and warmth that was now well beyond reach. Looking up towards the glassed-in observation balcony Amile gave a slight nod of acknowledgement to Lieutenant Melnyk and Detective Cravers. From their perch, the Lieutenant and Detective would be held safe from the gore soon to be exposed before them. The Doc would begin her journey of discovery. She would peel away the skin, layer by layer, until Jane was opened in grisly detail before their eyes. They wouldn't have to feel the rubber skin, nor smell the puff of gas as it escaped from the wound that the Doc would make in Jane's flat stomach. They could stay detached, behind their glass wall. Their only job was to witness. It was Dr. Amile's job to inflict and Janes' job to receive.

As she pulled back Jane's cover, Anna stopped as the familiar wave swept over her. From earlier career performance reviews with her boss, words returned to her. 'Dr Amile, Anna,' in the voice of a caring father, 'you must learn to distance yourself from the body. The body isn't your client. It didn't come here to have a stomach or headache fixed. It's been brought here for you to use the professional skills you have, to bring meaning, justice to the death. I've been in this profession for many years, and there's one thing I've learned the hard way, you must protect yourself. If you keep thinking of people rather than objects, it will change you. You can't keep doing what we do day in day out, carrying the tragedies of these people on your shoulders. The weight will build up to a point where you won't be able to bear it anymore. It will take over and the change will be devastating.'

Anna couldn't help herself. Her wave brought feelings of anger and hopelessness to her. She wasn't a particularly religious person. Childhood lessons had long left her. If there was a deity, a supreme loving being watching over us, why did he allow Jane to be here? What purpose did it serve? Was her life stolen from her when God looked away, or was it that God just didn't think Jane had any value? For a brief moment, Anna lowered her head, closed her eyes and said a short prayer to herself... 'Lord, if you do exist, help me to help Jane. Help me to bring justice to this fragile spirit. I don't understand, I simply don't understand how you could let this happen. If you didn't do your job, then give me the strength to do mine. It's the least that Jane deserves.'

Tom from his tower saw what was happening. He recognized the tell tales signs of caring that Anna was experiencing. Quietly clenching his fists, he felt the pain return to him. He too carried the weight from years of needless killings, of lives lost. He remembered how he openly wept over the small body of a boy, lying in the street, shot by some coward. He felt the feelings of utter uselessness as he tried to give some degree of comfort to the grieving mother when there was no comfort to give. It's a memory he's never forgotten. But now he had to do his job. He had to witness. He too prayed for the strength he needed to bring the peace to Jane, that now only justice could provide.

Chapter 12

Monday, November 11th
Afternoon
Police Services, Holding Cells

By the time Ken was returned to his holding cell, the plain white box, with the label 'Lunch' stuck to the outside, was already there. It had been there long enough to be cold. Although the coffee in its styrofoam cup had managed somehow to stay slightly warm, the cheeseburger, french fries and brownie had in fact arrived cold. Ken had the feeling that someone, playing smart with the contract for supplying food to the cells, must have been making a fortune. Probably listed as an urban meal perfect for the man on the go, this lunch had no doubt been charged at two to three times what it was really worth. Ken recognized the potential for a scam when he saw it. Scams like this had made Ken a lot of money.

This wasn't the type of food that he was used to eating. He had paid, or rather Spirling World had paid, a lot to learn the proper foods to eat and the correct way to eat them. He learned these lessons from Susan, a stanchly vegetarian dietitian that he used regularly. Ken hadn't given up meat, at least not yet. No fat, no grease, modest portions, plenty of veggies, eat with class not with vigor, as Susan would say. Susan ran a 'Lifestyle' consulting business out of a modest office downtown, just off of Bagley Avenue. She had set up a discrete consulting practice for the upwardly mobile executive. Not cheap, but not to worry, he had Jeff writing it all off as 'Business Consulting'. It was here that Ken first met the rather attractive Vivian Mooney. Both enrolled in expensive classes trying to learn the formula of 'Looking Good' plus 'Feeling Good' projected 'Confidence' which equaled 'Success'. If he kept eating this kind of food, the looking good part of the equation would be going right out the window. How long could they keep him here? He wanted, he needed to go home. Home to martini lunches, caesar salads, home to just about anything as long as it was home.

He needed a shower. Now in the second day of wearing his tracksuit even he could smell himself over the rank stench left in the cells by those before him. It would be hard enough to eat this food in front of him as it was, the smell certainly didn't improve his appetite, but the rumbling noises coming from his stomach told him he had to eat.

'*Clang*' the metal cell door opened, "Harris, your lawyer's here."

When he entered the briefing room, he could see Cohan, had his briefcase open and papers were spread out across the table.

"What's all this?"

"These are notes that I worked on last night to send to my partners and your uncle to keep them abreast of what's going on. Don't worry about them, we need to talk and there isn't much time. I have a meeting this evening with my partners to decide what course of action needs to be taken in your best interest, but I want to be honest with you, you are in one hell of a spot."

Ken still couldn't come to grips with the fact that people didn't believe him. He was telling the truth. That's all he could do. To hear these words coming from his own lawyer didn't sound right.

"You do believe me, don't you, Jonathan?"

"Ken, it doesn't matter if I believe you or not. What matters is, if you are charged with murder, and the chances are high that you will be, will a jury believe you?"

"They can't possibly charge me with murder, I didn't do anything. Why won't you believe me? I didn't do anything."

"Raising your voice isn't going to change anything. Between us, we need to stay calm and focused. Everything depends on keeping our heads and not getting angry or frightened." Jonathan knew that the prisons were filled with prisoners who spent their days, locked in cells, and nights screaming their heads off that they were innocent.

"The police can hold you for seventy-two hours, then they either have to charge you or release you. Let's see, today is Monday, they took you yesterday, so that means they have until Wednesday to gather enough evidence to convince the county DA that you are guilty. Our first task is to make sure that doesn't happen. You mentioned Jeff and this woman Vivian. Tell me about them, I need to talk with the two of them as soon as possible, hopefully before the police do."

Ken gave a sigh of relief. As soon as the police talked with Jeff and Vivian, they would hear that everything he said was the truth. This nightmare would be over.

Jonathan couldn't say anything about Jeff Hughes until he talked with him, but Vivian was another matter. He was worried about her. In Ken's story he was in a drunken stupor. He vaguely remembered Vivian crashing his birthday party, fighting with his guests, and then being carried out by her hair. She had sent Ken all those texts in desperation. Vivian could be a problem. There was no telling what a woman in her state would do. Vivian might just be the one who locks the cell door on Ken. He had to talk with her fast before the police talked to her.

"Is there anything you need?" asked Jonathan.

"I need to go home."

"I told you, seventy-two hours."

"I could use a clean pair of clothes."

"I'll get my assistant to run out and get something for you. Now remember, stay focused and we'll get through this."

Being locked back in his cell Ken muttered under his breath, "He keeps saying we'll. There is no we. It's me, only me."

Evening
Offices of Peters, Peters & Cohan

"Sorry I had to cancel out of this morning's meeting," Jonathan said as he crossed the office heading to his customary leather chair beside Arnold, "but I put in a full day at the city jail." With those words, both Alister and Arnold sat up. Jonathan hoped the city jail might rate as being important enough to miss a morning meeting according to the Alister Peters yardstick. "I've got an impending situation that we need to discuss."

"Go ahead, you've got the floor" Alister said as he sat back, crossing his hands in front of him. Arnold squirmed, making himself comfortable.

"I received an urgent call at home yesterday," Jonathan began, "from Simon Spirling, you know, of Spirling World Supply."

"Yes, one of our biggest clients, continue."

"Well, his nephew, Ken Harris," at the sound of the name Arnold instantly perked up, "the Head of Business Development for his company, has managed to get himself involved in a horrific murder."

"Clarify yourself, what do you mean involved in a murder?"

"He woke up Sunday morning and found a blood-soaked body of a girl lying on his bathroom floor, and according to him, he claims he can't remember any of it."

Alister, thought for a moment, "And do you believe him?" Alister remembered back to the martini lunches with Simon. Two stalwarts of business, huddled together, where Simon would drag on about his disappointment in his nephew.

"Right now, that's not the point." Jonathan answered.

I know I sure as hell wouldn't believe him, Arnold was thinking, having recently been on the receiving end of one of Ken's gifts. He had managed to squeeze out a trip to the Amalfi coast of Italy on the pretext of following the trail of missing marble. So far, it had been one of the highlights of his boring career. He and his wife lay on the beach, went shopping and experienced the Italian way of life, all on the Spirling tab.

"Well, what is the point?" asked Alister.

"This man is in serious trouble, far outside any of our expertise. He's going to need real help from someone knowledgeable in criminal law. Let's face it, it's been a long time since any of us has seen the inside of a courtroom. Why already the police have been trying to pull the wool over my eyes. I overheard them being criticized by the M.E. for contaminating the crime scene. Then they—"

"Hold on, spare me the details." Alister knew that Jonathan had a point. He hadn't been inside a courtroom in years. The majority of contract law that the firm handled could just as easily be handled by the bank of secretaries working away on the other side of his office door.

"Simon Spirling is demanding a face to face with us in the morning."

Alister looked to his son, "And what do you think Arnold?" As if Arnold could ever give his father any advice to be taken seriously.

"Dad, this could be just the opportunity I, or rather we, have been looking for. We've had our heads buried for so long in stacks of paper, dotting every i, crossing every t that we have lost sight of our true profession."

"Be careful, those i's and t's have provided a very good life for you and that trophy wife of yours."

"I know dad, and I'm grateful, but this could be just the windfall we've been waiting for. This could carry us into the new expanded offices you wanted." He's right, Alister was thinking. If handled properly there could be a lot of money here. Money he could use.

"Here's what we'll do," Alister had made his decision. "Jonathan, you tell Simon to give us some time to think this through. Arnold, I want you to put together a brief lay out of what we would need to do to stay involved with this. You can use two of our secretaries to help you. Before I fully commit to this, I want to see a clear plan." Arnold's head was already swimming with ideas of Private Investigators, Medical Experts, Consultants who would be added to the payroll.

"What about our responsibility to provide the best legal defense available for Ken Harris? What about our ethics?" Jonathan was starting to get worried. The Bar Association was an immensely powerful watchdog of ethics, and he wasn't prepared to be disbarred at this late stage of his career.

"Hold on, I'm not saying we are or are not committing to this. All I'm just saying is that before we make any rash decisions the pros and cons need to be thoroughly thought out. You got that Arnold?"

"Yes dad, leave it to me."

"Jonathan, you handle the police station and stay with our client. Try to keep on top of the police so they don't pull anymore fast ones on you."

"And what about Spirling?"

"Leave him to me. When the time's right, I'll go over and sit with him. We've had a long relationship; it wouldn't take much to keep him trusting our firm."

Chapter 13

Tuesday, November 12th
Morning
Police Services

Gathered in the Room with their ranks now swelled by the two additional detectives Melnyk had added, the briefing began.

"Where are we with the identification of the victim?"

"Lieutenant," the one addition started, "we've searched the missing person's database for any female declared missing in the county in the last forty-eight hours and have come up empty. Then we expanded our search efforts to the state level, but still no luck. We're now waiting on the FBI to tell us if they get a hit from the fingerprints the M.E. took. A search of dental records provided no matches from the dental database.

"Stay on it. The M.E. will only hold Jane for five days then the disposal process will kick in."

Russ had never heard of a disposal process. He leaned over to Karen and asked in a faint voice, "What does he mean, disposal process?"

"After five days, if a body isn't identified or claimed by a relative, the M.E. has no choice but to send it for cremation, then the ashes are kept in storage for three years. If no one still claims the ashes, then they are scattered in the municipal cemetery."

"God, that seems rather cold doesn't it" Russ remarked.

"Sergeant, what have you learned?" Melnyk asked.

"I told you earlier about my meeting with the building super and his wife. We now have the data from the building security system," related Karen.

Melnyk addressed the two detectives, "While you're waiting for feedback from the FBI, you two see if you can make any sense from it. Have a real good look at the security footage from the lobby camera. If you need help, have Carol get you someone from IT. What else?"

"I've been going over the forms from the uniform building knock check, the majority are as you would expect, nothing. But there is one thing that might be of interest. On the top floor of the building, opposite the 10B crime scene, I would have expected more from 10A. The reports show that the husband, Frederick Upton took the interview, but there is no mention of his wife, Eleanor. Now from the little bit I saw of her the other day, I got the distinct impression that there wasn't much that happened on the tenth floor that she didn't know about. Even Harris called her an old busy body. I'm going to go over there this afternoon to see if I can talk with her alone, without her husband being there. It could prove to be very interesting," Karen smiled.

"Alright, the Detective and I have interviewed Harris twice and so far, we haven't been able to break him. He's sticking to his story. And his lawyer's getting a little smug, reminded me we only have till Wednesday and if we don't have anything beyond the circumstantial evidence we have now, we'll have to release his client. He's pretty sharp for just a business lawyer," said a surprised lieutenant.

"Detective, how about you go upstairs to the 'Hot House' and see if you can shake the bushes a bit and get them moving along. The clock's ticking."

*****

Hearing the light tap tap on his door frame, Doctor Eric Cornell looked up from his paperwork. Working in this cramped and under-equipped workspace was the daily bain of the Doctor. He knew, through contact with his peers, from other city police labs, that his facilities were sadly lacking.

"The lieutenant sent me to check with you to see where you were with your examination of the evidence collected from the 10B crime scene."

"I've just started my preliminary report for you." Glancing around his office, "I might have had it done sooner, but you know..." Someday when the new Police Services Building, that every department head was crying for, was finally built, by God, he'd have a lab that would be second to none, or his name wasn't Eric Cornell. "You're lucky. It's been quiet so I've been able to have the whole team working on it and there's a couple of things that I can tell you."

Russ pulled his notepad from his pocket "Okay shoot."

"I'll include it all in my report that you should have by later this afternoon. First, from the bedding, I can confirm the presence of semen stains. When compared to the swab taken from your subject at the hospital, it's his. There was no other semen present. Second, we detected three separate pieces of female hair on the bedding. One was from the victim, so she, along with two others, were on the bed. There was only one sample of male hair on the bedding and that appears to be from your suspect."

"Okay, wait a minute. What you're saying is that Ken Harris was on his bed with three women. He claims to have had afternoon sex with his girlfriend, so that leaves two women unaccounted for and one of the women was definitely Jane Doe #6," Russ said in surprise.

"Correct. But what I can't say is when. I can't say if the women were all on the bed at the same time or if the women were there at different times."

"Can you say if the sex that occurred on the bed was with our Jane Doe?"

"No, unfortunately. I need to wait until the M.E. releases her report to see if I can get any matches from her examination," reported the doctor.

"What else?"

"From the samples of blood on the bathroom floor and the bathroom toilet lip, we detected only the blood of the victim. There were no other traces of blood found anywhere in the bathroom. And you'll find this interesting. From the swab taken from the bathroom sink, I can confirm that Ken Harris did urinate in the sink. Since it takes approximately 60 to 80 minutes for a puddle of blood to start to congeal, and with the footprint being on top of the hardened blood when it was entirely congealed on the floor, Ken Harris's story of urinating in the sink after he discovered the body is true. He was in there at least a couple of hours after the death. Which also means the traces of dried blood on Harris's shoes were not the cause of the bloody footprint stains on the carpet. They came from a different pair of shoes."

"The lieutenant isn't going to like that. Are you sure?"

"One hundred percent. If I had better equipment, I could even tell you exactly how much after the death Harris stepped on the hardened blood on the bathroom floor, but it was definitely after the death of that girl. But that's not the best part" reported Dr. Cornell.

"You mean there's more?" asked Russ in surprise.

"Oh yeah, there's the big one that's going to blow your lieutenant away. From the urine swab, we also found the slight trace of Rohypnol, you know it as the 'date rape' drug."

"But I saw the blood sample results the sergeant had them take at the hospital and I don't remember seeing anything like that." Russ stated.

"Well, you wouldn't. It's very powerful and dissipates in the blood quickly. Your best chance to find evidence is through a urine sample. It stays detectable in the body urine for up to three days. I suggest we get a fresh sample from Mr. Harris immediately."

Back in Melnyk's office Russ broke the news. News that the lieutenant wasn't happy to hear.

"Lieutenant, you're gonna get the preliminary forensics report later this afternoon, Dr. Cornell is in the process of finishing it up. There's a number of things in it you're not going to like."

The lieutenant had been half listening to his detective as he continued trying, without much success, to bring some sort of organization to the chaos of files in front of him. The words 'not going to like' stopped the desk chore in mid sweep. Russ had his full attention now.

"First, the footprints in the blood and urine in the sink prove that Harris told the truth. He entered the bathroom sometime after the girl died. The footprint stains on the carpet prove there was a third person who was in the bathroom at the time of the death. And you're really not going to like this, urine testing proved what he told us could be true. The sample the doc just took shows the presence of Rohypnol, which combined with the amount of alcohol that he had in his system would have knocked him out well into tomorrow land. He's lucky he even remembers his name."

"Is Cornell sure of this?" demanded Melnyk.

"He says one hundred percent. We might very well be focusing on the wrong guy."

With disgust grabbing hold of his brain the lieutenant couldn't hide the sarcasm in his voice, "You think so detective, you bloody well think so?"

10:30AM
Spirling World Supply

Handing his gold embossed card to Betty that carried the feel of a professional to her hand before she even read it, "Alister Peters to see Mr. Spirling. I believe he's expecting me."

"Yes Mr. Peters, I'll let him know you're here."

"Don't bother." With a slight tap on the closed door, Alister walked right in. "Simon, so good to see you."

Two men of business that couldn't have been more different in their appearance if they tried. Alister was dapper, in his freshly pressed, dark pinstriped suit, shiny black shoes. A full head of trimmed white hair was held in place with just the slightest touch of styling gel. Although a little on the short side, he was standing straight, stiff. His presence gave an immediate look that held your attention. The other, Simon, sat slouched behind his old battle scratched desk. He wore no jacket, a crumpled white shirt supporting a loosely knotted tie. He had thinning hair allowing a lot of forehead to shine through. His gray five o'clock shadow, even though it was morning, screamed of being a work horse.

"Where's your man, Cohan? I thought he was going to be here." Simon waved his hand directing Alister to sit down.

"This is rather a messy situation you have here, Simon. I thought it better if just the two of us talk, put our heads together."

"It's more than a messy situation. It's a Goddamn nightmare. I told Molly about it last night and she hasn't stopped crying yet. She went on, and on, all night, demanding that I fix it. She didn't care how I fixed it or how much it cost but I had better well fix it and get it fixed fast. You'd think Ken was my son rather than my nephew."

Alister loved the words, 'didn't care how much it cost'. "I'm sorry that Molly is distressed, I know how much she loves that boy."

"That boy, that boy! It's time that boy grew up and became a man." Every time Simon made any mention of his nephew lately his face would flush red from his rising blood pressure. "I've done nothing but fix up his screw ups."

"Calm down Simon, this needs thinking not reacting," Alister said calmly.

"Well, other than costing me a lot of money, what's your brilliant idea? This is far more than the last bit of fraud he got himself into that I had to get you to straighten out. And that cost me a small fortune. This is murder. For the life of me I can't figure out how someone could have a dead girl in his bathroom and not know anything about it. I know he's lying; he's always lying. He has to be." Simon responded loudly.

"I can't comment on that. For the time being, I think we need to take him at his word. It's either that or we have to throw in the towel and we both know that Molly wouldn't like that." And besides, thought Alister, throwing in the towel would shut off the money tap before we even got it flowing. "Simon, we've known each other for an awfully long time and I like to think that during this time our business relationship has been beneficial for both of us. It's because we've known each other for so long that I want to be very upfront with you. This, no matter how you slice it, is going to be a long, drawn out, exhausting, expensive effort."

"You think I don't know that? You think I haven't already got my accounting group looking into how big a hit we could afford to take right off the top and still survive?" huffed Simon.

It was time Alister started laying the foundation for his plan. A way out might just be possible that could solve both Simon's dilemma, and possibly remove a gnawing problem that he had. It was risky, Simon might blow up, throw him out of his office and he'd lose one of his firm's most profitable customers. But if it did work, why, it could turn out to be a stroke of pure genius.

"I know how much this company means to you. You've worked so hard to build it, to keep it viable. It's a shame that this had to happen. I feel heartbroken. I can only imagine what you and your dear wife Molly must be going through."

"Well, let me be honest with you" Simon said. "Before this disaster was dumped into my lap, I mulled around the thought of cutting my nephew loose, but when I discussed it with Molly, she would have no part in it. And now, I'm stuck between a rock and a hard place."

"I understand. It's hard to have to make the choice between your spoiled, privileged, nephew who's taken advantage of his position, your company and your trust against what you've spent your whole life working for, your company."

Betty, in the outer room, heard the men talking. With the word murder being said, she moved closer to the door to make sure she didn't miss anything. She knew the old man was upset on Sunday, but murder?

"Simon, as I see it, you have a couple of options. Now hear me out, you may not like what I'm about to say, but I say it only as a friend." Now to deliver. Be straight. Tell him exactly how it's going to be, then he'll either jump or fireworks. Alister began to lay out his plan.

"We can move forward. Hire a top-notch criminal firm and turn the defense completely over to them.

And, to be sure, that's what we should do. A good criminal group could end up stretching this out for years, at prices that even I can't believe. The sky's the limit. And you know Molly would want to keep going as long as there was even the slightest glimmer of hope. Your company would be slowly and steadily bled to death. And remember, there's no guarantee that Ken would be found innocent after you spend all that money. Let's face it, this case is doomed before it starts. Or.." wait for it, "Or we can accept the fact that Ken, by his very nature, is guilty."

"Okay, we both know that Ken has to be lying and that he's guilty. How does that help me?"

He's interested. The hook is in his mouth. Now slowly reel him in, not too fast or you'll scare him, and he'll get away thought Alister. "Simple, we let the inevitable happen. We let Ken get what he deserves and he deserves to go to jail, without, yes, I said it, without you spending a fortune," except to us Alister thought. "We let Ken go to jail. We continue to have Ken be represented by Jonathan Cohan, at reasonable prices, over a short period of time. This fulfills the responsibility you have Simon. Ken gets legal guidance, and your beloved company isn't bled to death. While Jonathan isn't one of the ridiculous priced criminal lawyers, he'll put up a good show. We both agree that this case, if it does go to trial, is unwinnable. Worst case scenario, Ken gets twenty years, but with good behavior he gains parole after ten. He's what, thirty-six now, he'll get paroled at forty-six."

"Is that legal?" asked Simon hesitantly.

"Strictly speaking, no. But if he's going to jail anyway, why spend all the money fighting a losing cause? Think about it, you get free of the burden of your nephew. Molly sees that you are doing everything possible for him. And Ken really doesn't suffer."

"What if someone finds out that we decided to let Ken get what he deserves?"

Alister lowered his voice "Only you and I will know, but consider this, before you decide to go down this road. Once we start this, we have to see it through to the end. There'll be no stopping it."

Betty, outside the door, was stunned. She couldn't believe what she was hearing. Not only was Simon's nephew guilty of murder, but his very own uncle was willing to let him go to jail without barely lifting a finger. 'Wait till Jeff hears about this. He's never going to believe it.' But maybe Jeff would believe it. After all, Simon had already told him of the murder. Now Betty would tell him of the plan to guarantee Ken gets sent to jail. Just maybe, Jeff would be happy after all.

Mid-day
Roxworth Towers Apartment 10A

Karen's eyes were having a tough time seeing the road ahead of her as she drove through the city, heading towards Roxworth Towers. If the department would have allowed it, she'd preferred to be driving her own SUV. Its darkly tinted windows would have at least stopped the afternoon sun from blinding her. On this rare November day, the sun brought a degree of heat to the front seat. It was vastly different from the usual damp chill which normally accompanied the constant clouds of fall. It felt good. If the sun was shining, it always lifted her spirts no matter what horrors her homicide job exposed her to. She would have adjusted the sun visor, but, on this department pool car it was broken, and with all the budget cuts the likely hood of it ever getting fixed amounted from slim to none.

*****

"Yes," as the wooden door opened just a crack.

"Mrs. Upton, its Sergeant Karen Langdon. Do you remember me? I talked to you briefly the other day."

With a quick comeback that surprised Karen, "Of course I remember you. Just because I'm old doesn't mean I'm senile, you know." It bothered Eleanor that everyone thought of her as senile, especially her husband Fredrick. He always told her she imagined things, but she proved him wrong, didn't she? She knew right from the start that trouble lived across the hall.

"Mrs. Upton, is it ok if I come inside so we can talk?"

'Come inside'. No one ever came inside. Fredrick had given her strict instructions to never let anyone in when he wasn't home. You could never tell which people out there were trying to trick you. Eleanor knew all too well what would happen if Fredrick found out she had let strangers in his house. Well, Fredrick wasn't here right now, and as long as he didn't find out,,, Eleanor took the chance. "Yes dear, come in. Why, I haven't had a visitor in some time. It'd be nice to have someone to chat with."

In front of Karen stood her grandmother, or rather her great grandmother. Mrs. Upton had the paper-thin skin, colored the color of milk. Not the pure white of whole rich milk. This was the blueish white of watered down skim milk, exposing purple veins running up and down the arms and legs. It was skin that hadn't seen any sun in a long, long time. Karen towered above Eleanor, who was shrunken by age, and easily outweighed her by a good fifty pounds.

"Here, come over and sit on the couch, I'll make us a nice pot of tea."

"You don't have to do that, I'm fine."

"Don't be silly. You can't visit without a cup of tea. I'm afraid I haven't got any cookies or cake though; my husband doesn't like it when I have sweets in the house."

"That's alright, I just had lunch a little while ago and I couldn't eat another bite." Karen was just being kind. Like most days lately, she never seemed to have enough time to squeeze in lunch. A cookie or two might have tasted really good.

The overstuffed couch with matching chair, worn oriental rug and heavy floral drapes combined with family pictures displayed on the walls gave the room the feel and smell that an old person lived here. This was starkly different from the Harris apartment across the way. This was a home that has been lived in over the years. 10B was an apartment that you took photos in, but you never really lived there.

The tea arrived in silver rimmed bone china cups balanced on a large silver tray. Karen hadn't drunk from china teacups in quite some time. She and Matt didn't even own a set of china. Mismatched coffee-stained mugs, carrying sayings like, State Fair 02, and Worlds Best Dad, filled her cupboard and suited their lifestyle just fine.

"Mrs. Upton,"

"Eleanor, dear. Call me Eleanor."

"Alright, Eleanor, you're aware that there has been an unfortunate incident in Apartment 10B."

"I know, I saw it on the news that night when you were first here. Murder. I can scarcely believe it. But with the goings on over there, nothing surprises me. I told my husband Fredrick, you mark my words, something bad is going to happen, and I was right."

"Eleanor, when our officers were here doing their interviewing, I see that it was your husband who answered, and there was no mention of you in their statement."

"Fredrick's like that. He doesn't like me answering the door to anyone," sighed Eleanor.

"I wanted to come to see you to ask if there's anything you can tell me about last Saturday night. Did you see or hear anything unusual?" asked Karen.

"I'll say I did" as she sat back in the chair as if to tell a bedtime story. "I was in bed sleeping when I was awakened by the sound of the elevator doors opening. I got out of bed in my night dress and peeked out into the hallway. You'll never guess who I saw, sheepishly creeping into 10B."

"Did you recognize this person?"

"Yes, I hadn't seen him since the summer, but it was that man Harris had working in his apartment. Fredrick didn't like it when there was dust everywhere."

Hearing this, the penny didn't drop for Karen, not yet, but when it did, she was going to be in for the shock of her life.

"I was just falling back to sleep when I was wakened up again. This time when I looked out, there was Mr. Harris, so drunk he couldn't stand, being dragged into his apartment by another man and a scantily dressed young girl. Then behind them, right in the middle of the hallway was a second girl. She began laughing hysterically, taking off her clothes and tossing them away. Then you know what I did?"

"No, tell me"

"Once they were all in the apartment and had their music blasting, I went out into the hallway and picked up all the clothes. I couldn't leave such unmentionables out there in the open for Fredrick to see." Eleanor had learned to made sure she kept unmentionables out of Fredrick's sight. "What would he think?"

Karen had finally found the missing clothes. Eleanor Upton had them all this time and nobody had thought to ask her.

"Do you still have these clothes?" hope upon hope.

"Why yes, I washed them, and they are folded in my closet. I was waiting for the girl to come back to get them. Then I was going to give her some motherly advice. She shouldn't be running around naked in front of men; she's going to get a very bad name and you never know what men will do."

Eleanor was right about one thing. The girl did get a bad name, Jane Doe #6.

"Did you see them when they left the apartment? Did they all leave at the same time?"

"I don't know, Fredrick got mad at me. He made me take one of my pills to help me sleep. He said it was none of my business."

Chapter 14

Wednesday, November 13th
Early Morning
Police Services

The Homicide team's briefing area now took on the personality of being a war room. Pictures of Jane Doe #6 and Ken Harris occupied the center positions of honor. A city street map complete with red and green push pins showed the location of the Roxworth Apartments, Elmo's Restaurant and the Envy Night Club.

Melnyk asked the pool detectives for an update of the apartment building security system findings.

"We've gone through all the security data retrieved from the Morrisons and I think we finally have it figured out. During last Saturday night to early Sunday morning there was a lot of activity happening at the mover's side door. Without a working video camera in the area, we can't see who is coming and going but it is registering as being opened using the private key code assigned to Apartment 10B. There is some good news, the camera in the front lobby shows movement happening in the distant background. At mid-night, a single male enters and goes to the elevator. Then early

Sunday morning at 1:00AM a male and a female can be seen carrying what looks like another male followed by a second female. Now here's the really interesting part, an hour later, only one male and one female are seen leaving the elevator and exiting the building followed about ten minutes later by the first male who had gone in. Unfortunately, the figures are too far in the background, and we can't make out for sure who any of these people are."

Russ asked, "Can IT enhance the video?"

"It's a cheap camera and the pictures turned grainy when we tried."

Karen checked her notes, "That corresponds with what Eleanor Upton said she saw. She identified the first man as the contractor who did the summer renovations to 10B, and the carried man as being Ken Harris."

"We need to identify those other people," the lieutenant said. "The missing female has to be our Jane Doe."

"I'm working on that today" Russ said, "I'm going over to Club Envy this morning before they open to talk with the manager, Bernie Habers. I checked our records, and this Bernie has a lengthy list of priors."

Melnyk looked at the two pool detectives "One of you two check with the taxis. Find out if any of them had any fares in the area of the Towers. The other, start working on Harris's phone. I want to know anything on that phone from Saturday morning right through until the Sergeant retrieved it on Monday. I've talked to the County Assistant DA, and with this being an election year, she's unwilling to go to trial in a high-profile murder case she might not win with only the circumstantial evidence we have so far."

"But lieutenant," Russ said, "She's right. The forensic evidence is telling us that Harris isn't the killer, if she went to trial with him, she'd lose."

"I don't care what the forensics tells us, I can feel he's guilty, and until we can prove someone else is the killer, he's our best suspect. Today being the end of our 72-hour window, we're going to have to release him at noon. Sergeant, this is our last chance to question him before we have to let him go. You and I are going to break this act of his this morning."

Early Morning
Office of Peters, Peters & Cohan

Clouds hid any trace of the morning sun as Jonathan drove. The automatic headlights of his Mercedes had triggered themselves on showing him the way ahead into the eerie calm of a city that hadn't yet decided to wake itself. Only Jonathan's Mercedes and the garbage trucks picking up last night's refuse from the shops along the way, were on the road. The car was silent as it slipped forward, street by street. Inside Jonathan kept the radio off. He stared straight ahead, not seeing the odd bits of trash that had spilled out onto the streets, showing the tell-tale signs of being picked over by dogs, cats or maybe even a stray raccoon looking for some man-made delicacy during the dark of night. At the office, only a scattering of people had arrived early, dropped off by a husband or boyfriend on their way to work. Like him, they had no choice but to be early, they by necessity, he by need. It wouldn't be long before the office would fill and the din of near silent computer keys *click, click, clicking* would be heard. Monitors would awaken, shining their blue glow into some eyes that were bloodshot from too much, and some that were bleary from sleeping angrily on their couch.

From his office he could hear Arnold arrive, no doubt anxious for his big day.

"Good morning Mr. Peters"

"Good morning" Arnold replied to his personal assistant as he passed by her desk.

"The color for today is blue," she said, passing him the blue tie and pocket puff she had retrieved from her desk. Arnold Peters and his assistant had developed the morning color of the day routine when Arnold first became a partner. In order to please his father, and it was a hard enough thing to do, before every morning meeting, he would make it a point to be wearing the same-colored tie and pocket puff, in the same dark blue pinstriped suit as his father. His assistant kept hidden in her desk a full assortment of ties and pocket puffs. The standard joke around the water cooler was that if the old man wore purple polka-dot boxers, Margaret would have a pair in her desk waiting for Arnold to put on.

Dad had asked Arnold for a presentation, and Arnold wasn't going to disappoint. It didn't really matter what plan Arnold came up with. Alister, along with his co-conspirator Simon had already agreed to what was going to happen. Dad was merely now letting his son go through the motions. It was a tactic designed to sooth Jonathan, but, when he realized what was going on, have his anger directed to Arnold. Then Alister could bring Jonathon into the devious deception, knowing that once he knew what was at stake, he would have no choice. No choice if he knew what was good for him.

At this morning's meeting, Alister and Jonathan were witness to a presentation of epic proportions. Color slides flashed across the screen before their eyes. Dramatic music rang out emphasizing this point then that point. Flash, flash, flash. Arnold, with the help of his two assistants had pulled out all the stops. If there were any kind of award for presentations, this one surely would be on the receiving end. Arnold on his feet, with his blue tie and matching pocket puff acted as Master of Ceremonies for this game show. The only thing missing was the buttered popcorn.

"You've got to be kidding" Jonathan sneered.

"Now Jonathan, give Arnold a chance."

"But Alister, this is insane. Do you realize what he's saying?" Jonathan couldn't believe what he heard. At the core of Arnold's so-called plan, it was clear Jonathan would be the one hung out to dry. Emergency support was one thing. It would be like putting a tourniquet on an open wound until a surgeon, who knew what he was doing, could step in and save the patient. It was entirely different from thinking that he could do the surgery.

"Arnold, continue."

"Yes, Dad. As I was saying, I researched the average length of billable time in this state, from first involvement to trial completion, and it amounts to roughly one and a half to two years. If you take that amount of time, minus various items such as consultants, expert witnesses, office resources, it still leaves quite a hefty profit for our firm."

"This is far more than profit and loss. This is a man's life we're talking about," Jonathan stated.

“I’m well aware of what we are talking about, and I don’t need to be reminded by you.” Alister snapped.

“I’m sorry Alister, but someone here needs to be reminded of what's at stake. All I’m hearing from Arnold is that the firm makes a lot of money while I am thrown into the front line as cannon fodder.”

“Now Jonathan, don’t you think you’re being a tad bit dramatic?”

“No, I most certainly do not. Have you even taken five minutes to read any of the notes I’ve sent you? This is nearly an impossible case to win. Think about it. Our client goes out to a seedy club, a club known to the police for drugs and easy women, to celebrate his birthday. Somehow, he arrives back at his apartment, totally out of his mind, with a bunch of party women. He passes out and wakes up in the morning alone. Then he finds a dead girl brutally murdered in his bathroom and all he can offer as a defense is that he doesn't remember. What jury in the world is going to believe a story like that?”

Alister asked, “I’ve asked you this once before. Do you believe Harris?”

“Honestly, I don’t know. This is a guy, living way beyond his means, with an ego that could choke a horse. He thinks of himself as a giant of business, wheeling and dealing his way through life. And we’ve seen some of the deals that his uncle has had us get their company out of. I don’t know if I believe him or just feel sorry for him. But I do know, either way, he deserves legal help far greater than I can give him.”

“Jonathon, I don’t think you’re giving yourself enough credit. You graduated top of your class from Freemont, and we wouldn’t have taken you in as a partner unless you were one of the best. Both Arnold and I have confidence in you even if you don't have confidence in yourself. Isn't that right, Arnold?"

"Yes Dad. We have confidence in you Jonathan."

Jonathan didn't give a damn if Arnold had confidence in him. Anyone who would put together a plan solely based on profit, with no regard for moral ethics, let alone legal ethics was an idiot. Jonathan knew the total amount of ethics Arnold had amounted to zero. Arnold showed that to everyone when he came back from his supposedly investigative trip to Italy, bringing a bag full of souvenirs for all the women in the office. He knew that Alister knew it was all a sham, and he kicked himself for not saying something then, but Arnold was the son, and he, Jonathan, just a partner. Not this time. He couldn't and wouldn't stay quiet this time. He didn't care what these two did, but he had to face himself in the mirror every day.

"Alister, I'm sorry. I can't go along with this."

Alister looked right down on Jonathan, eyes boring directly through him, "Explain yourself. What do you mean you can't go along with this?"

"If this firm moves forward with this ridiculous plan, a plan that is morally and ethically wrong, I will have no choice but to tender my resignation."

Jonathan resigning was not part of the deal that Alister and his co-conspirator Simon had hatched. It was core to the plan that Jonathan remained. He had to lead the legal efforts to support the client, Ken.

"Arnold," said Alister turning to his son, "thank you for all the wonderful work you did. Very impressive, but could you leave us for a couple of minutes? Jonathan and I need to have a private chat."

Arnold nodded to the two men then obediently left the room.

For a long time, Alister and Jonathan sat there looking at each other. Alister often used this tactic to disarm his opponent during negotiations. Had used it for years. Sit and wait while watching for the tell-tale signs of uneasiness in his prey. There, he could see it. Jonathan was making slight adjustments in his chair. The shifting of his weight, the movement of his shoulders. Alister knew Jonathan would cave. His victims always did.

"Jonathan, I've been meaning to have a heart-to-heart talk with you for some time, and I guess now is as good a time as any. Answer me this. What is the prime purpose of this firm?"

"Why, to provide the best legal advice to our clients, of course."

"Wrong. That's the mechanics of what we do. That's not why we do it. If our prime purpose was to do as you suggest, we would be operating a store front like the one you volunteer at. Our prime purpose is to make money, pure and simple. We make money so we can have these wood- paneled offices with staff to do our bidding. We make money so that you can send your son off to that high-priced military school, and your wife can have a housekeeper to do her work. We make money so you can swim in your pool and drive your Mercedes. Everything we do, for ourselves and for our families takes money, and the more money we make, the better it is for everyone. From the first moment you started at this firm, you have benefited, and as a partner, benefited far more than most. Your family, your wife, your son. They've all benefited, haven't they?"

"Yes, but that's not the point."

"That's entirely the point. I know Arnold is window dressing, but he's family and I value family. You have the talent and skill necessary for this that he doesn't possess. Now I have to wonder if you value family as much as I do. What will you tell your lovely wife when you go home tonight, and you no longer have a position here because you decided to resign? How will you tell her that your son can no longer attend military school as her family has for years?"

"I'll get another position in another firm."

"Think about it. What firm would hire you when they find you resigned from such a prestigious firm as this one? You'll be spoiled goods and no one other than the store fronts will have anything to do with you. Now you don't really want that, do you?"

Jonathan realized he was being blackmailed into doing what he knew was unethical and wrong, but he also wondered how many heroes in the past had nobly lost everything for a principle? Wasn't his family important? Would his wife rally around him with unquestioning support or would she go crying to her daddy, slipping away to the safety of her family? Before he had principles. Now he had to think of family.

Mid-morning
Club Envy, Bernie Habers' Office

Russ recognized sleaze when he saw it and this man sitting behind the desk in front of him definitely earned that title. Slicked-back black hair shone in the office light, a throw back in time. Russ didn't think anyone used that much oil on their hair anymore. He was afraid that if Habers got too close to a candle his head would probably go up in a flaming ball of fire.

"Why are you cops hassling me? I run a respectable establishment. My security at the door checks every single person for proper age. All my fire codes are up to date, I pay all my taxes. What more can I do?"

"Mr. Habers, my name is Detective Russell Cravers and I'm not here to hassle you. I'm from Homicide and I need to ask you a few questions. Now I can either ask the questions here or maybe you'd be more obliging answering them back at the station. It's your choice."

"No, here's fine. Ask away," mumbled Mr. Habers.

"Do you know a Ken Harris?"

"Never heard of him."

"Did you host a birthday party here last Saturday night for a Ken Harris?"

"Now why would I run a birthday party for someone I don't even know?"

"So, you had no birthday party here?"

"Detective, on any given Saturday night we are packed to the rafters. With that many people jumping all around, you expect me to know if some of them have birthdays?"

"Do you have any security cameras on the premises that I could check the footage from?"

"You know I have security cameras; I'd be a fool not to have them. As for you viewing them, I have to think of the privacy of my loyal patrons. You never know what some of them might be telling their wives or husbands while they are here. So no, if you want to see the video you need to come back another time with a search warrant. And I want you to know I pay a lot of money to lawyers to keep club happenings from prying eyes."

Russ was growing tired of this cat and mouse game. "Mr. Habers, we are investigating a horrific murder, and your so-called respectable establishment is right in the middle of it. So I ask you again. Are you going to be a good citizen and cooperate with our investigation, or are you going to risk being charged with obstruction of justice?"

"Like I've already told you, I pay a lot of money for lawyers. So unless there's something else Detective, I'm a busy man. You can see yourself out."

As soon as Russ had cleared the doorway, Bernie picked up his phone and called Jeff. What the hell was Jeff thinking? There's no way he's getting tied up in a murder case. A little party fun, a little slap and tickle was one thing. But if Jeff thought he was going to drag him or his club into murder, then Bernie had some people that would be visiting Jeff real soon.

Police Services, Lieutenant Melnyk's Office

Ken Harris's phone showed him to be a remarkably busy individual, revealing a mountain of incoming and outgoing calls and texts, locally and internationally. Ken chased deals and opportunities that made him money, lots of money. All this back and forth produced a stack of data that the police had to sort through. Although being able to narrow the search field to last Friday through to Sunday helped make the task manageable. Tracing the phone numbers showed over 50% originated from a Vivian Mooney and a few were from Jeff Hughes, as well as a large number of confusing texts on Sunday from Mooney.

"Lieutenant, from everything I can see, the phone records confirm exactly what Harris has been telling us. While I can't obviously tell what the conversations were about, the dates and times are right on the mark. What I can see though is the content of the texts Mooney sent him early Sunday morning, and there's a flood of them. She went on and on about being sorry. How she got jealous. How she didn't mean to do it, whatever 'do it' means. And also, there is something about a note."

Lieutenant Melnyk searched his memory and couldn't recall any note among the evidence that had been collected from the crime scene. "Get word out to Detective Cravers to pick up Mooney and bring her in for an interview. Tell him to treat her nicely, she might just hold the key we need to finish off that arrogant Harris." Melnyk couldn't contain himself, and the smile that broke out on his face said it all, "there's nothing better than a pissed-off woman."

"About the note, when we were looking through the front lobby video from the Towers, just before the doorman locked the front doors for the night around midnight, we did see a woman give something to the doorman that he put in the mail pigeon holes."

"Drop what you're doing and get over there right away. If that's the note Mooney texted about, it'll still be there. Harris hasn't had time to pick it up yet. He's been in our cells since Sunday afternoon. I want it before he gets it." Melnyk ordered.

Mid-morning
Police Services, Interview Room #2

"Mr. Harris, I want to remind you, for the record, that we are being recorded and you have been read your rights."

"Lieutenant," Jonathan Cohan added, "For the record, I want to remind you, that you have detained my client, unjustly I might add, for the 72 hours you're legally allowed. It is now time to either charge my client or set him free."

Lieutenant Melnyk, taken by surprise by the strength in Cohan's voice, wasn't going to be threatened by a Business Lawyer, not while he still had a little time left to nail his client. He paid no heed to the lawyer warning.

"Joining us today is Sergeant Karen Langdon."

Ken's eyes popped open, "What did you say her name was?"

"Sergeant Karen Langdon." Karen replied.

The lieutenant recognized that the atmosphere in the room had for some reason changed. He could see at the sound of the Sergeant's name, the cloak of fear, desperation, and hopelessness that had covered Harris for these last three days had been lifted. If he didn't know better, he'd swear that Harris had the slightest trace of a smirk on his face.

Ken relaxed back in his plastic chair. He realized he was now in control. With a calm voice he said, "Lieutenant, I've put up with this treatment long enough. You forcibly removed me from my home.

You've subjected me to countless hours of questions. You've tried without success to fool my lawyer and you've fed me nothing but garbage the whole time I've been here. As my lawyer has clearly said, and for the recording I might add, charge me now or we are leaving. This madness you have with me, has come to an end, right here, right now." Ken loved the feeling of being in control. It felt good to be back in the driver's seat.

Lieutenant Melnyk, in all the years of questionings, had never witnessed such a dramatic change in a suspect before. He sat stunned in his chair. In his mind, he quickly ran through the options, deciding that it was better to fight this battle another day. "Sergeant, please take Mr. Harris downstairs and release him. For the present, your apartment remains a sealed active crime scene, so you will need to find other accommodations in the meantime."

Reaching the door, for the first time in three days, Ken felt the afternoon sun on his face. Free, the slight smirk on his face blossomed to a full-grown smile. What had started out as a crappy morning had changed into a sunny afternoon for him, and he liked it when things turned out sunny for him.

"What happened in there?" Cohan couldn't figure out why Ken had become a different man.

"Didn't you recognize the Sergeant's name? Langdon. Your firm is in the process of suing Eastgate Family Construction, which is owned by Matt Langdon, for theft and fraud. The cop has a big-time crook for a husband."

As Karen approached her cubicle, she could see the lieutenant standing, waiting for her. He needed some answers. "I want to see you in my office."

Sitting down behind his desk, he reached into his side drawer and pulled out a large economy sized bottle of antiacid tablets. It had been a while since he last had to use these, but his stomach was on fire. Popping two in his mouth, his jaw began working, chomping down on the tabs.

"Close the door and sit down. Tell me why, as soon as Harris heard your name, he changed. We had him dead to rights, then with your name he broke free. Now I want to know why!" he demanded.

"Don't you try laying the blame on me. We had no case against him. You said it yourself that the assistant DA wouldn't bring charges against him. Releasing him had nothing to do with my name; we simply didn't have enough evidence to hold him." Karen didn't like having to defend herself against what she felt was a ridicules accusation. She knew the blame landed right at the feet of the lieutenant himself. It was a mistake, right from the start, to think that he could bully a confession out of someone like Harris. Harris made his living manipulating the system, attempting to brow beat him was a joke.

Melnyk wasn't buying what Karen was trying to sell him. Harris was guilty as sin and Melnyk knew it, even if everything else pointed the other way. The fire in his belly told him something was wrong here. Right now, he didn't know what it was, but he would. He needed to find the link between the sergeant and Harris. He needed to figure out if his sergeant had something to hide. Could she be trusted? If the sergeant had turned rogue, there's no way he was going to have a bad cop on his team.

Afternoon
Vivian Mooney's Apartment

Three days ago, she called in sick to her boss, unable to function. For Vivian, holed up in her one-bedroom apartment, the world around her seemed small and dark. Curtains were drawn shut, keeping the daylight outside, not allowing any sign of happiness in. She had been happy once, filled with thoughts of a future where she was Mrs. Ken Harris, living in the bright sun filled 10B apartment, high above the city. But now her future had no room for sunshine. Dishes, dirty with dry food crusted on them, filled the kitchen sink waiting to be washed. They had been there for three days, they would probably be waiting for a long time to come. Vivian's emotions ran the whole gamut from thoughts of poor Ken, her love, needing her, wanting her, through to the evil Ken, the abuser, the user, who didn't deserve to be in her future. She couldn't help herself though. She loved him. As simple as that. She loved him. Curled up on her bed, the only light in the room coming from the single lamp on her bedside dresser, she watched her phone. For three days she had been watching her phone, waiting for it to ring, hoping for Ken to call. Would he say he was sorry? Did he want to bring her back into his life like it used to be, like it should be? They could be so happy together living on the tenth floor in apartment 10B.

Buzz...Buzz. The screen of her phone glowed as it came to life from its three days of hibernation.

"Ken, Ken, I'm so happy you've finally called."

"Miss Mooney, I'm sorry, this isn't Ken. My name is Jonathon Cohan. I'm Mr. Harris's lawyer."

Stunned, shocked, the only word she heard was lawyer. It wasn't Ken, it was a lawyer calling her. What would a lawyer want with her? She still hadn't said a word into her phone. She was trying to digest the meaning of the word lawyer.

"Miss Mooney, are you there?"

"Yes."

"I'm Mr. Harris's lawyer and I need to talk with you."

Now Vivian was now really confused. Why would Ken have his lawyer calling her? Was Ken so upset with her tirade at the club that he had a lawyer taking some sort of legal action against her? She had said she was sorry. Surely Ken understood and had forgiven her, hadn't he?

"What do you want from me? I explained everything to Ken. It wasn't my fault."

"Miss Mooney, I don't think you understand. I'm calling you because Ken needs your help."

"Ken needs my help?" Curtains were opening, and the sun started creeping in. Ken needed her help. Life began to return to Vivian.

"Miss Mooney, you do know Ken is in serious trouble, don't you?"

"Yes, I know. I was there at Envy's and saw him. He was trapped by a group of man hungry girls unable to defend himself. I tried to help him, but he pushed me away."

"Miss Mooney, Ken is caught in the middle of a horrific murder."

With that, Vivian lay stunned on her bed. How could her beautiful Ken throw away their perfect future by committing murder?

“Hello, hello, Miss Mooney.” Jonathan's phone was silent, and all his pleadings weren’t going to rouse Vivian from her trauma. Confused, rubbing first his chin, then scratching his head, he had a hard time trying to figure out what to do next. Did she hang up out of anger? Would she be a threat to Ken’s defense? Or did she hang up out of fear with being involved in a murder investigation and trial?

At the same time, Detective Cravers in his car outside Vivian Mooney’s apartment building, had started to lose it. Normally things didn’t bother him. Being easy going, most things simply rolled off his back. But the more he thought about it, his so called interview with Bernie Habers had gotten under his skin. His hands were clamped so tightly around the steering wheel, his fingers were becoming numb. He struggled to find a parking spot in front of the building. Habers might just as well gotten up from behind his desk and kicked him squarely in the backside out the door. The Lieutenant, the Sergeant, and now Habers. No one showed him the respect he deserved. ‘Take the lead’ the Lieutenant had said. Ha! The lieutenant was fixated on Harris. The Sergeant took control whenever she could and that sleaze ball Habers treated him as if he was a no account kid. And now, he had been told to treat this Vivian Mooney, ‘especially nice’. Well, it was just too much. Maybe that’s my problem, he thought, by being too nice I’m letting every one of them walk all over me.

Ring...Ring...Ring, Vivians's doorbell screamed as Russ pushed...pushed...pushed the button. The doorbell’s response to Russ’s demand to be answered brought Vivian back to consciousness. Opening the door, Vivian found herself confronted by a huge man, standing firm, feet placed solidly apart, shoulders squared, head erect. She cowered before him. What else did this day from Hell have to reveal?

"Miss Vivian Mooney? My name is Detective Russell Cravers from Homicide."

That's it. Murder now appeared in person at her door. The little bit of blood that flowed in Vivian raced to her feet, leaving her face ghost white.

"We have reason to believe that you are an acquaintance of a Mr. Ken Harris?"

So now she had been demoted to an acquaintance, a long way down the list from lover, partner, wife. Her knees already trembling, Vivian came close to collapsing. Unsure of how to answer, and too weak to challenge the label of acquaintance, all she could say was "Yes."

"Please get your coat. I'm here to escort you to the station for questioning." Russ left no room for debate in his voice. He was clear. You're coming with me, and you're coming now.

With no resistance, resigned to accept this new role that Ken had imposed upon her, all this acquaintance of an accused murderer could say was "Yes."

Afternoon
Spirling Mansion

Knowing that his Uncle Simon would be at his office, Ken didn't bother to knock on the huge oak double front doors. He stood in the foyer on tiled floors sparkling from meticulous cleaning given to them by his uncle's housekeeping staff. The smell of wax permeated the open space.

"Aunt Molly, Aunt Molly" Ken's voice echoed through the chamber. From the side, a middle-aged woman appeared.

"Excuse me, can I help you?"

"I haven't seen you before, who are you?"

"I'm Miss Molly's maid, and can I ask you who you are, sir?"

"I'm Ken, and your Miss Molly is my aunt." It was difficult to keep up with the constant change of faces in the Spirling staff. Few could endure for long, the gruff treatment dished out by Uncle Simon. In the office, Simon was demanding. In his own home, Simon was brutal. "Where is my aunt?" Ken asked.

"She's upstairs having her afternoon nap."

"Would you go and tell her I'm here please?" Not waiting for an answer, Ken wandered into the sitting room. Two large, leather, high back chairs straddled either side of the cold fireplace. Making up the set, a beige love seat took up position at the top of the red oriental rug, directly in front of the fireplace. To the right, colored bottles rested on the glass top of the sideboard. Not wanting his aunts first vision of him to be one of lounging with a drink in his hand, he walked over to the mantle and struck a pose.

At an amazing pace for a woman of her years and girth, Molly sprinted directly to Ken. Wrapping him in her arms, she coddled him to her ample breast, rocking back and forth.

"Are you alright? I've been so worried about you. They didn't hurt you, did they?" Stroking the back of his head as a loving mother would do to her baby, tears began to form in the corners of Molly's eyes. "Ken, Ken" she whispered, rocking back and forth. Her nightly prayers answered, her Ken was safe. Stepping back to look at him, "When your uncle told me about the terrible mistake the police had made in thinking you were capable of murder, I couldn't believe it. You look thin. Do you want something to eat? Let me get the cook to bring you out something."

"I'm okay, Aunt Molly, it's just so good to be home." Ken slipped a childish tone into his voice. He knew how to play his aunt, and now he needed a favor from her. He needed her to act as the go between, to convince Uncle Simon to allow him to stay here until the police released his apartment. When Uncle Simon finally came home from work, he didn't want to be the one asking him for the favor. Uncle Simon would be in no mood for favors. In all likelihood Ken would need to brace himself for the onslaught his uncle would unleash upon him.

Late Afternoon
Police Services, Interview Room #1

Russ and Karen sat opposite Vivian. Before going in, the sergeant had suggested that she be the one to interview Vivian, woman to woman. Russ never responded to Karen's suggestion; he only shook his head no, and walked in. This woman was his, and he would lead the interview.

Vivian sat there, straight as a board, just like she had sat in the Principal's Office. That was back in high school, when she was caught cheating on her chemistry exam. This was way more serious. She wished Ken was here at her side, giving her the support she needed to get through this.

"Miss Mooney, we're going to be asking you some questions. We want you to take your time answering. Answer them truthfully, do you understand?"

Vivian nodded her head.

"For the recording, I have to ask you to speak up when you answer."

"Yes, sir"

That was more like it. She was showing some respect. Russ continued with his questions, short, blunt, to the point. The tone and directness of the questions, intimidated Vivian. She answered as best she could. She wanted this to be over. When asked about the present status of her relationship with Ken Harris, she couldn't answer. During the course of these last couple of days, she'd been a companion, a lover, a hopeful, a cast off, and now she was reduced to the lowest setting on the relationship scale. An acquaintance of a murderer.

"Miss Mooney, last Saturday night, did you go to Roxworth apartments at approximately midnight and leave a note with the doorman for your lover, Ken Harris?"

My God, they had the letter she left for Ken in a fit of rage. How could she explain it to them. Then her brain kicked in. Stepping through the sequence she realized, that if they had the letter, that meant Ken didn't have the letter. And if Ken didn't have the letter, he wouldn't have read the letter. And if Ken hadn't read the letter, she had nothing to worry about.

Russ reached into his jacket pocket and placed the letter in front of Vivian. On it, only two words, in bold block letters... 'YOU BASTARD'

"Miss Mooney, can you explain what you meant when you wrote this letter?"

"Detective, you need to understand what I was going through when I wrote that note. I never intended to write a note like that, far from it. I originally started out wanting to write Ken explaining my feelings for him. I wanted to explain to him I still loved him even though he pushed me away at the club.

The sergeant wanted to know what exactly happened at the club, from a firsthand eyewitness. "You mentioned the club. Can you walk us though what happened that night at Envy's?"

Vivian went through step by step everything she experienced at Envy's, holding nothing back. She hoped her truth could help Ken. At the mention of Ken's condition, the sergeant stopped her.

"Are you sure Mr. Harris was totally incapacitated? It's very important that you're sure he wasn't faking it?"

"Sergeant, I grew up with a drunken lout of a father. I know when someone is way beyond being able to take care of themself. There's no way Ken was faking."

Evening
Spirling Mansion

Up in his old room, the same one he had as a kid, after his parents' unexpected deaths, Ken missed his own apartment. This room depressed him. With the bikini girl posters still stuck on the wall in the same place he put them years ago, his past was being held captive. Growing up here he couldn't breathe. His aunt always on him, hugging him, squeezing him, trying to make up for the affection missing in her life from her workhorse husband. He knew his Aunt Molly couldn't help it, and he felt kind of sorry for her, but why did he have to suffocate because of his uncle? Aunt Molly had told him to wait in his room. It was always his room, never the guest room or the extra room. Since the day he left for college, this space had been declared his room, whether he lived in this house or a hundred miles away.

Lying back on his old single bed with his legs stretched out, hands crossed behind his head, staring at the ceiling, his thoughts ran to Vivian. From what he remembered about the club; he treated her terribly when all she wanted to do was help him. Maybe, if she had been the one to take him home that night, rather than Jeff, he might not be in the mess he's in now. He might have wakened up with Vivian in his bed, instead of finding a woman dead on his bathroom floor. All this dreaming about what might have been wasn't going to help him. He had to get serious. Searching the devious side of his brain, he hunted for a way to use the Langdon connection to his advantage. It was obvious during his last interrogation, the sergeant wife of that sap Langdon, wasn't aware of her husband's predicament. He saw it in the way she reacted.

*****

"Dear, I have great news" Molly greeted Simon, returning home after another long day. "Ken is going to be staying with us for a few days." There was no asking for permission, it was fact. Her Ken needed a place to stay, and Molly happily obliged. "He's up in his room resting. The ordeal he's been through these last three days has worn the poor dear out."

Molly wasn't telling Simon anything new. In his office, he had been receiving daily, blow by blow reports from the lawyer Cohan. The latest report told of his nephew's release from jail which surprised him. He certainly didn't expect Ken to show up here at his doorstep. Although he was antsy to talk with Ken, he would have to wait till Molly went to bed. There was no point trying to get any truth out of his nephew with Molly around.

Around the dinner table Molly beamed. Fussing over Ken as if he'd never grown up, it was like old times. Quizzing him if he had enough to eat, was he feeling okay, did he need more carrots. She was in her element. She never once asked Simon how his day went, or if anything interesting happened at the office today. Dinner was all about Ken. Simon ate his food in silence, waiting for his turn to quiz Ken, and it wouldn't be about dinner. Simon needed answers, firsthand, right from the horse's mouth. A lot depended on those answers.

Chapter 15

Thursday, November 14th
Early Morning
Cohan Household

The warmth of the house this morning allowed Jonathan to be sitting at the breakfast table without his slippers, wearing his dressing robe tied tightly around his waist.

"I think I better have some oatmeal this morning, Mrs. Dodds." He probably would end up missing lunch again today so oatmeal would have to hold him over till dinner.

Mrs. Dodds, the family chief cook and bottle washer ever since forever, her position being more than just a hired servant, had no problem speaking up. "Oatmeal's far better for you than the pancakes or waffles you usually have."

"Thank you, Mrs. Dodds, also some orange juice and coffee, and none of that fake sweetener you try to slip past me, I want real sugar," then added "Please."

Through the bow windows of the morning room the trees were waving final goodbyes to the few remaining leaves that fell down to the ground to join in a swirling dance across the back lawn.

"Is Mrs. Cohan joining you?"

"I think so. She should be here in a couple of minutes. She's finishing up her hair. Just bring me the coffee while I wait for her."

He had only Dolly to wait for. Their son had been packed up and returned to Military School at the start of the term. Dolly had insisted. It was part of her family heritage going back all the way back to the Civil War. Boys were sent to Military School to have their heads filled with hopes of leading men into glorious battles for noble causes. Having been born and raised in the south to one of its grand olde families, Dolly had some extraordinarily strong ideas embedded into her. Just because they had moved to the East Coast for Jonathan's work, there was no reason to change tradition.

Jonathan's family had vastly different traditions, but over time these relaxed, evolved and were lost. Having arrived as landed Jewish Immigrants, steeped in centuries old culture, they were thrown into the melting pot of America. What evolved was a mish mash of Jewish-Americanization. His father-in-law, had taken a firm stance when Jonathan asked him for permission to marry his daughter. Presbyterian. The family was Presbyterian, and if Jonathon wanted to marry into the family, he had to become Presbyterian. It wasn't Dolly marrying into the Cohan family, it was the other way around.

"You came home rather late last night," Dolly said as she floated across the floor towards the breakfast table. She looked exactly as she did some fifteen odd years ago when Jonathon married her. At least she did in his eyes. Tall, slender, a southern belle with a grace that couldn't be learned. It was only inherited at birth, by the rare few women of breeding.

"I tried not to wake you."

"I wasn't sleeping, I was reading the letter David sent from school."

"That's nice. How's he doing?"

"The usual complaints, marching here, marching there, waving a lot of silly flags around."

"We could bring him home."

"We've been through this Jonathan. When I mentioned it to daddy on the phone last Tuesday, daddy said it was all part of the growing process. He went through it and so will David."

Although he was more than a hundred miles away, daddy still held influence over his daughter, and by default, over Jonathan. The rules of the 'Grand Ole Families' were simple. A dutiful daughter lived with her husband, but obeyed her father, and Jonathan knew what he was getting into when he married Dolly.

"Remember we're playing bridge at the Wilkinson's this evening."

"I don't know if I can make it. I have so much work to do if I want to get ahead in this case." And Jonathon did have an awful lot of work to do. The daily demands of spending time at the police station with his client Ken. Time updating his partner Alister, Uncle Simon and dealing with the constant police tricks, were wearing thin on him. That's not counting the amount of time he locked himself away in his office scouring through old law books trying to change himself from a lawyer of business to one of homicide. It was hopeless. You don't change yourself in a day, a week or even a year. Criminal law demanded a lifetime of commitment, and he was far too old to be starting all over again from scratch. He knew it but he couldn't understand why such a senior lawyer as Alister didn't know it and why Uncle Simon would even put up with it. Playing bridge with the Wilkinson's didn't come close to something he needed to be doing.

"Jonathan, we have so few friends now as it is. We can't disappoint the Wilkinson's. Why the only other real friends we have are Alister and JoAnna Peters, and you know what a pompous ass Alister is."

Jonathan had often felt that one of the main reasons he was offered a partnership with the firm was because of Dolly. He could tell right from their first meeting, Alister looked upon Dolly as an asset to the firm. She would bring the style and grace to business cocktail parties and civic functions that were beyond what Arnold could bring. She was an asset far greater than Arnold's wife, the trophy that had to be watched around the Martini bar.

"Alright, I can't promise but I'll try." He hated disappointing his wife. She was the main reason he kept trying to be Ken's lawyer. He hadn't told her. He didn't want to worry her, or have her phoning daddy. Alister had given him the clear picture that representing Ken was good for the firm, and lawyers who wanted to be partners, knew what was good for the firm. Everything was at stake. The message, although never formally said, couldn't have been clearer. You were either in with what was good for the firm, or you were out. The Georgian style house, the Mercedes, David's Military School, the pool and the tennis court, even the wide lawns with their swirling leaves all depended on him being something that he was not, a Criminal Lawyer. He volunteered once a month doing Pro Bono work at the city storefront walk-in legal office. Saw the people struggling with their lives, most existing day to day. He couldn't subject Dolly to that kind of life, and he couldn't imagine being without her.

"Here, you better take your umbrella today Mr. Cohan," said Mrs. Dodds as she handed it to him. "The sky is starting to look pretty dark out there. It might rain soon." Mrs. Dodds didn't know just how right she was. For the last couple of days, rain had been falling pretty steadily on Jonathan, and he didn't see any sun coming his way in the foreseeable future.

Early Morning
Spirling World Supply

"Betty, I don't want to be disturbed." Simon, back in the familiar setting of his office, needed time to think. He did his best thinking here, behind his old desk, by himself. He had an office at home, all fitted out, but that was more for show. This office was where he worked.

His last night's talk with his nephew had given him a lot to think about. During the late evening, after Molly retired to her bed, he and Ken sat, face to face, in the high back leather chairs with the embers of the evening fire slowly dying out. He grilled Ken very carefully, making him go through every single event over the last days, right from the Saturday wakeup call from that girl Vivian to finally being released from custody. Knowing his nephew's skill at manipulating the truth whenever he felt it to his advantage, he made Ken do it again. This time stopping him at every stage with questions. Ken had anticipated his uncles probing well in advance and prepared himself. His story was solid. There was no need to lie or change it. He told his uncle exactly what he told the police. He knew nothing about a dead girl. What he did have to add and get his uncle to focus on was the Langdon connection.

In his most sincere voice, "Uncle Simon, I've told you everything I know. I can't help it if I can't remember. You can ask me the same things over and over but it's no use. You're doing the same thing that crooked cop Langdon was trying to do to me."

"What do you mean crooked cop? And where have I heard the name Langdon before?"

"Don't you remember? Matt Langdon is the owner of Eastgate Family Construction. He's the guy you had your lawyers investigate for the Fraud and Theft. He committed it against our company and tried to cast the blame over onto me. Now his wife, the sergeant leading the investigation, is threating me that unless I get her husband off the hook, she'll see me fry."

After listening to the story, then the questions and finally the possibility that a crooked cop on the police team had swayed their determination to charge Ken, Simon believed him. Now he had to take time to figure out what to do. Think it through, slowly and methodically.

He knew Ken to be a screw up who hadn't lived up to the dreams he had for him. He needed to let that go, not let his nephew's past failings cloud his thinking. Maybe this experience would ultimately change Ken, he couldn't tell. But for now, the whole crooked Langdon family had to be dealt with.

Sitting behind his desk, not moving, staring out into space, he thought, and thought, and thought. His mind churned, lost to the passage of time. He had to keep thinking until the way forward revealed itself to him. Picking up his phone, he put a call through to his mid-west distribution office. He needed one more piece of information. Then he would be ready to act.

"Hello, Oklahoma Distribution Center, how can I direct your call?"

"This is Simon Spirling," The receptionist put her magazine away. "I want to speak with that on-site lawyer we have down there."

"That would be Mr. Norman, sir, let me connect you."

Simon, during one of his yearly inspection trips of his Spirling North American Distribution Outlets had met the young Alex Norman and was impressed with him. Although technically he worked as part of the Peters, Peters & Cohan network of lawyers, Simon found him to be a free thinking, competent lawyer, and thought he would answer his question truthfully as an unbiased third party.

"Alex here, how can I help you?"

"This is Simon Spirling. You might not remember me, but we met last summer."

"Of course, I remember you sir. You're not someone a person could easily forget."

"I have a hypothetical question to put to you and I need an honest answer."

"If I can be of any help, go ahead, I'm listening." Alex said, expecting a question of business.

Simon had to be careful how he phrased his question, not wanting to reveal that it concerned him and his family personally. "If someone was suspected of a serious crime, and one of the lead police investigators had, without a doubt, a personal connection with a criminal involved in the case. What impact would it have on the investigation?"

Alex read national newspapers and watched national news broadcasts, "Does this have anything to do with the murder of a young woman recently up there? Because I wouldn't want to be giving advice from down here, so far removed from the investigation."

"Never mind that, just give me your opinion."

"Well, if I was involved, I would see this as a clear conflict of interest on behalf of the police, and as such, I'd be pushing to have any evidence presented by the police ruled as inadmissible. We tend to call it the fruit of the poison tree. Remember, I'm only talking hypothetically."

"Thank you, that's all I need to know."

Armed with this tidbit of information Simon was now ready to talk to Alister.

"Betty," he bellowed out to his assistant, "Get hold of Alister Peters and tell him I need to see him immediately."

I wonder, Betty thought to herself, would he'd even notice if I ripped the Intercom system right off his desk and gave him a bull horn to use instead.

Early morning
Police Services.

Russ stood at the bulletin board intently studying the array of crime scene photos pinned to it as Lieutenant Melnyk entered the briefing room area.

"Any thing standing out for you Detective?"

"Not yet, but there has to be something here that I'm just not seeing."

The rest of the team filed in, and Russ took his place beside his sergeant.

"Okay, hold it down," the lieutenant said, drawing everyone's attention to him. "We all know that unless we are able to solve this murder soon, it has the potential to turn into an endurance test. It could last months or maybe years, so we have to buckle down and get to work. I know it was a setback having to release Harris, but we had no choice. Our holding time had run out. So, we need to regroup. We must find out where we stand and figure out where we go from here. Who wants to start?"

One by one each of them gave their report, and with each report more questions emerged instead of answers. The autopsy report confirmed the time and method of death, but it didn't lead to Jane Doe #6's identity. She had no birthmarks, scars or tattoos to follow up on and her fingerprints were a dead end.

"Somebody's got to know she's missing. The M.E. says in her report the blood contained a high amount of alcohol and recreational drugs. We know, according to Harris, he, along with others, spent most of the evening at Club Envy. Detective, how did you make out interviewing Habers?"

“Bernie Habers is a sleaze ball. He completely stonewalled me with threats of high-priced lawyers. I wouldn’t trust a word that came out of his mouth. He claims to know nothing of the Harris birthday party. There are video tapes of club action, but we’ll need a search warrant to get at them. Habers isn’t going to volunteer anything.”

“Okay, if he wants a search warrant, get him a search warrant. We need to see those tapes.”

“Sergeant, you were following up a hunch about the old woman in the apartment opposite Harris.”

“I met with Eleanor Upton; she confirmed the shapes we saw in the background of the lobby camera. She also had possession of the missing clothes. Unfortunately, she took it upon herself to wash the clothes.”

“Why in the world would she do a thing like that?”

“I’m not completely sure. Partly because she’s an old fuddy duddy, and, this part I don’t understand, partly because she said she had to keep them out of sight of her husband. He wasn’t there when I interviewed Eleanor. I’m going back when he’s at home so I can interview him. I can tell you, from the little bit that Eleanor let slip in our conversation, her husband has some real problems.”

“What about Harris’s girlfriend, Vivian Mooney?”

“When the sergeant and I interviewed her, it became clear she is in love with Harris. Everything she said supports Harris's version of the night in the club. She is solid that Harris was completely unable to function in any way on his own.”

"Damn," Lieutenant Melnyk had expected a lot more from Vivian. He had hoped she'd be willing to lash out at her lost lover. She could've been a valuable tool in his quest to deliver Ken to a new home behind bars for a long, long time. "Are you sure she wasn't putting on an act?"

"Lieutenant," Karen said, "If she was ever put on a witness stand, in my opinion, Ken Harris would walk out a free man."

Looking to the two pool detectives of the team, "You two track down that friend of Harris's, Jeff Hughes. We haven't talked to him yet, and we need to, bring him in. Don't take no for an answer. Bring him in. If he gives you any trouble, get some uniforms and arrest him. Harris said he was at the club with him, and he may very well be the one that the Upton woman saw carrying Harris into his apartment."

Morning
Jeff Hughes Apartment.

At the open door to the apartment, both detectives instinctively grimaced. Jeff's multicolored right eye, combined with his cracked puffed lower lip looked painful. A glance over Jeff's shoulder at the broken table lamp and overturned chair showed the detectives unmistakable evidence of a recent struggle.

"Are you alright?"

With the taste of fresh blood still in his mouth, "Yeah, I just ran into a door." A 250lb door, complete with fists like concrete blocks for door knobs, named Maurice, a business partner sent from Bernie Habers. Maurice carried a message delivered to Jeff in a way he knew Jeff would understand. Bernie wasn't happy being linked to a murder. By the time Maurice left, Jeff had received the message and he understood. Involving Bernie in murder was a mistake that Jeff didn't want to repeat, that is, if he knew what was good for him.

"Mr. Hughes, we're from Homicide. We've been sent to escort you to the station to answer a few questions. If you'd like to get your coat, we'll wait here for you."

After his recent heart to heart discussion with Maurice, Jeff wasn't in any mood to answer questions. Answering questions could lead to another visit from Maurice with even greater consequences. "I'm not going anywhere or answering any of your questions."

"Not answering questions is your choice, but you are coming with us. We have instructions to arrest you if we have to." the detective answered as he slipped his hand behind his back to retrieve a waiting pair of handcuffs.

"I need to make a phone call." Jeff said hurriedly.

"Go ahead, but make it quick."

"Spirling World Supply" chirped cheerfully in Jeff's ear.

"Betty, it's me, Jeff. Tell Mr. Spirling I won't be in today, I have some personal problems that I have to deal with."

"Is there anything I can do to help?" Betty would be more than happy to help Jeff, hoping he'd see her as something other than just Simon's gofer.

"No, it's alright, just give Spirling the message." and with that, Jeff disconnected, and Betty sighed.

Ok, get your coat, let's go." with a subtle jangle of the cuffs the detective started for the door.

Mid-morning
Bernie Habers' Office

Flanked by two uniforms and with a search warrant tucked away in his inside jacket pocket, Detective Cravers burst into Bernie Habers office.

"Didn't they teach you any manners at police school? You're supposed to knock when you want to enter" yelled Bernie in anger.

"Oh, they taught me a lot" Russ said as he reached inside his jacket for the warrant. "They taught me that carrying this little piece of paper was a magic key to get in anywhere I want." He dropped the warrant on Bernie's desk.

"Well, well, what have we here, Detective?"

"It's the warrant you requested for the club video tapes." Russ relished having the upper hand. This sleaze ball might have thought he was funny at their last get together, but who was laughing now?

Bernie picked up his phone, "Hailey, can you come in here for a moment darling?"

Through the side door, a tall, long legged red head, wearing the shortest dress Russ had ever seen swayed up to Bernie's desk. "Hailey darling, can you escort these fine gentlemen to the security room and give them any video tapes they want?"

The deep throated "Follow me Gentlemen" caused a slight shiver to run through Russ.

“Now don’t be surprised if you see your missus on the tape enjoying herself, will you?” Bernie laughed out loud as Russ exited the office, eyes glued to the side-to-side wobble in front of him. Russ had a challenging time watching the stairs as he stumbled, going up the steep, black metal staircase, leading to the upper level, way up above the empty dance floor.

The tightness of the security room allowed for no escaping the brushing hips of Hailey.

“Now which tapes are you interested in?” This voice resonated with Russ. This was a voice for a warm Saturday evening, sipping wine under a star filled sky.

“Last Saturday evening, Sunday morning.”

“Here, let me make a copy for you” the slender fingers picked out a couple of tapes from the overhead rack.

Outside, with the tape copies secured under his arm, Russ turned to the two uniforms beside him and they all grinned, that silly grin of little boys with a crush on their teacher.

Back inside, “You didn’t give them the party room tapes, did you?’”

“Of course not Mr. Habers,” Hailey said with a smile.

“Good Girl.”

Noon
Spirling World Supply

“Simon, what’s so important? Your girl told me I had to drop what I was doing and rush right over?

Everything's on track, going to plan, just like we wanted. If you had a question or concern, you could've just called me, you know."

Simon rubbed his eyes. He had been blankly staring at the top of his desk for too long, and now his eyes burned. Alister saw the red eyes as he sat down.

"Has something got you worked up?"

"I called you over because we need to talk," Simon said in a low thoughtful voice. The voice of a man who despised corruption and now had to correct it. "Alister," he took a long pause, "we need to adjust our plan," another long pause, "there's a crooked cop."

"Of course, there are crooked cops. What has that got to do with our plan? We agreed to let my man Cohan represent Ken and let the chips fall where they may. A crooked cop doesn't change anything."

"I agreed to have Cohan represent Ken, but it has to be done fairly. I've run into enough greedy, crooked people trying to squeeze me over my career and there's no way I'm going to let one get her claws on my nephew. He may have killed that girl. I don't think either one of us can say for certain. And if he did, he should pay. But, if he's innocent and convicted by blackmail, that's another matter."

"Simon, what's gotten into you? We're dealing with a possible murder case and the best way to protect your company. You can't go off halfcocked tilting at windmills at a time like this. How is this supposedly crooked cop mixed up with your nephew anyway?"

Simon went on in flourishing detail of the Langdon connection. He explained how Ken had told him of been threatened with blackmail by the lead detective, Karen Langdon, unless all action against her husband was stopped.

Alister remembered the Langdon affair and the shoddy investigation done by his son Arnold and decided he didn't want to open that can of worms. What to do, what to do. Alister was stumped. There was no point in trying to argue or plead with Simon, he could see that. The red eyes looking at him told him it was done. "It's your decision. What do you want to do?"

Simon leaned forward, "I've been thinking about this all morning. Ken tells me he likes Cohan; feels he is doing an excellent job looking out for his interests, so we need to keep him working with Ken."

"Cohan is a good man, highly skilled. We can trust that he'll do everything humanly possible to represent Ken." That part's good, now what else?

"I want you to talk with Cohan. Get him to dig into this sergeant, and if what Ken is telling me is true, we should be able to use that to our advantage. We could use something like 'Fruit from the Poison Tree'."

It was strange hearing that phrase coming out of the mouth of Simon. But Alister knew if true, it could be used to Ken's advantage. There might be a chance out of this after all.

Afternoon
Vivian Mooney's Apartment

At the small kitchen table, Jonathan sat on one of the only two chairs available. Although the curtains were open, the gray afternoon had no sun to spare for Vivian's apartment. Jonathan noticed a musty smell, as if the place had been closed up tight with no air circulating for some time.

"Do you take anything in your coffee?" Vivian played the part of being a gracious host to her guest. This man sitting at her table was Ken's lawyer, and she felt relaxed. This man's job was to help Ken through the trouble he was in. And Vivian wanted to help, in any way she could, any way that Ken needed.

"Just black with a little sugar." Jonathan didn't have a lot of time to visit and chit-chat. He had received a call from Alister informing him that he would be staying late at the office to see him. "Miss Mooney, even though Ken was released from police custody yesterday, he's not out of the woods yet. They still have him as their prime person of interest. It would be extremely helpful to me and to Ken if you could tell me everything you remember from last Saturday through to Sunday morning."

Vivian went through all the events as she remembered them. The breakfast was described in great detail, the Eggs Benedict with the wonderful warm sauce, how happy she and Ken were being there together. She described the waitress as being a plain girl, actually quite snippy, who pestered Ken as he tried to eat. The rude phone call Ken received that forced him to have to spend the evening with some people from his office even though she had a whole day planned out for the two of them. Vivian skipped over the afternoon dessert she and her lover enjoyed together, thinking some things were way too personal to share with strangers.

"And what about the club? Ken tells me you were there. Did you see or hear anything?" Jonathan asked.

"Yes, I was at Club Envy Saturday night. I found Ken in one of the private party rooms, totally intoxicated. He was being taken advantage of by that so called friend of his, Jeff Hughes and a number of women. When I tried to get Ken out of there and take him home, Jeff had me forcibly removed from the club.

"You remember Ken being heavily intoxicated? Do you remember anything about the people he was with? Who they were, or how many were with him?"

"Like I said, Ken was there along with Jeff Hughes and a number of strange women, I'm not sure how many as they were crawling all over the place."

"Miss Mooney, have you been interviewed by the police yet?"

"Yes. Yesterday, one of them came here and drove me to the police station."

Perfect. Vivian's recollection of the evening events were completely identical to what Ken recalled. Jonathan had the feeling that she was telling the truth, and any statement she gave to the police vindicated his client.

"Thank you, Miss. Mooney, you've been an immense help."

"I hope so. A person like Ken couldn't have killed anyone."

saw a man and a woman carry Harris into the apartment along with a dancing girl. She was sure Eleanor would be able to identify the man as Hughes, that is if her husband Fredrick would let her. She still had to meet with Fredrick. Something was not quite right there, and in the pit of her stomach it bothered her.

"Well of course I took him to his apartment. What'd you expect me to do? Drop him off on the lobby floor."

"After you dropped him off in his apartment, then what did you do?"

"I left and went home."

"And what about the two girls, what did they do?" Karen asked.

"I have no idea; they were with Ken. He's a handsome guy. He got lucky and picked the two of them up. They have nothing to do with me."

"What were their names?" The lieutenant had a strong interest to find out the true name of Jane Doe #6. Ever since seeing her on the autopsy table, when Dr. Amile held a personal moment over her, he was determined to give Jane her name back.

"Lieutenant, I already told you, those girls had nothing to do with me. I know nothing about them."

Karen wanted to try one more question. "When you left the apartment, did you and the two girls leave together?" Fredrick had sent Eleanor to bed, so unfortunately, she didn't see anyone leave the apartment.

Jeff picked up on the sergeant's uncertainty. The police didn't know when or who left.

"The girls were Ken's. How many times do I have to tell you, I had nothing to do with them? I left by myself." Game, set, match. The smirk was now a hurting smile. They had nothing on him and he knew it.

The sergeant had now caught him lying for the second time, "Mr. Hughes, you need to stop lying to us. You're only digging yourself a bigger hole. We have positive evidence that you didn't leave alone. In fact, the lobby camera shows you left the building sometime later accompanied by only one female. You went into the building with two females and left with only one. Where was the second female and what is her name? The truth this time Mr. Hughes, the truth."

The smile dissolved; the know-it-all smirk now replaced by worry lines stretched across his forehead. He couldn't tell them about his plan to use shameful pictures to squeeze Ken out. He couldn't tell them about the girls for fear of what Bernie would do to him, but, if he didn't say something, he could be the one facing a murder charge.

"Okay, I've been lying to try to protect Ken Harris from his uncle. Ken and I brought the women back to his apartment for an evening of enjoyment, nothing other than that. Ken had gotten himself so liquored up that he and the one girl, I don't know her name, both passed out on the bed. I took my girl and left to go back to my place instead. Now I have no idea what Ken and his girl did after I left, or why Ken murdered the girl. Believe me, they were both passed out on the bed when we left."

The sergeant didn't believe him for a minute, but the lieutenant took this as a major boost for his quest to put Harris behind bars.

"Alright, Mr. Hughes, you can go for now, but don't leave the area, we may have more questions for you." Melnyk said, despite what his sergeant was thinking of doing.

Late evening
Offices of Peters, Peters & Cohan

Using his pass key Jonathan slipped inside out of the damp air and turned a few of the overhead lights on. He had banged his shins enough as it was weaving through the maze of work desks during the day. Now with the dark empty office, he wanted some light. Alister's desk lamp still burned, and so did Alister. He hated having to wait for anything. So far, it hadn't been a good day for him. It started off by being summoned to Simon's office as a lowly minion and now having had to wait for his partner, didn't sit well with him.

"When I told you I'd wait for you, I didn't mean I wanted to be here all night."

Jonathan took his time returning to the office on purpose. After his promising interview with Vivian Mooney, he decided to go home. He felt he needed to rest. He wanted to spend some time with his wife over a warm meal, be reminded why he was letting Alister subject him to this turmoil. The stress he had been operating under during these last couple of days had begun to take its toll. The last thing he needed was to be sitting here, listening to Alister whine about how his life was being disturbed.

"Alister, you wanted to see me, I'm awfully tired. What is it you want?"

Seeing his partner slumped in the chair in front of him looking worn out, Alister thought he better change his tact. Time to dust off his coaching hat. He tried to hold a comforting smile on his face, but that proved difficult. It wanted to turn back into the normal sneer it was used to.

"I had an interesting meeting this morning with Simon Spirling I wanted to share with you. Apparently, Simon had a real heart to heart with his nephew last night. Ken told him you were doing a good job in representing him, and he didn't want to change lawyers. He's happy with you and wants you to continue. I took that as really good news; it confirms the confidence I have in you."

Jonathan didn't need to be buttered up. He knew why he was doing this. It was for his wife, his son, his lifestyle. But it was nice to hear that Ken appreciated the efforts he had been putting in.

"And there was something else he said that I didn't quite understand. What's this business of a senior police detective having a husband we're gearing up to charge with Fraud and Theft?"

"It was sprung on me yesterday as Ken was being released from custody. One of the lead police investigators, Sergeant Karen Langdon, is married to Matt Langdon, the owner of Eastgate Family Construction. That's the boon dongle that Arnold charged his Italian holiday against. We sent Eastgate a notice instructing them they had 90 days to repay all monies illegally obtained during the supposed work performed at Spirling World Supplies or we would begin legal proceedings against them."

Alister sat back in his heavily padded chair and stared at the ceiling. "And where do we stand on this?"

"I'm not totally sure. If I launch a formal complaint to Police Services, I'm libel to come across as a desperate lawyer trying to tarnish the good name of a senior officer. If that happens the complaint will be dismissed."

"You're probably right, but this is too good to let go. I'm attending a civic function this weekend where the Police Commissioner will be present. If I were to subtly drop a word in her ear, it may work in our favor. The complaint would appear to be coming from her, not from us, and that won't so easily be dismissed."

Chapter 16

Friday, November 15th
6:30AM
Hedge Street, Eastgate, the suburbs

All during this past week, Russ watched his murder case move from front page national news status, to being lost in a column buried at the bottom of the local news page. Beside the spread-out paper on the breakfast table his coffee sat growing cold. On the first day of reporting, the front-page articles were filled with describing all the known details of the city's twenty-first homicide of the year. Russ actually cut out and saved his picture from its center of page place of honor, showing him being interviewed by Rick Hanna. Had his mother still been around, she would have saved it in her scrap filled book. Without her, Russ had it resting between two pairs of jeans, in his bedroom dresser. He wasn't sure what he'd ever do with it but cutting it out just seemed the thing to do.

Today's small blurb, for those that could find it, regurgitated the same words as yesterday. The police were working on clues left by the killer and expected to make an arrest any day now. If the police were destined to make an arrest, that was news to Russ. At every stage of the investigation, he found himself no further ahead than he was the day before. Working every night late had his wife riding his back. Why wasn't he home to help with the kids? Why wasn't the front porch light fixed? Why was she having to do everything by herself? Russ knew the sooner this case could be solved, the better. He was working as hard as he could, searching, studying, interviewing, yet the way forward remained cloudy, hidden out of his reach.

*****

Wanting to arrive early, to get a jump on viewing the video tapes he had retrieved from Club Envy, Russ left home before the kids were up from their beds. The smudgy streaks that spread across his car window, left by squeaking wiper blades as they battled the steady downpour of rain, did little to improve his mood. Something else to be piled on his to-do list. Driving while thinking, having the case turning over and over in his head had him going faster than the wet road allowed. While he was taking the corner, his back wheels had started to skid towards the ditch, jolting him back. It was going to be one of those days.

In his cubicle, with his first hot coffee in his hand, he hit PLAY on the recorder. Knowing the case appeared to get its start at Envy's, told him clues had to be hidden somewhere on these tapes. If studied really hard, the clues might reveal themselves to him. Immediately he had to mute the volume. The pounding music drowned out any chance of hearing anything of value. On the screen the packed dance floor showed throngs of young people gyrating wildly to the ear-splitting music. Every time the dance lights strobed, the screen flashed bright, causing it to be nearly impossible to see anything clearly. These tapes were useless. There had to be others. A scumbag like Habers would have tapes, better than these, capable of being used to further his means.

Russ stared at the snow filled screen. It was the first sign of another late night ahead, and another late call home. Even this early in the morning he started to brace himself against the oncoming barrage from his wife. 'The kids tracked mud throughout the house. It's too wet to play outside after school. They were fighting over their video games. Katey had gotten into her makeup. Why wasn't he home?' Russ hated rainy days.

Morning
Police Services

Pacing back and forth at the front of the briefing room, Lieutenant Melnyk tried to get his thoughts together. He wasn't happy with how the investigation was progressing. At every lead, they seemed to be slipping backward instead of moving forward. Having to release his prime suspect didn't sit well with him, and this latest interview with Jeff Hughes... "Sergeant, how do you think the interview with Hughes went?"

"We were played, pure and simple. From everything we know so far, only three or four people, other than the girls, were in that apartment, Harris, Hughes, some unknown contractor and possibly a fourth person with blood-stained shoes. All the forensic evidence points away from Harris. He was drugged to the point of unconsciousness. Jeff Hughes knows more or is involved far deeper in this then he is trying to make us believe. And his story of running into a door, he's hiding something, and it must be big. That beating he took wasn't just a coincidence. My instincts tell me we need to find out a lot more about this Jeff Hughes. I'm planning to return to the Towers to try to interview the husband 'Fredrick' in 10A this morning. I'm interested in his story. Maybe the detective here can follow up with Hughes?" Karen suggested.

"No problem. The tapes we got from Habers were useless. I'm going back there to find the real tapes that he must be hiding. While I'm there I can press him about Hughes and the girls that supposedly came from his club."

"Good idea. Also, look through our records and see if we have anything on Hughes. Then go over to where he works and start asking questions. Don't be discrete. Let him know we have an interest in him. Let's see if we can shake that arrogant ass of his. Put a little fear into him. It could prove interesting to see what he does with some heat on him."

"And Sergeant, once you're through with 10A, start hunting down this unknown contractor. Who is he, and why was he there in the apartment?" Melnyk ordered.

In his cubicle, Russ took a minute to run a quick background check on Jeff Hughes. A few small hits came up. He had a DUI when he was seventeen and a Disturbing the Peace at a rowdy college party. Nothing of any consequence. He called downstairs to the Day Watch Commander to put in his request for a sizable uniform presence to carry out a full search at Club Envy. This time he was going in prepared for battle. Bernie Habers was going to do what he was told.

Behind his desk, Melnyk debated. Was he wrong about his sergeant? Everything she'd said this morning was right on track. Maybe it had nothing to do with her and he was just looking for a scapegoat to blame, but something about her got Harris released.

"Melnyk here" the lieutenant said into his desk phone.

"Lieutenant, this is Dr. Amile."

A pleasant voice from an interesting young woman, "What can I do for you Dr. Amile."

"I'm following up on how you're doing finding out the identity of Jane Doe #6, the girl we retrieved from Roxworth Towers. It's been five days and time has run out, I'm going to have to send her for processing soon. I don't want to do it if there's any chance at all you can get her identified."

The impact of those words went right to the pit of his stomach. He was no farther ahead in finding out the girl's identity now than when he had started. Elbows on his desk, shoulders sagging "Can you give me a couple more days, say till Monday? Something might break by then."

Disappointed to hear Jane was still an unknown, Dr. Amile sighed, "Just till Monday, I can't hold her any longer than that."

Morning
365 Maple Row, Eastgate, the suburbs

When he left Roxworth Towers early last Sunday morning, Matt had felt pretty pleased with himself. For the first time since receiving the letter threating legal action for Fraud and Theft from Peters, Peters & Cohan, he believed he had a way out. On his phone, he carried proven evidence Jeff Hughes along with two girls were setting up to blackmail Ken Harris. If his instincts were right, he had the one picture he felt sure Harris would pay anything to get his hands on. But it wasn't money that Matt needed, he needed Ken Harris to call off the lawyers.

With the discovery of a murdered body, everything changed. Being the last one to leave the apartment would by default, make him the prime suspect of murder. At night, when his wife Karen came home late from work, exhausted, he tried to find out how the investigation was proceeding. He asked a few casual questions, here and there, sprinkled in, nothing direct enough to cause Karen to question his motive. So far it looked like the police were stumbling, unable to put together the puzzle. Knowing his wife's determination, it wouldn't be much longer before his secret would be exposed.

Five days had lapsed since the body was discovered and still not hearing a word from Jeff worried him. As far as he knew, only Jeff could place him inside the apartment the night of the murder. Unknowing was starting to drive him crazy. He didn't want to, but he'd have to make contact with Jeff. If need be, he could use the blackmail photo as leverage to force Jeff to stay silent.

10AM
Club Envy

Three black and whites, with sirens blaring, flashing lights bouncing off the wet pavement followed Detective Cravers as he pulled up in front of the club. Russ had instructed them to make their presence known. Marching in step the six uniforms burst through the door of Habers office.

His hot morning coffee spilled across his desk as he jumped up in surprise. "What the hell!" he shouted as he tried to contain the black liquid now dripping down onto the floor.

Russ slipped through the formation to the front. "Remember me Mr. Habers? The last time I was here I asked for the club videos from the night of the Harris party."

"I gave you what you wanted; you have no right to barge in here with your storm troopers. I'm going to have my lawyers file a formal complaint for harassment."

"The tapes you gave me were garbage and you know it. I'm sure a man of your caliber would have real tapes that are useable, and my friends here are going to rip this place apart to find them. Starting at the top going right through to the bottom, we're going to find where you've hidden them. And I bet they might just stumble upon a number of other interesting things you have tucked away."

Wiping his coffee-soaked hands on his pant legs, Bernie had some quick thinking to do. If they did a search, as this pumped-up cop suggested, it could lead to a lot of pain for him. "Hold on, I'm sure we can come to some kind of understanding. Hailey must have just forgotten to give you the party room tapes. It's a simple mistake." He called for his assistant, "Hailey, can you come in here for a moment?"

Try as he might, Russ couldn't help licking his lips at the thought of witnessing the red headed bombshell Hailey again. She strutted in to her boss. You could hear the slight gasp from the gawking troop of men.

"Yes Mr. Habers." the heavy voice exactly as Russ had remembered.

"Hailey, darling. These fine gentlemen tell me you didn't give them all the video tapes. Is that true?"

Hailey might have looked as if she had a light brain, but she picked up perfectly on the line Bernie was sending her. "I'm sorry Mr. Habers, but the handsome detective here was standing so close to me, I must have gotten rattled."

"That's alright darling. See I told you, just a simple mistake."

Russ had to focus on Habers and get his mind off Hailey. He had been fooled once; he wasn't going to be fooled again. "We'll wait here. You've two minutes to produce those tapes."

"Hustle along and get the tapes for our friends." Bernie directed.

With a wobble, Hailey moved towards the door, making sure a hip here and a hip there were nudged as she passed through the group of men.

"Here you go Detective. It was so nice to see you again." Her seductive smile locked on till she left the room.

Wanting to be sure this time he had the real goods, "Put the tapes in and lets you and I watch them together." Turning to his waiting crew, "Thank you officers, you won't be needed and can return to the station now." Exiting the office, from the connecting hallway, Russ could hear the excited chatter of his men. The marvelous Hailey had struck again.

"Okay, stop it there" Russ commanded. On the screen clear as a bell, Russ could make out Jeff

Hughes aided by a heavy set sparkly dressed woman carrying Harris out the door followed by a second nymph. “I want the names of those two women.”

“That’s impossible.” Bernie wasn’t giving up his people. “How do you possibly expect me to know them? They must be friends of either Jeff there or his passed-out partner. You’ll have to ask them who they are.”

Bernie recognized the heavier of the two women as Rochelle, one of the club regulars he sometime used for parties. He'd have to do something about her. He didn’t recognize the other, deciding she must either be a friend of Jeff’s or a club hanger-on that crashed the party room.

Late Morning
Roxworth Towers Apartment 10A

Exiting the elevator, Karen ran her fingers through her wet hair. Then she attempted to shake the dripping rain off her jacket. Squeaks from the soles of her shoes echoed through the empty hallway as she approached the large wooden door of apartment 10A. From the little bit of information Eleanor had let slip during her last visit to this apartment, she had formed an opinion in her head of Fredrick Upton, and now it was time to put a face on the imagined form. Her instincts, nurtured for over past years and countless interviews, brought her here. The time had come to see if those instincts were right.

At the first ring of the doorbell the door swung completely open, so different from the crack when Eleanor had answered. In front of her stood a figure, nearly exactly as she had imagined. A small rotund man, a bully of a man wearing the small man syndrome chip on his shoulder. Gray hair, longer than it should be, accompanied the bristled unshaven face. Thick soled shoes trying to gain the extra inch in height were the only things clean and shiny. Karen felt sorry for Eleanor. An aging grandma should have a comforting companion to spend her declining days together with, not this little sour form in front of her.

"Well?" No hello, no can I help you. Direct, blunt and annoying, just Well?

Karen pulled out her badge and started her customary introduction.

"I know who you are. Your whole crew have been pestering us. What is it you want this time?" sneered Mr. Upton.

Karen fought to hold the dislike for this man from her voice. "I'd like to ask you a few questions if you don't mind. Maybe I could come inside?" as she took a half step forward towards the opening.

There was no movement, he stood his ground. Leaning forward, he stopped Karen mid-step, "I know you were here the other day, pretending to be nice to my wife by drinking tea with her, trying to pry into our affairs. You have no right; our business is of no concern of you."

"Mr. Upton, we are investigating a horrific murder of a young female directly across the hall from your apartment. I have every right to be asking questions, and I will keep asking questions until I get the answers I need."

"You're not looking for answers, I know your type. You're looking at ways to continually harass good people like us, and I'm telling you it's not going to happen here. Now go away and leave us alone." With that the door started to close.

A thin voice called out from inside, "Fredrick, who's there?"

Staring through the annoyance in front of him, "Now see what you've done. I hope you're happy with yourself." He called back to his wife, "It's no one you need to be concerned about. Go back to watching your tv. They're leaving."

Eleanor, now stood behind her husband, blocked from Karens view and peeked around his mass, "Oh, it's you Karen. Why don't you invite her in?"

Stern and direct, "I said she's leaving."

"Mr. Upton, this isn't done. I'll come back and you will talk with me."

Slam. Behind the door Karen could hear the shout, "Just leave us alone."

Afternoon
Spirling World Supply

Russ sat in the parking lot, waiting for the cloud burst of rain to ease up, as local news played on the car radio. With nothing special going on, the radio acted as mindless background noise along with the steady *tap..tap..tap* of rain bouncing off the hood of his car. The Spirling World Supply office consisted of a small one floor aged red brick building. It was different from the slapped together prefab glass front buildings downtown. Occupying the lone Visitors spot, he counted six cars, all parked orderly in their own designated space. Russ pulled his jacket collar up and sprinted around the puddles to the front door.

The noisy hum from the overhead fluorescent lights dated the office. Sitting behind the desk, directly in front of him, the chubby woman looked surprised to see him. Few people just walked into the building off the street. Her thick brown hair pulled back tight showed a face devoid of any makeup.

"Yes. Can I help you?" Betty said, looking up at him.

"My name is Detective Russell Cravers. I'm from the Police Homicide division, and I'm here to speak to someone in authority." Russ wasn't sure who he should be asking for.

Wanting to look a little professional, Betty pressed down the page button on her desk intercom. "Mr. Spirling. There's a police Detective here who would like to speak with you." No reply. Trying to keep her composure, she tried again, "Mr. Spirling. There is a police Detective here who wishes to speak with you." Still no reply. Giving up she went over to the door behind her, stuck her head in and spoke directly to Simon.

Simon had been expecting a visit from the police. He wondered why it had taken so long for them to finally get around to talking to him.

"I assume you're here to talk about my nephew Ken." Simon asked Russ, who was seated in one of the two wooden chairs in front of the desk.

"No, Mr. Spirling, I'm here to ask some questions about one of your employees, a Jeff Hughes."

"Why in the world would you want to talk about Jeff Hughes? It's Ken you're interested in, isn't it?"

"Your nephew is a person of interest, but right now, we're looking for background information on Mr. Hughes. I'm not sure how much you know of the role Mr. Hughes played last Saturday into early Sunday morning along with your nephew Ken."

From his fireside talk with Ken, Simon knew that Jeff had thrown a birthday party for Ken. Then at the end of the night, Jeff, being the good buddy that he was, considering the condition Ken was in, had made sure he got home safely. Ken had told him everything he remembered, and Simon believed him, but maybe it would be wise to hear what the police knew.

Russ remembered the lieutenant gave him instructions to shake things up for Jeff Hughes. "From evidence we have gathered so far, not only did Mr. Hughes take your nephew home, when he was completely inebriated, he did it with two, how should I say it, two women of very dubious character. When we questioned Mr. Hughes, he claimed he had nothing to do with these women. They were there for Ken. And we also now believe that one of these women was the murdered woman found on the bathroom floor."

This bit of information puzzled Simon. Sure, Ken was a virial young man, and his uncle understood that young men went about spreading their wild oats. But if Ken was totally out of it, why would Jeff bring women into Ken's apartment. Jeff had never mentioned any of this to him.

"Betty" the sudden bellow from Simon startled Russ. "Find Jeff and tell him I need to see him." He looked at Russ, "We'll get to the bottom of this right now."

Glancing out the office window, over Simon's shoulder, Russ detected sudden movement. A man, with his coat pulled up over his head to protect from the rain, dashed across to the side of a truck, parked at the back of the lot. Russ couldn't quite make out what was going on. With arms flailing about, it looked like an intense argument was taking place. Interested, Russ got up out of his chair and moved over to the window. With the rain beating down heavily, it was hard to make out, but he was sure he'd seen that truck before. He recognized the color of the truck with bright letters on its side, 'Eastgate Family Construction'. Why in the world would Eastgate be here? This place hasn't seen any construction activity in years. The surprising realization hit him. Eastgate Family Construction was owned by Sergeant Karen Langton's husband.

"Who's that out there by that truck?"

Simon turned to look, "Can't tell, too much rain."

Standing beside the truck, being pelted by the driving rain, Jeff yelled through the rolled down window, "Don't you dare try to threaten me."

"You promised me. If I broke into the apartment to retrieve the original work invoices, you would make the charges go away. I haven't heard from you in five days." Matt yelled back.

"But you didn't get the papers, did you?"

Matt was fast reaching his breaking point arguing with this drenched rat. "I didn't get the papers because they weren't there. I looked everywhere. It took me so long looking, I was still in the apartment when you and your friends carried Harris in. I saw what you were doing."

Jeff was alarmed that someone had seen him. He had left the apartment that night satisfied his plan was a complete success. With Ken committing the murder of one of Bernie's girls, and now to have this nobody tell him he had been seen setting up the blackmail, his perfect plan had unraveled into a twisted train wreck he no longer had control of.

"Not only did I see you, I took a picture. A picture showing you and those women preparing to blackmail Harris. You've got till Tuesday then I'll be using this picture."

As Russ continued to watch, the driver gunned his motor, the tires squealed on wet pavement. The lone man shook his fist, and yelled as the truck roared away.

A brief time later, a rain-soaked Jeff, with his swollen face, walked into Simon's office.

"What the hell's happened to you." a startled Simon yelled out.

Jeff looked at the police detective, surprised to see him sitting there, waiting to hear the answer.

"Oh, you mean my face," trying to make light of his black and blue markings. "It's nothing, a personal disagreement that got a little out of hand." He didn't want to use the 'ran into a door' excuse in front of his boss fearing it would raise more unwanted questions.

"Jeff, I want you to sit down here. The detective and I have a few questions we need truthful answers to."

"You know I've always told you the truth, and I resent the police trying to intimidate me in front of you. I have nothing to hide."

Russ sat and listened; pleased Jeff felt intimidated in front of his boss. Simon spelled out in detail everything Ken had revealed to him for Jeff to hear. Then he added the sordid information the detective had just shared with him.

Uneasiness settled in on Jeff, knowing this to be the first-time Simon had been made aware of the girls. Fate continued to deal him a rotten hand and showed no sign of letting up. It was bad enough when he realized his plan to force Ken out was lost due to a murder. Now he had Matt, in the parking lot, threaten him, of all people, with blackmail. He needed to choose his words carefully or he might end up the one being forced out, or worse yet, be the one accused of murdering that wasted girl.

"I'm sorry. Knowing how much Ken means to you, and with him being my best friend, I felt I needed to spare you the tawdry details of yet another one of Ken's affairs. The girls in the apartment were there because Ken brought them there. I tried to stop him, but you know how he is. As I told the police, I had nothing to do with the girls being there, I don't even know those girls. If you ask me, this is just another case of Ken being caught and trying to shift the blame onto someone else. It hurts me, and I'm sorry that I'm the one to have to tell you, but that's the truth."

Russ watched with delight as Jeff squirmed and weaseled, trying to talk his way out. The lieutenant's idea of squeezing Jeff in front of his boss was paying off.

Listening to Jeff's speech tightened Simon's shoulders and turned his face cold. He had seen enough in his vast dealings over countless years to recognize a bold-faced lie when it played out in front of him. That fatal night, Ken was in no condition to be bringing girls back to his apartment for any reason. The only one attempting to shift blame sat right in front of him. The question Simon had now was why. What was Jeff hiding up his sleeve?

"Okay, Jeff, I appreciate everything you've told me today. You can go back to work now."

With Jeff out of the room, "Detective, I don't know about you, but I'm more confused than ever. If Ken was inebriated to the point he has no recollection of the events from that night, why in the world would Jeff say Ken was the one bringing those girls into the apartment? And if Ken didn't bring them, it had to be Jeff. Why would Jeff be lying to us? What's he trying to hide? After listening to this, I imagine you're not done with him yet. Am I right?"

Evening
Police Services

At the end of the day's debriefing the lieutenant gave his team some welcome news. "Everyone's worked hard this past week, staying late most nights. I think we all need a break; I want everyone to go home on time tonight. Have a good weekend with your families. Rest up and come back Monday, ready to go again."

To Russ, this was especially good news. Home life these last couple of days had been testy to say the least. An uninterrupted weekend with him taking care of the kids. Giving his wife the needed relief, she'd been needling him about, was just what they both needed right now.

"Lieutenant, before we go, could I talk with you for a minute?" Russ asked as the others started to disband.

In the lieutenant's office, Russ didn't know quite how to begin. He was on the verge of shaking the 'Blue Wall'. The members of the force were expected to live by the unwritten code of sticking up for their partner officer, no matter what. Anyone caught breaking the code would be ostracized, thrown out into the cold by themselves. He hoped a quiet word with the lieutenant would be enough to quell his uneasiness.

"Lieutenant, I didn't want to say anything in front of the others, but I need to tell someone."

Melnyk, not sure where this was going, listened.

"When I gave my report about shaking Hughes up at his workplace, I didn't say everything that happened."

"How so?" If his detective had something to say, why would he pass up the opportunity to primp himself in front of the others.

"When I questioned Bernie Habers at his club, he claimed he didn't know the women that left Envy's that night with Hughes and Harris. He claimed they had to be friends of either Hughes or Harris. But when I questioned Jeff Hughes at his workplace in front of his boss Simon Spirling, he said the girls were brought to the apartment by Ken Harris. When I watched the video tape from that night, you can clearly see there's no way Ken could have brought any girls back with him. He was so drunk he couldn't bring himself back. Jeff Hughes is lying. He's hiding something that may very well have led up to the murder."

"Good work, that's exactly what I hoped would happen. So, what's the problem? You have to keep questioning your suspects until one of them cracks and you catch them in a lie. It looks to me like we hit a raw nerve. On Monday, we'll go back after Hughes."

"But then something else happened that seems a little strange to me. It might not have anything to do with the case, but it just didn't feel right with me. While I was sitting in Simon Spirling's office, just by chance mind you, I saw Jeff Hughes outside in the pouring rain having an argument with someone sitting in a truck with the label Eastgate Family Construction on it. Now I couldn't see for sure who was in the truck, but I do know that's the company owned by the Sergeant's husband. And it wasn't just an argument, I'd say it was heated way past the boiling point."

"Are you sure? It's important that you're damn sure you recognized the truck."

"No mistake, it clearly said Eastgate Family Construction."

"What did Hughes say when you confronted him with it?"

"I never mentioned it. I didn't want to say anything in front of Harris's uncle, or until I at least had a chance to talk with you."

Was this the missing piece of the puzzle that got Harris released? Was the sergeant trying to shield her husband? When she was asked to start looking into the unidentified contractor, why didn't she say something then if she knew the contractor was her husband? The fire in his belly burst into flames. Reaching for his anti-acid tablets, he started chewing feverously.

"Okay, leave this with me, and don't say anything to anybody, especially the sergeant."

Chapter 17

Saturday, November 16th
Night
365 Maple Row, Eastgate, the suburbs

While his wife softly gurgled away beside him, Matt, unable to sleep, tossed and turned for most of the night. Grabbing his robe as silently as he could, he crept downstairs to the small nook under the front stairs he called his office. With unfocused eyes staring out, a hot coffee resting untouched in front of him, he sat. Time had become his enemy. Time till the lawyers' threats turned to formal charges. Time till his wife learned of his involvement with Harris and Hughes. Time till she realized he had been in the apartment where the dead girl was found. Time till he ended up as a prime suspect in her murder. His one and only hope pinned to the single picture hidden on his phone. Connecting to his aged bulky desk top computer, he downloaded a copy of the picture. He thought he'd better protect it in a safe place just in case something weird were to happen. He'd only get one chance to use it, but where? Slowly it dawned on him, everything happening to him revolved around the Spirling company. Ken, with his illegal use of company funds and resources, blamed on him. Jeff with his blackmailing of Ken for personal gain at the company, placed him in the crosshairs of a murder investigation. If Jeff didn't come through and get the charges against him stopped, he'd have to cut this all off at the head. He'd have to take the picture to Harris. Plead with Ken to let him off the hook and turn his rage over onto Jeff. It was his only chance.

"Honey, why are you up so early? Why are you on your computer, it's Saturday?" asked his bleary-eyed wife, wrapped tightly in her housecoat.

"I'm sorry, I didn't mean to wake you. I just have a lot on my mind and couldn't sleep."

Sitting down beside him, Karen stole a sip from his cooling coffee. "What's the matter? You've been sulking around here all week. Now tell me what's on your mind. Is my having to work late every night this week bothering you?"

"No, it's not that."

"Well tell me. Is it something with your work? Are you overdrawn at the bank again? I can't help you unless you tell me." Hearing no reply, Karen resigned herself. If he wasn't going to tell her what his problem was, later when he went out, she'd have to check his computer to see what he'd been playing with.

Matt would love to be able to tell her everything, but he knew he couldn't. She carried a badge, and until he got himself free from the grip tightening around his throat, he had to keep his problems secret. He looked at her, "Do you love me?" In his troubled mind, it all might boil down to the answer to this simple question.

"That's a silly question. You're my husband. Of course I love you. Stop fooling around and come on back to bed" Now she knew she had to check the computer. Why would he ask a question like that unless he's done something he's ashamed of?

Matt finally started to drink his cool coffee. Tuesday morning, one way or another, something was going to happen.

Night
Club Envy

Scanning the dance floor through the one-way mirror hidden on the back wall of his office, always put a smile on Bernie's face. Another Saturday night and another packed house. The dance floor was filled with nimble bodies gyrating in time to the waves of pounding music. Flashing colored lights, rebounding off shiny dresses, bounced back into overly made-up eyes. In the corners and around the walls, couples were locked in deep embraces, oblivious to their surroundings. At each end, the crowded bars served out the watered-down booze. The regulars were there, eagerly dishing out their weekly mad money, held in tight jean pockets and tiny clutch purses, desperate to feel the release from their mundane work-a-day lives. In the mixture wandering around, a nice assortment of newbies, chattered, wide eyed, soaking it all in. Bernie never tired watching the constant struggle of life that kept a steady flow of money pouring into his pocket. Over on the side, he spied Rochelle, one of his girls, slowly sipping from a tall plastic glass searching out a target for the night. Bernie, reached behind him and pushed the small button on his desk. One of his security guards hustled in, quick to respond to the silent summons.

"Yes Mr. Habers."

Pointing out through the mirror, "Go over there and tell Rochelle I want to see her."

"Come on in darling" as Rochelle nervously inched through the office door. "Sit down, we haven't chatted for a while, have we?" She knew when Bernie wanted to chat, you kept your mouth shut and listened. Bernie didn't chat to be sociable. "I haven't had time to see how things went with you last Saturday night." Bernie wanted to find out some details to fill in the holes of what he knew. He and that dumb detective had watched the start of the evening, all recorded on the private party room tapes, and he knew somehow the evening ended with a murder. "Now don't hold back, I want you to tell me everything."

"Nothing much happened. I did as you wanted. I slipped the poor sap a little party favor and he passed out. Your friend and I carried him back to his place. He took a bunch of pictures as we made nice with the passed out guy on the bed. Then we left. All pretty boring. I came back and closed the evening out here at the club by myself."

"Now darling," Bernie rose and stood beside the girl, gently stroking her hair. "A little more than that happened." He wrapped his hand around a clump of hair and started to twist as he continued to chat with a smooth voice. "I told you, I want you to tell me everything."

"That's all that happened, I swear" with her head now pulled back, forcing her to look up at her tormentor.

"A little bird told me that somehow, your partner went and got herself killed."

"She wasn't my partner," Rochelle was quick to shut down any ties with the dead woman. "I never saw her before. I thought she came with your friend. Honest. When we left, she stayed behind. I didn't know she went and got herself killed. I thought she stayed behind, passed out on the bed beside the stiff."

Back to gently stroking the mane of hair, "You wouldn't lie to me now would you darling?"

"Never, Bernie, that's the truth. You can ask your friend, he'll tell you."

Bernie was going to more than ask Jeff, just as soon as he was safely clear of the police.

"Okay, darling, you go back inside and have a good time. Tell them at the bar tonight's on me."

Bernie had one more thing he had to do. He pressed the button again.

As the security hulk entered, "I want you to take Rochelle on a little trip. Take her to our club in Glendale and see that she stays there until I call her back. No rough stuff, I just need for her to be out of reach for the next couple of days. Understood?"

"Yes sir Mr. Habers."

"Good boy."

Chapter 18

Monday, November 18th
Morning
Police Services

The lieutenant mysteriously informed his waiting team, "We'll hold off with this morning's briefing. There are a few things I have to deal with first. Everyone, just pick up where you left off on Friday."

Russ danced gingerly around his sergeant, guiltily not wanting to get into any kind of dialogue with her. He had work to do. Early this morning, when he first arrived, he dispatched a couple of uniforms to pick up Jeff Hughes who was now waiting upstairs. He hoped to ease his conscience by getting some answers out of Jeff about his Eastgate dealings.

Karen, at her desk, livened up her computer. In the records search field, she began typing in 'Fredrick Upton' then 'Fred Upton', then 'Rick Upton'. Slowly the machine typed back to her. I knew it, she thought, proud of herself, reading the blocks of texts scrolling across the screen.

- Aggravated Assault
- Stalking
- Indecent Behavior

The list went on covering several years. There were no convictions. Charge after charge dismissed.

"Lieutenant, I'm going back out to 10A to question Fredrick Upton again." With the background info she had now, she wouldn't be so nice. The bully Upton was going to talk with her or come back in cuffs.

"Hold on for a minute Sergeant, I'd like a quick word with you in private."

*****

Upstairs in interview room #3 Russ sat opposite an aggravated Jeff. Driving his fist onto the table, "You can't keep dragging me in here every time you feel like it. I've got an important job I have to do. I don't have time for this." Jeff said. The swelling of his lip had receded, but his eye maintained its purple hue. He was growing tired of being yanked around whenever the police felt like it. Friday's stunt of trying to scare him at his workplace in front of his boss, had almost succeeded, but he was too clever for them. He had his boss Simon totally fooled. This dumb ass detective didn't have a chance.

Russ had to use all his strength to hold it in. If he started to crack even the slightest smile, he knew he would break out into an all-out belly laugh. Jeff's days on his so-called important job were numbered. As far as Russ was concerned, this was a dead man walking. Pointing to the cameras in the corners with their red blinking lights dark, "I'm not recording this. There's only you and me here, so cut the crap. Your bravado isn't fooling anyone. Everything we say is completely off the record. I need some straight answers."

Jeff slouched back in his chair, not sure what to make of this new tactic. When you're talking with the police nothing is off the record. What is it the detectives' after? Weary about any accusations of trying to set up Ken for blackmail that might arise from Matt Langdon. After the questions from Simon on Friday, he took preemptive measures and deleted all the pictures of that night from his phone. He had no worries of Bernie getting involved. That's all-ancient history now. The only thing left on the table was the murder. There's no way Ken was going to be laying that on him. Ken had to have killed the girl sometime in the night after he left.

"On Friday, I witnessed you having a heated argument in the parking lot with someone sitting in an 'Eastgate Family Construction' truck. I need to know who you were arguing with and what it was about?"

So that's it, a little office loyalty going on. This guy's probing to see if his partner, through her husband, is somehow linked into the murder. Well, isn't that nice. Matt's going to be sent down not only for Fraud but also possibly murder, and when he does, the wife is going to be traveling with him.

"Listen, I was arguing with Matt Langdon, the owner of 'Eastgate'. Our firm is on the verge of suing him for Fraud and Theft. It was fully investigated by our company lawyers, and they found evidence proving him guilty. In desperation, he's begging me, trying to bribe me, into cooking our books to get him off the hook. The argument you saw was him not taking no for an answer. I couldn't do that to my company. They're a good company and have always treated me fairly."

Russ took in all Jeff had to say. It was a little half-truth buried in a whole lot of lies. But he found out what he wanted to know. The sergeant's husband was involved, but did she know about it and in knowing, try to point the investigation away from the truth. Satisfied he did the right thing in reporting the argument to his lieutenant. His conscience was clear. It was now out of his hands. Maybe the lieutenant might be forced to turn this over into the hands of Internal Affairs.

*****

In the lieutenant's office with the door closed tight, Karen couldn't think what he wanted her for that was so secret.

"Sergeant, have you started looking into the unknown contractor your Eleanor Upton claims to have seen the night of the murder?"

To Karen, it was a curious question to ask. "No, not yet. At the briefing I told you I wanted to chase down Eleanor Upton's husband Fredrick first. I'm only one person, I can't do two things at once, and my instincts are telling me somethings not right with Upton."

"Are your instincts telling you that or are you avoiding looking into who the contractor is?"

"Why would you say something like that? I'm going to get to the contractor right after I have Fredrick Upton straightened out." The lieutenant wasn't making any sense. Why would she possibly be avoiding looking into the contractor. It was on her things to do list and it'll get done soon enough.

The lieutenant wanted to make sure he was giving his sergeant every opportunity to come clean if she had any inkling of what her husband was up to. Hearing no acknowledgement, he had no choice. He'd have to now go to Internal Affairs and leave the matter in their laps. "Okay Sergeant, I just wanted to give you the chance to discuss any problem you might have."

Karen stood to leave "I've no problem I can't handle by myself."

Mid-Morning
Jeff Hughes Apartment

Climbing out from the back seat of the police cruiser that returned him home, Jeff noticed a familiar car parked on the other side of the street with its engine running. It had visited his apartment once before. Sprinting, he headed towards the front door and the safety within.

"Hold on" Maurice called out. "Mr. Habers wants to see you."

Jeff pretended not to hear the beckoning command and continued trying for safety.

"Don't make me come to get ya. You wouldn't want to keep Mr. Haber's waiting now, would you?"

It was no use trying to escape the inevitable. When Bernie wanted something, it was better to comply. Much better for your health.

Bernie was seated in his office, while his assistant Hailey, stood behind him, using her long strong fingers to dig into her boss's pliable shoulder muscles. "Thank you darling, that was wonderful. If you can leave us now, Jeff and I have a little business to discuss." Without saying a word, giving a broad seductive smile towards Maurice and Jeff, Hailey wobbled out. As she passed Jeff, he smelled the light hint of jasmine from her lingering perfume.

"That's a lovely shade of purple you're wearing on your one eye. Maurice told me how you ran into a door. You have to be more careful. There's a lot of doors out there, aren't there Maurice?"

Jeff half turned to see Maurice, a stone pillar, standing in front of the only escape.

"Jeff my friend, do you remember what I said to you when you asked me to set up a special birthday party for your friend? I believe I said something like... 'if this blows up in your face, it has nothing to do with me'... do you remember me saying that?"

Jeff meekly nodded his head.

"Then why Jeff, why have I had the police here, interviewing me, crawling around my club demanding copies of my video tapes. Threating my whole operation. And why am I being linked into your murder."

"I'm sorry, Bernie. The murder was a shock to me too. It's all the fault of Ken Harris. I have it all under control now. You won't be bothered anymore, I promise."

"Oh, I wish I could believe you; don't you wish you could believe him Maurice?" The stone pillar never moved.

"It's true. I was dragged in by the police this morning. I was questioned all about Ken. They're in the final stages of wrapping the case up. Ken is going to be arrested and charged with the murder of that girl any day now. Even the papers are reporting it." Jeff saying anything, desperately trying to try to talk his way out of this.

Bernie pondered Jeff's haggard response "I asked Rochelle who the dead girl was. She told me she didn't know. Said the girl was one of your friends. I've had to take Rochelle and put her in hiding till all this blows over. What kind of game do you think you're playing with me?"

Oh God, could this get any worse? Now Bernie believes the murdered girl is a friend of mine and I'm trying to set him up for her murder. "Honest Bernie, I don't know who the girl was. She just followed Rochelle and I when we deposited Ken at his home. It had to be Ken who murdered her. She was alive when Rochelle and I left the apartment. Honest." The sound of pleading mixed heavily with a dose of fear filled his voice.

"You better be right, for your sake." Turning to Maurice, "Don't you think our friend here better be right?" Maurice stood silently, rubbing his concrete hands together. "Ok, get him out of here." As Maurice hauled Jeff out of the office, "If I have to see you again, I won't be so nice."

Noon
Jackson County Crematorium

Two men, dressed in their standard undertaker's uniforms, black slacks, shoes and jacket worn over a white shirt with dark tie, pushed the squeaky wheeled gurney carrying Jane Doe#6 off the loading dock into the center of the holding area. Jane rested quietly inside her six-foot white cardboard box with bold black letters stenciled on the top 'Human Remains'. Back at the M.E. Mortuary, Dr. Amile had dressed Jane for her voyage in an open backed blue hospital gown, then imaging she might get cold on her trip, covered her with a fresh crisp white sheet. Before securing the lid, she slipped a single flower from her desk into the box. Anna hated this. Her job was to use the special skills she learned from years of studying combined with months of hands-on training to bring meaning to senseless loss of life. She worked through the blood and gore of broken bodies searching for clues vital in determining causes of death. Dr. Amile wanted to give the grieving families a sense of peace. With Jane, there was no grieving family to receive peace.

Unable to bear the thought of sending Jane on her final journey alone, Dr. Amile, waited in the holding area beside the white cardboard box. The slight sound of an organ playing drifted around the pair. As if on que, Alice Jacobs approached. "Good afternoon, Dr. Amile." she greeted in a hushed voice. Anna nodded but didn't say anything. She knew Ms. Jacobs through their ongoing mutual work relationship. Jacobs was a middle-aged woman of average height, wearing short stubbed heels, dark hair pulled back tight which revealed a cream face that required little makeup. "Who have we here?" Dr. Amile reached into her valise, handed Jane's paperwork over. "If you can just give me a moment" Alice said retreating to her office to complete the required legal formalities.

Dr. Amile stood, silently taking more of the personal weight on her shoulders. Weight, she had been warned not to place upon herself. The hypnotizing drone of the background organ music caused her to drift, making her place her hand on Jane's container for support.

"Everything's in order, we'll take her from here." Alice said. Then as an afterthought, "You never found out her name?"

"No."

“Pity.”

Outside the entrance doors, Anna stopped to fasten her jacket, bracing against the cold November breeze blowing across the steps. Lieutenant Melnyk, red faced, huffing climbed the stairway, “Am I too late?”

“Yes, it’s all done now.”

Taking her hand, he squeezed it gently. “I tried Anna, I really tried.” All formalities gone.

“I know you did, Tom, but it doesn't matter now” squeezing his hand in return.

Afternoon
Roxworth Towers, Apartment 10A

Bracing herself, Karen pressed the doorbell. The dark wooden door stayed defiantly closed to her command. Karen knew Fredrick had to be home. If Eleanor was alone, the crack in the door with the watery eyes peering out, would have showed as the sergeant stepped from the elevator. She wasn’t going to be deterred. She’d stand here ringing this damn bell all afternoon if she had to. *Ring...Ring...Ring*, she commanded as the door never moved. *Ring...Ring...Ring*, and again *Ring...Ring...Ring*. The sudden swiftness of the wooden barrier as it sprung open startled her. A grubby rotund Fredrick stood in the gaping doorway, and menacingly stared at her. Prepared as she was, she couldn’t help the feeling of dread that women get, while walking down a dark deserted street at night, hearing *clip, clip, clip* from shoes approaching behind them.

“Mr. Upton, —” Karen abruptly cut off.

“Who do you think you are ringing my doorbell like that? I told you once before to leave us alone. What part of leave us alone can’t that little female brain of yours understand?”

The thought of this bully attempting to belittle her, infuriated Karen. All through her progression in the force she had been subjected to it. She didn’t take it then, from people far greater than this beast, and she wasn’t going to take it now. “Mr. Upton, I’ve had just about all I’m going to take from you, so you might as well stop. You’re one step away from being arrested for Obstruction of Justice as it is.”

At the threat of being arrested, Fredrick notched down his stance. He’d spent nights sitting in cells in many different places because of women trying to push him around. A bully knows when he’s being pushed and when to push back. The firmness of this woman police officer told him now was not the time to push.

“I’ve checked into your background, and you’ve been rather busy. There’re charges dating back over the last several years of Aggravated Assault, Stalking, Indecent Behavior.”

“None of them proven. All those charges were from women that lead you on then go screaming foul to the police. I’m an innocent man. Women like you won’t leave me alone.”

The sergeant's skin developed a creepy crawly feeling spreading over her as she listened to Upton’s attempt to rationalize his long running behavior.

“My past has nothing to do with you investigating a murder” he defended himself.

"True but adding your past with your unwillingness to co-operate, makes me wonder what it is you're trying to hide."

Fredrick wanted to put an end to the harassment from this overbearing woman before he did something he knew he'd regret. "All right, ask your question. Then get out of here."

Karen really couldn't think of one. This man just ticked every one of her dangerous boxes. She wanted him to know she knew what kind of a man he really was. He wasn't going to get away with anything as long as she could stop him.

"Mr. Upton, I'm going to be keeping my eye on you."

'*Slam*', so hard the door frame jiggled.

On the ride down the elevator Karen thought to herself, while it didn't add anything to the murder investigation, it was something she had to do. Tomorrow she'd buckle down and search out the mysterious contractor. Maybe she had delayed the contractor search as the lieutenant indicated, but to her it was worth it. If a short delay in the investigation stopped one creep from preying on women, she felt she did the right thing.

Evening
365 Maple Row, Eastgate, the suburbs

Parking in her empty driveway Karen could tell her husband Matt wasn't home yet. He must be still out somewhere on a job or giving an estimate for possible upcoming work. Lord knows he needed any work he could get. Just as well, it'd been a long day and after her time with Fredrick Upton she felt the need for a good hot cleansing shower.

Stepping out from the shower in her steam filled bathroom, warm droplets of water streaked down her tight body onto the floor. Wiping away the fog coating, she pondered the aging woman in the vanity mirror looking back at her. Using her fingers, she tried to bring some order to her damp mess of hair, but the attempt proved futile. Karen didn't do it often, or often enough for her husband's liking, but the old lady in the mirror told her she had a need to girly herself up. Pulling on her thick cotton robe, she sat down at the small decorative makeup table Matt had made for Valentine's Day several years ago. Applying makeup was never a skill she was any good at. As an art, it took plenty of practice to perfect. Working in the heavily testosterone laden police force she learned it was better to hide her femininity away and approach the male herd as an equal.

Making her way downstairs she couldn't help feeling a little foolish. Having painted her face ready for a night on the town, she chose to remain inside the comfort of her robe and didn't get dressed. Passing the small office nook under the front stairs, she remembered Matt had been toying with his computer instead of snoring in bed beside her. Curious why he asked the dumb 'Do you love me' question, she sat down and turned the bulky black computer on. All during this past week, whenever Karen would sit back, done for the day, in her padded recliner with feet up trying to wind down, she'd been subjected to a steady stream of little questions from Matt. Her husband might have thought he was being coy by shading his questions as, 'How was your day?'... 'What did you do today?'... 'Who'd you talk to today?' but Karen knew when she was being probed. She herself was a master of the subtle technique. It was unlike her husband to show any interest in her job. He never had an interest before, but for whatever the reason, he was showing an increased interest in her Roxworth Towers' murder now. The last thing she sure didn't want to do was to spend her evenings rehashing her workday struggles.

Thinking she couldn't help him, as she always had done in the past, unless she knew what his problem was, she opened the file folder tagged as Recent. There were two items resting inside of the folder. A letter from the legal office of Peters, Peters and Cohan, and a photo. Knowing the lawyer Cohan to be acting as legal counsel for the murder suspect Ken Harris, she clicked on the letter.

'To Eastgate Family Construction.

Sir,

This is to inform you that our client, Spirling World Supply, after an exhaustive investigation, has determined you have dealt fraudulently...'

It went on. Karens' eyes followed the words displayed on the flickering screen, having a hard time absorbing what was being told.

'... unless there is full restitution of all funds within ninety days, we will have no other recourse other than to bring formal charges of Fraud and Theft against both you and your company....'

Clicking on the photo it opened in full vivid color. A single picture filled the screen, revealing far more than she had ever expected. She recognized the participants instantly, Harris, Hughes, a strange naked woman and Jane Doe #6, all in the bedroom of apartment 10B. She didn't know why this revealing photo now resided on her husbands' computer. The photo time stamp placed the picture shortly before the murder of Jane. This made no sense to her. Pulling the robe tighter around, trying to fend off the iceberg growing inside her, she went through the alarming letter again, hoping she made a mistake in what she had read.

This had to be what the lieutenant was hinting at when he questioned her about her delay in not investigating the mysterious contractor lead Eleanor Upton had given them. The lieutenant already had to have known the contractor skulking around the crime scene was her husband. There'd be no sleep tonight. When Matt finally got home, Sergeant Karen Langdon was going to need a lot of answers before she could go into work in the morning. She headed upstairs to wash the damn makeup off her face and get dressed. Karen knew you didn't interview a potential murder suspect in your bathrobe.

Evening
Police Services.

Leaving his half eaten microwaved dinner for his dog to finish, Lieutenant Melnyk cruised back into work. The phone call he received made it clear he was being summoned by Internal Affairs to discuss a disturbing allegation against one of his officers. An allegation serious enough it couldn't wait till the morning. Earlier, after hearing the 'Eastgate' truck argument from his detective, then hearing no adequate response for the delay in finding the murder scene contractor from his sergeant, he had made up his mind. First thing in the morning he was going up to the fourth floor to Internal Affairs. Now that task had been taken out of his hands, someone had beaten him to it.

Approaching the door, he heard the '*click*' as the lock released. As he stepped inside a commanding voice called out from the end of the hallway. "Lieutenant Melnyk, down here."

What struck the lieutenant the most was the silence. Having just transitioned from the outer chaotic hum of the police offices into this eerily quiet internal chamber was un-nerving.

"Sit down Lieutenant."

Taking his seat across from two I.A. officers who didn't have the curtesy to introduce themselves, Melnyk looked around the barren room. In the top corner he recognized the blinking red eye. Realizing this whole twilight scene was meant to instill a touch of fear, the lieutenant sat back feeling his stiffness ease away.

"What can you tell us about the Sergeant Karen Langdon issue?"

Direct, to the point, but a little too broad based for the lieutenant. He was going to make them narrow down their search. He did not want to release a can of worms by accident. "You'll have to be a little more specific. What issue are you referring to?"

Leaning intimidatingly forward the suit to the left snapped "This is no time to play smart Lieutenant. One of the officers under your immediate command has been accused of very serious actions. Actions, let me point out, you apparently did nothing about."

"I deal with all kinds of issues every shift, so be careful with what you're saying." Not wanting to get pushed around the lieutenant responded defiantly. “Now what exact issue are you talking about?”

The hefty investigator to the right, was squeezed uncomfortably into a brown suit two sizes too small for his bulk. “The issue we’re interested in concerns the apparent tie your sergeant has directly linking her, through her husband, with one of your prime suspects in the Roxworth murder. You need to tell us what you know about this link. When were you made aware of the possible conflict of interest from one of your lead investigators in the case and what have you done, if anything, about it.”

Melnyk didn’t like the insinuation they were throwing at him of him being incompetent in his responsibilities. “I first became concerned with my sergeant, when in the middle of an interrogation with the suspect Ken Harris, his demeaner changed from being worried to being cocky when Sergeant Langdon was introduced to him. This link later surfaced again when my detective, Russell Cravers, witnessed a heated argument that occurred between someone in an Eastgate construction truck and our second suspect Jeff Hughes. I had given the assignment to locate a potential third suspect to the sergeant. A witness recognized him as a contractor being at the crime scene the night of the murder. An assignment she appeared to deliberately stall in favor of a personal gut feeling she claimed to have gotten from the witness’s husband. With this information I confronted Langdon to give her the opportunity to defend herself. Upon hearing no valid explanation, I planned to notify Internal Affairs first thing this morning.”

“Well lucky for you we were notified personally by the Police Commissioner. You can go now but remember this is a confidential matter not to be disclosed with anyone, especially Sergeant Langdon."

On his drive home in the dark, Melnyk was irked by the high-handed dealings of the two suits. Telling him he 'could go now' as if he were some kind of lap dog they could summon and dismiss as they please. Why was the Police commissioner personally involved? How did she know about the daily interactions going on amongst his squad?

Late Evening
365 Maple Row, Eastgate, the suburbs

The headlights from his truck swept across the wall above her head as she sat in the dark waiting. During the course of her career, she had interrogated hundreds of suspects, but this was going to be different. She had to keep reminding herself. The man coming in the door wasn't the man she married. He was a suspect whose dark secrets she had to pry out, without mercy, if necessary, to get to the truth. She had solid evidence her husband was not only on the verge of being charged with Fraud and Theft, but worse, he was present at her crime scene moments before the murder was committed. In this interrogation, Karen Langdon's first question was to herself; did she even know who her husband was?

"Hi Hun, sorry I'm late." Matt said as he fastened his truck keys to the hooks behind the back door. "Why are you sitting in the dark?"

Karen took a long moment to size up her husband, thinking back to the 'Do you love me?' question he had asked. It was a question that didn't seem so foolish now.

Making himself a coffee, "Would you like one?"

"No, I need for you to sit down here and answer some questions. And I want truthful answers." Only with truthful answers could she determine what her next steps would be.

By the tone of her voice and the seriousness in her eyes, Matt realized his wife finally knew his dreadful secret. Sitting opposite her, filled with trepidation, he let out an audible sigh, "You know, don't you? I'm so sorry. I never meant this to happen, but once it started, it continued to snowball, and I couldn't stop it."

"Being sorry now doesn't help. If you had come to me right at the start, maybe I could have done something. But you didn't, and now it's far too late. Now tell me everything, leave nothing out, and for God's sake don't lie to me."

Matt took a deep breath and began his story. It was a story detailing his descent from being a loving husband down to a despicable, lying, dishonest murder suspect. He held nothing back, and only stopped occasionally to wipe the tears of shame that flowed down his cheeks.

Karen understood the fraud and theft. Her husband, trying to stupidly seize the chance to finally improve, was taken advantage of, set up to take the fall for a devious Ken Harris. Having dealt with Harris, she was well aware of Ken's mastery of manipulation to anyone who was vulnerable enough for him to use. These were crimes of business. Crimes that could be handled by contracts, lawyers and courts.

But she needed to hear all the details around the murder.

"....and while I searched for the missing invoices, I witnessed Jeff Hughes using a couple of naked women, preparing to blackmail a passed-out Ken Harris. That's where the picture came from. I secretly took the photo that night. I hoped to be able to use it to get all my problems wiped clean. I met with Hughes, told him I had the picture and gave him till tomorrow morning or else I was going to take the picture to Harris myself."

"And what did you expect Harris to do for you?" Karen asked in disbelief.

"Once I was able to prove to Ken what Jeff was attempting to do I thought he'd be grateful and call off his company's lawyers. I could be free and out of this death spiral he started me on."

Karen recognized the crazy logic reasoning her husband put forward. And some parts of it made sense. That is if you were dealing with normal people, but neither Ken nor Jeff were normal. "How many times must you get bitten by a snake to recognize a snake? Both Harris and Hughes are snakes, and neither one of them can be trusted. Can't you see, dealing with those two has just gotten you in deeper and deeper?"

"But what else could I do? I had no choice."

"You should have come to me. I could've stopped this."

It was always Karen as the breadwinner, controller of the purse, and Matt always had to accept it. He accepted he would never be the leader of his family; he was just part of Karen's team. He struggled through his days wearing the skirt, until Karen came home from work, wearing the pants. How could he come crawling to her for help on his knees again? There had to be a time when he stood on his own feet. "I couldn't, I just couldn't. I got myself in this mess and I thought I could get myself out of it, for once, without you having to always bail me out."

She had a lot to think about. As a police sergeant she had enough cause to drag Matt down to the station and throw him in a cell. As a wife she had to figure out if there was a way to get her husband out of the mess, he'd gotten himself into.

"Listen to me, this is what I want you to do." Karen had made her decision. Putting her career on the line, for right or wrong, the wife had won the debate. "You're going to stop dealing with either Harris or Hughes. Tomorrow morning, I want you to take this picture to the law office of Peters, Peters and Cohan. I want you to talk only with Jonathan Cohan. Tell him everything you've just told me and give him the picture. Do you understand? Give the photo only to Cohan, no one else. Then leave it to him. From what I've seen of him, he's smart enough, he might just pull you out of this."

Chapter 19

Tuesday, November 19th
Mid-Morning
Police Services, Second Floor.

In the briefing room, the number of investigators working on the case had grown. The lieutenant, not wanting to give up on the search for Jane's true identity, had some of the crew continuing the hopeless chase of missing persons. Others were kept busy with the never-ending questioning of taxi drivers, store owners, people on the streets, looking for anyone who might know something. "We need to break this case. I know all of you have been putting in a lot of hours, but it's not enough. We're dancing around when I need solid evidence to take to the assistant D.A." Melnyk said to his team.

That's all Russ needed to hear. Lately home life teetered between tense and unbearable as it was. If he had to tell his wife Mary his workload had increased, lord only knows what she would say. Tonight, when he'd finally be able to go home, he'd have to make it a point to get the porch light fixed, even if it took him till midnight. It least that'd be one less thing she'd be able to jab him about.

Sticking her head into the room, “Lieutenant, sorry for the interruption, but there’s a gentleman downstairs, a Jonathan Cohan, claims he’s Ken Harris’s lawyer. Says he has to speak with you urgently.” Carol informed her leader.

Karen knew exactly what the urgent matter was. She had sent her husband Matt to Cohan's office first thing this morning and now the savvy lawyer had the tell all picture and he was running with it. She'd have to wait till this evening to find out how the discussion went and whether or not Cohan was willing to erase the pending legal actions against her husband.

Already Lieutenant Melnyk’s stomach had started to churn. “Send him up to my office.” Then he mumbled under his breath, ‘I’m not done with his client, no matter how much he complains’.

Washing a couple of anti-acid tablets down with a mouthful of cold coffee, Melnyk tried to make himself comfortable in his chair.

“Good morning, Lieutenant, thanks for agreeing to see me.” Jonathan greeted from the office doorway.

“Morning” the terse response as he waved the lawyer towards a chair, “What can I do for you, Mr. Cohan?”

“I’ve recently come into possession of what I believe to be critical evidence in the murder case of that unfortunate young woman who was found in my client's apartment. Evidence, I’m happy to say that proves beyond the shadow of any reasonable doubt my client, Ken Harris, is not guilty of having performed murder. In fact, it proves, like the dead woman, he too is an innocent victim in this tragic affair.”

Melnyk felt Cohan was getting a little ahead of himself by claiming Harris to be an innocent victim similar to the murdered woman, "Hold on Councilor, we're not in a court room here. Before you start claiming your client not guilty, I think you should at least have the decency to show me this so-called critical evidence."

Lifting his briefcase onto his lap, Jonathan retrieved the 8x10 glossy picture, surrendered to him by Matt Langdon earlier this morning, and handed it over to the lieutenant. "Here, see for yourself."

Melnyk took the picture and examined it for a moment. His eyes grew ever wider, "What am I supposed to be looking at?"

Jonathan was getting a little frustrated by the standoffish treatment he was receiving from the lieutenant. "There, right in front of you," he pointed his finger in the air towards the picture. "Can't you see it. It's as plain as the nose on your face."

The lieutenant had seen it. He quickly recognized precisely what it meant but didn't want to concede too easily.

"You can clearly see my client prone on his bed, utterly incapable of any movement. Standing at the end of the bed you can see Hughes directing the two naked girls as he's taking pictures of the action with his cell phone. This photo shows Jeff caught red handed in the middle of what I believe is a case for blackmail gone terribly wrong."

That was exactly what the lieutenant had seen. Holding the solid proof in his hands, he saw his murderer. This evidence placed Hughes in the apartment with Jane at the time of her death. And more, he now had a clear picture of Jane with someone who knew her alive as well as dead.

"Where did you get this picture? Who took it?"

"For now, I'm not saying. If this goes to court, I'll produce him. You'll have to trust me that he took no part in this. It's purely a matter of being in the wrong place at the right time."

Lieutenant Melnyk couldn't stop staring at the glossy he was holding. To see this young woman, Jane, alive, unsettled him. He'd had investigators scouring everywhere trying to pick up any trace of this woman, and now, he held her in his trembling hands. So close, so very close he thought. "Councilor, I have to ask you," he said as he leaned forward across the clutter on his desk, unable to mask the sound of pleading in his voice. "Can the person who took this photo, or your client Harris, identify either of these two women? I can see the one lying on the left of Harris is the murdered victim. Or can they tell us where these women came from? Anything at all would be helpful."

Jonathan felt empathy for the lieutenant. In front of him sat his adversary for over the past week. A man who had pushed him towards his limit in a dogged determination to charge his client with murder. At this moment, it wasn't a seasoned police investigator who asked these questions. It was just a man looking for the answer he desperately needed to free himself from a hidden burden he carried. If he could, Jonathan would have given the answer needed to bring the comforting relief the lieutenant was seeking. "I'm sorry, but I too have asked that very question. You know that my client has only a limited recollection of the events of that night. I would think your answer lies with Hughes. After seeing this picture, he's the one who I'd be asking."

Afternoon
Vivian Mooney's Apartment

It had been days since Vivian had heard anything from Ken. She'd been through a lot. She suffered the shock of being interviewed by the police and by Ken's own lawyer, in a murder investigation, and still Ken hadn't tried to connect with her. But in thinking about it, it wasn't all that unusual. Ken only made contact when it was convenient for him or if he wanted something. Most of the time she'd have to be the one to reach out. She didn't mind, she had accepted Ken's self-centered traits.

Vivian made it a point to carry her cell phone with her wherever she went, to work, grocery shopping, at home. She always wanted to be ready just in case Ken decided to call. The other day, when she was out doing a little window shopping for shoes, she accidently on purpose stopped by Kens' Roxworth apartment. All she found waiting for her was a large wooden door with a police seal on it.

The longer she waited, the more anxious she got. If he wasn't going to call her, she'd have to be the one to reach out and break the ice.

Buzz...Buzz...Buzz

No answer. She decided to let it ring a few more times, hoped he'd pick up, so she wouldn't have to leave a pleading voice message.

Buzz...Buzz...Buzz

"Hello" right at the failsafe hang-up point.

“Hi baby. It’s Vivian.” Ken knew who it was. His phone told him. He had debated whether or not to answer. “I haven’t heard from you in a while and I got concerned how you were holding up.” Vivian said.

“I’m doing okay, all things considered.” Ken was doing more than okay. One problem he had though was he was starting to put on a number of extra pounds. His Aunt Molly had the habit of continually pushing a steady flow of food at him.

“The other day I was in the neighborhood, so I dropped by your apartment, but you weren’t there.”

“No, the police still have me locked out. I’ve had to stay out in the country at my aunt and uncle’s place.”

Visions of country manors, rolling hills and babbling brooks danced through Vivians's thoughts. “That must be wonderful for you. Out in the fresh air, walking in the quiet of the woods whenever you want. Being out of the rat race of this city would be so nice,” she sighed wispily.

“It’s okay for a day or two, but I’m bored out of my mind. You can only walk by so many trees.”

“Oh, I’d love it. I could stroll around enjoying nature all day long.” In her mind she pictured Ken and her, wearing thick, hand knit, matching turtle neck sweaters, waltzing down a wooded pathway, hand in hand, kicking up leaves.

“Well, I can’t wait to get back into my own apartment just as soon as the police release it. In fact, I’m thinking of throwing a ‘Welcome Home’ party for myself.”

Vivian waited to see if Ken would invite her to his party right now. But with Ken, she'd have to wait a little longer until the mood struck him.

12:30PM
Salvador's Restaurant

"Good afternoon Mr. Spirling, so good of you to join us again." the welcoming Maitre'd Angelo greeted. "I've seated your guests at your usual table. Carlotta, come over here and take Mr. Spirling's coat for him." A chubby round-faced woman wearing a green peasant's dress scurried over to help Simon shed his heavy overcoat. Placing a menu under his arm Angelo moved forward. "Right this way." Seating his guest at the table in the chair facing the window, "Can I get you something from the bar while you look over the menu?"

Simon didn't need any time to look over the menu, Salvador's was his favorite place for lunch when he went out. The dwindling number of spare holes left in his belt told of him being out for a few too many lunches lately. Seeing Alister and Jonathan both holding drinks in front of them, "Bring me a bourbon, straight up."

"We have some delicious specials this afternoon" Angelo started into his lunch time spiel.

With the flick of his hand, Simon cut him off, "Later, later."

"Mr. Spirling," Jonathon greeted, anxious to get on to the reason he arranged this private lunch with the two kingpins. "I thought it was time we all sat down and discussed the most recent evidence that has come into my possession concerning your nephew, Ken."

Simon snapped, across the table to Alister, a little concerned with this statement from Cohan. "Alister, I thought you were keeping me up to date. Why is Cohan here saying he has evidence, and you haven't told me?"

"This is all news to me. Jonathan, you better have a damn good reason for springing this on us with no warning" Alister said. He wanted to be sure Simon understood that he had held nothing back and this lunch stunt was all Jonathan's doing.

Simon paid no attention to the banter Alister was rambling on about. instead, he sat with his eyes focused on Jonathan. When his drink came, he took a large gulp from the glass. He allowed the brown liquid to flow freely down his throat, bringing a sweet burn to his expanded belly.

Jonathan, holding his hand up, signaled for the two to stop, "I've invited you both to lunch because we need to talk. This morning I had an interesting guest drop by my office."

An intrigued Alister questioned, "Who would that have been?"

"I was visited by Matt Langdon. You remember him, don't you? He's the owner of Eastgate Family Construction, the one we are about to ruin."

Alister wanted to clarify, "No, that's the firm we investigated for alleged Fraud and Thief, and as we discussed, he's the husband to one of the lead investigators against your client in the murder case. And, just so you know, as we agreed, I did make contact with the Police Commissioner. She was very interested to hear of the link between one of her senior investigators and a potential crook. I believe she was going to put this whole matter in the hands of the Police Department's Internal Affairs. It wouldn't surprise me one bit if this sergeant was out pounding the pavement looking for a new job before this day's over," Alister announced with a great deal of pride at his accomplishment.

Jonathan took a swig of courage from his glass as he prepared to criticize his boss directly in front of their firm's biggest client. "I listened to Langdon's story this morning in my office. Something you should have done Alister." He took another swig of warmth from his glass. "And you know what? Unlike you, I learned the truth. Matt Langdon was tricked by a manipulative Ken. It was Ken who committed the fraud. By bribing your son Arnold with the all-expense trip through Italy, that Simon here paid for by the way, he succeeded in getting the blame thrown over onto Langdon. This whole fraud mess rests with us. If we had done what we were supposed to do, none of this would have happened."

"Now hold on Jonathan. We completed a very comprehensive investigation. That trip you mention was given to Arnold as a reward for the good work he did. I resent what you're implying."

"Resent all you want, I'm not here to accuse anybody of anything. That's all water under the bridge. Alister and Simon, I want both of you to immediately stop all action against Eastgate. We all were wrong, and we need to make it right."

Alister was sitting back in a huff as Simon responded, "If that's what you want, we can do that, but might this not hurt Ken in his legal battle? If there's no charges pending against Eastgate, we won't be able to use it as a way of removing all police evidence against Ken."

"That brings me to the most important point I learned that will interest you." Jonathon went on to describe the photo shooting events that occurred that fatal night. Producing a copy of Matt's picture, he handed it over to Simon. "You're holding a copy of a picture that Langdon took the night of the murder. It clearly proves that it would have been impossible for Ken to commit any murder. He couldn't even move. And the one standing at the end of the bed with the phone taking the sordid pictures is Jeff Hughes. He's the mastermind behind the whole grisly murder night."

"Have you shown this picture to the police?" an eager Simon asked.

"Yes, I thought it best to hand deliver it to Lieutenant Melnyk this morning. Now in all fairness, Alister, I believe you should call off your commissioner friend. If it wasn't for Matt Langdon, we wouldn't have this picture," announced Jonathan.

Simon nodded his head in agreement. "Alister, I think that's something you should do right away. By the look of this picture, Langdon has proven Ken innocent of murder." Looking to Cohan, "What did the lieutenant have to say about Jeff?"

"You don't need to be concerned with Hughes anymore. The lieutenant will be handling him."

A satisfied Simon, raised his hand towards Angelo, "Okay, I'm hungry, lets order."

Alister leaned back, sipped his drink. He had lost his appetite.

Noon
Police Services

After staring at the photo, the lieutenant settled on the next course of action.

At Russ's cubicle, he held the new evidence gingerly in his hand, "Detective."

A startled Russ popped his head up with embarrassment, "Oh, sorry Lieutenant, I didn't mean to doze off. It's just these last couple of late nights, then having to deal with the wife and kids is catching up on me."

"Have a look at this photo and tell me what you see."

Russ studied the photo, "I recognize the location, that's Harris's apartment 10B. Of course, the two are Harris and Hughes. The one girl, the heavier set one, I saw on the party room tapes we got from Club Envy. I didn't see the other one, Jane, on the club video though."

"That's what I thought. These girls definitely came from Habers' club. I want you to go over to the club, and nicely mind you, invite Habers to come visit us this afternoon. Don't take any uniforms. We need to treat Habers with kid gloves if we want to get any kind of truthful answers from him.

2:00PM
Police Services

When the lieutenant entered interview room #1, he was taken aback by the trio confronting him, sitting quietly at the table. In the middle of the group sat Bernie Habers, with his slicked back oiled hair and crème colored suit. Flanked on either side of him, perched two of the most startling women Melnyk had ever seen. On the left, a dark slim woman with a mass of blue-black glistening ringlets and curls that cascaded down to her shoulders. On the right, the complete opposite. A porcelain white skinned, red lipped blond with short, straight hair, complete with just the slightest sweep of bangs that fell across her forehead.

"Mr. Habers," the lieutenant started...

"Please Tom, you and I are old friends. Call me Bernie."

Lieutenant Melnyk and Bernie Habers had crossed paths many times, but he certainly wasn't a friend. Between the two it wasn't respect, rather a cautious awareness of each other.

"Alright, Bernie." the lieutenant said, wanting to keep his prey at ease, "you know my Detective here already."

"Yes, your detective has visited my club a number of times over the last couple of days." Then he added with a smirk, "Detective, my assistant Hailey said to say hello, and she's sorry she couldn't be here with us today."

Russ blushed while the lieutenant frowned.

Looking to the two women, the lieutenant asked, “And who have you brought with you Bernie?”

With a broad smile, Bernie stated. “These two, are two of the smartest lawyers you’ll ever come across. Don't let their good looks fool you, when it comes to law, they’re vicious. And Detective, don’t even bother looking at them, I’m not going to tell you how much their legal services cost, but let's just say you could drive a couple of high-priced cars with what I pay them. Isn’t that right girls?” Bernie chuckled.

The ladies slid their cards across the table to the lieutenant. Both white cards with charcoal embossing. ‘Roberts & Hyser, Attorneys at Law’

“Okay Bernie, you can cut it out.” the lieutenant directed. Pointing to the corner cameras with their red lights blinking, “everything we say is being recorded.”

With that, the curly haired lawyer to the left, Jo Anne Roberts, reached into her brief case and pulled out a small hand-held recorder and placed it in the middle of the table. “And Lieutenant, you should be aware, that in the interests of our client, we too will be recording.”

“Bernie,” the lieutenant said while looking at the blond lawyer on the right, “I’m going to show you a photo and I want you to have a real hard look at it. We want'a know the names of the people in the picture.” As he slides the photo across the table, it is intercepted by Roberts. She studied it then handed it over to her partner.

“Lieutenant,” the blond lawyer, Aida Hyser, started, realizing the picture has all the ear marks of a blackmail scene. “Our client has no knowledge of this, so I’m afraid he is unable to identify anyone as you request.”

“Come on Bernie, at least look at the picture. We're aware that it is an attempted blackmail setup that went wrong, our only interest is in the names of the participants.”

“It’s okay girls,” Bernie stated as he took the picture. “There’s no harm if we can help our good friend here out.” Bernie studied the picture. So that’s what that weasel Jeff was up to he thought. “Tom, of course I recognize Jeff Hughes, he did a little bookkeeping work for me, and in exchange, I let him use our club party room for a birthday party for his friend.”

“And what about the girls Bernie. What about the girls?”

“To be honest with you,” Bernie said as he glanced at his lawyers, ignoring their joint disapproval clearly displayed across their firm faces. “I’ve seen the heavy-set girl. She’s a regular who hangs around the club on most weekends. I believe her name’s Rochelle, or something like that, don’t know her last name though. As for the other one,” he paused, studied the photo, “Nope, she’s completely new to me.”

Hyser piped in, making sure a defensive statement was recorded, “Lieutenant, we realize that these young women are patrons of Club Envy, just as so many other young people are. That's the business our client is in, entertainment for the young. And while Mr. Habers may recognize different patrons, he has no ties with any of them. It is solely a business relationship in which our client provides a service to willing patrons, nothing more.”.

Melnyk, not wanting to give up yet, “Bernie, how would we get ahold of this Rochelle? We need to speak with her.”

"Tom, old buddy, the best I can do is have my security people keep an eye open for her, and if she comes to the club, I'll have them contact you." Knowing full well he had Rochelle securely tucked away so there'd be no contacting with the police.

Chapter 20

Wednesday, November 20th
Afternoon 1:30PM
Police Services.

Something was going on. At first Karen thought she was imagining things, but now, she was sure. Any doubt erased. It was blatant. She definitely was being isolated from the mainstream. All morning she watched the lieutenant spend time discussing the case with the detective, and whenever she came around, the discussion stopped or moved into the lieutenant's office. She no longer had any input when the next steps in the investigation were being hashed out. She could feel she had intentionally been moved from the front-line team towards the sidelines. Even Carol, normally quick to jump on any request, now appeared to drag her feet whenever Karen asked for anything, said she'd have to run it by the lieutenant first. Why? What's happened? Has the old boys club decided now was the time to close ranks and squeeze her out? Was there a promotion in the air that someone has decided she wasn't going to be allowed to receive? She hadn't heard of any. Yes, she thought of herself as determined but certainly not aggressive. Looking back, she didn't think she had ruffled anyone's feathers, at least no one who didn't deserve it. Her coworkers, friends, some she had been working with for years were now treating her like a leper. No one wanted to be near her let alone be seen with her. Her husband had assured her the lawyer Cohan was going to clean up the Fraud and Theft mess, so it couldn't be that.

Worry began to bring back memories of high school. Memories of having to endure the pointing and whispering behind her back. Being pregnant at seventeen, forced her to quit school, ashamed, trying to hide away. She needed to take action to get to the bottom of whatever was going on. Her first step, she had to find out why, because this time she wasn't seventeen and pregnant, this time she wasn't quitting. At fifty-six, she had earned her place, put in her time and she had no plans to let anyone push her out of the way.

"Okay, spill it, what the hell's going on?" She cornered Carol by the coffee machine, and she needed an answer, no matter how long it took.

Nervously Carol looked around, "I'm not comfortable with this. You need to talk with the Lieutenant, not me."

"I'm going to be talking with the Lieutenant, but right now I'm talking with you, and I know you know everything that goes on. So, spill it."

"Don't tell anyone you heard it from me. I don't want to be linked into this in any way," holding her coffee cup with two hands trying to stop the shaking that had started.

"What are you so afraid of? I need to know." This has got to be really serious. What could make old reliable Carol so uneasy?

"I know the lieutenant was ordered in last Monday night, especially to talk with Internal Affairs and since then, they've started asking questions about you. They've been poking around, looking through your reports. That's all I know."

With the words, 'Internal Affairs', Karen could feel the blood draining from her face. Shock, speech left her for a moment. "Why would Internal Affairs be looking into me?"

"I don't know, and I don't want to know. Whatever you've done, I want no part of."

Guilty. If Internal Affairs were looking at you, you were automatically branded a 'Bad Cop'. No innocent till proven guilty. With them quite the opposite. You were guilty and the chances of being proved innocent were slim to none. No wonder everyone had been avoiding her. They all had something to hide. You couldn't do police work without having a few secrets buried away, and no one wanted to fall under the Internal Affairs microscope to have their secrets dug up, exposed to the light.

Internal Affairs worked out of the top floor and were a force unto themselves. They were the cops of the cops. They only reported to the State Department of Justice. They worked in secret with free reign to go anywhere, look into anything and not have to justify their actions to anyone. They kept to themselves. No going out for a beer after work with the boys, no going for a hot dog at the ballpark with the team. Never a piece of cake when Officer Jones or Smith retired. Karen wasn't even sure how many of them were up on the top floor. She just knew they were there, in the shadows and she was here and as long as it stayed that way everything was good.

Karen stormed into the lieutenant's office causing the pane of glass to rattle when she slammed the door. Hearing the bang, Russ shrank down in his desk. Carol turned away. No one wanted to be a witness to what was going to be happening,

"When were you going to tell me? Carol tells me you came in Monday night to talk with Internal Affairs. You once told me if there were ever a problem you were more than man enough to tell me face to face. What's the matter, did you lose your guts? I'm here. Tell me right to my face or are you going to keep playing this game of hide and seek?" Karen, face flame red, was spitting as she talked. If it were possible there would actually be steam blowing out her ears from the pressure built up inside her.

"Sergeant, I just got off the phone with the Commissioner, and was coming to get you." Lieutenant Tom Melnyk was cold. Cold enough that Karen's heated rage wasn't going to melt him. He was man enough to do the job he now had to do. He didn't like it. No lieutenant ever liked it, but he was man enough.

"Sergeant, as of now, you are suspended with pay until this investigation by Internal Affairs is completed."

"What investigation?"

"I've been instructed to inform you today, at four o'clock, you have an appointment with Internal Affairs on the fourth floor, and I'd strongly advise you to get hold of your Union Representative to obtain legal representation before you go."

"And you're not even going to tell me why you're doing this to me?" Karen screamed directly into Lieutenant Melnyk's face.

"It's not me doing this to you. This is coming directly from the Police Commissioner herself. Until they get to the bottom of this, I have to ask you to surrender your gun and badge to me now. They will be returned to you as soon as this matter is cleared up."

This was unbelievable. In all her twenty plus years on the force she had played by the rules. She never once strayed over to the dark side. Oh, she'd had chances. She'd been tempted, but she had been through too much to be seduced. She had given everything she had to the job and now couldn't believe it that this was how the job was planning on repaying her. Guilty, no reason, she hadn't done anything, but the Police Commissioner, from her high office had decided to strike her down. Slowly she reached into her jacket pocket and pulled out her badge. This time not to show in honor, but to surrender in shame. Karen laid her gun down on the desk in pure defiance rather than place it in Melnyk's outstretched hand.

"Make sure you keep them for me. You're not getting rid of me this easily. As soon as this mistake is cleared up, I'll be coming back to get them."

I really don't think so, thought the Chief. Ever since he had been forced to release Harris, he'd been trying to find the connection between the two of them. And now, with her husband being linked directly with the main suspects, Internal Affairs had a lot to go through. All he needed to do was sit back and wait. Once they got their teeth into something, no one ever came back.

Afternoon 2:30PM
Roxworth Towers, Apartment 10B

Ken stood in his doorway, feeling at first a little apprehensive to step inside. Earlier this morning, at his aunt and uncle's mansion, he was overjoyed to receive the call releasing his crime scene apartment. Although, he had to admit, staying at the mansion rather than a hotel was okay in the interim. Now he was able to at last go home. It finally freed him to get back to his life. He missed the city. Missed his routine. Wasting his days walking in the countryside wasn't how he wanted to spend his time. He needed to be among people. People who would be impressed when he walked down the street, dressed in his finery, sipping his drink, heading to the subway. There was no point dressing up going for a morning latte with the trees. The trees didn't care. He was an intruder in the country. The silence of the fallen leaves told him he didn't belong.

The hustle, bustle and chaotic noise of the city eagerly welcomed him back. He loved the city, but right now he didn't love his apartment. It had been violated. Strangers had plodded through. They had touched, poked, searched, moved all his belongings. And the girl. He still didn't understand the girl. Why'd she have to choose his bathroom to die in, his white tiled floor to ooze her dark blood over? Inhaling a deep breath, steadying his will power, he stepped inside. He was home, but strangely it didn't feel like home. Everything was there. It was just different than he remembered. He had to first retrieve the cushions someone left scattered on the floor before he could sit on his couch. The blood-stained footprints on his carpet were still there. While he was absent time hadn't removed them. Slumped back into the padding of his couch, surrounded by the quiet stillness of his apartment, he waited.

Buzz...Buzz...Buzz

It was Vivian. If he answered, what would he tell her?

Buzz...Buzz...Buzz

"Hello"

"Hi baby. It's me, Viv."

"I know."

Late Afternoon 4:00PM
Police Services.

Outside the locked door of Internal Affairs, Karen sat on one of the two plastic chairs pressed tight up against the wall. The sign on the door made it clear, 'No Unauthorized Entry', so she sat and waited, and waited, and waited. Across the hall she could hear the sounds of activity escaping from the Police Commissioner's Office. The muted hum of lighthearted people chattering away combined with the piercing ringing of phones, only heightened her feeling of being out in the cold, alone. In her mind, she played with a dozen different scenarios. So much depended on the outcome of this inquisition. She knew she had done nothing wrong. Her fault lies with being pulled into a whirlpool of greed, deceit, blackmail and murder, all piled on her from her husband. How could he have been so damn stupid and gullible to be used by Harris and Hughes. He had been manipulated for their personal gain, then tossed, and now she was paying the price.

'*Click*' the door lock woke, "Sergeant Langdon, please step inside," an ominous voice crackled from the speaker above the door. On the other side of the opening stood a large man, much bigger than the suit he wore. "Follow me" he commanded. No greeting, just an order as he moved with silent footsteps down the hallway. Close behind, the clacking of Karens stub heeled shoes, the only sounds to break the silence, echoed off the walls.

"Sergeant Langdon," the grey-haired woman, in a dark blue form fitted suit sitting opposite her started in a drawn out monotoned voice, "My name is Lieutenant April Kirby and I've been assigned to look into some rather startling irregularities put forward against you by the Police Commissioner. Allegations concerning you and your handling of the Jane Doe #6 murder investigation." April noticed the sergeant was alone, "You were informed, were you not, of your right to have your Police Union Representative present at this interview?"

"Yes"

"And you choose to proceed on your own?"

"Yes"

"You do understand the seriousness of your situation? These are grave allegations raised against you by very senior ranking officers of your command" the puzzled woman asked, wanting to make sure all her bases were covered.

Now was the time for Karen to firmly state her objection to this whole farce. "I have heard no allegation or charge against me. I am the innocent victim of malicious gossip, false innuendo," and thinking of her lieutenant, "politically motivated slander. I stand on my spotless record of over twenty years of service in the force, and I strongly resent the action you people have wrongly taken by suspending me from my duties."

"Well, Sergeant, that's a nice speech, but we both know that's not quite true, don't we?" The monotoned voice had heard statements like that before. Kirby fumbled through her stack of papers, picked up a pink colored sheet "Let's see what we have here, and feel free to correct me if I'm wrong. You are the lead police officer investigating the sudden violent death of a female, later classified as Jane Doe #6, found in apartment 10B of Roxworth Towers. The apartment is occupied by the primary suspect, a Mr. Ken Harris ..." she continued with the details. "... and your husband Matt Langdon is in the process of being charged with both Fraud and Theft by the suspect's company, Spirling World Supply."

"Stop right there," Karen interrupted. "There are no charges being laid against my husband. Spirling Supply is in the process of correcting a mistake they made."

"Interesting" the investigator said as she scribbled a note on the side of the pink paper. An item to be checked into later. "Let's move on, shall we? A simple review of your husbands' bank account records showed he recently was paid a sizeable amount from the Spirling Company. Money he used to purchase a brand-new SUV for you. Now this looks to us like a little bit of old-fashioned kick back. And there's more. During the night of the murder, a witness, a Mrs. Eleanor Upton, clearly saw your husband enter the crime scene. And when your lieutenant instructed you to investigate this, you stalled. You preferred instead to harass the witness's husband, a Fredrick Upton, possibly trying to discredit a viable witness against your husband."

"That's not true" Karen slammed her fist down on the table. "Fredrick Upton's' record shows him to be a violent threat to innocent women. I wanted to scare him from committing any more atrocities against unsuspecting women."

"Sergeant, the records show there has never been any formal charge laid against Mr. Upton."

"That's because he intimidated his victims, and crafty lawyers get him freed." A cold shiver ran across the back of her neck as she remembered her confrontation with Upton. "All you have to do is look at him and you can see he's evil."

"Sergeant, I can tell you, the charges we have against you are mounting with every rock we turn over. So far, we've got Kick-back, Dereliction of duty, and the Harassment of a witness." Captain Kirby folded her papers into a neat pile. "Your suspension stands until the completion of our investigation. You are to have no contact in any way with this murder investigation, or with the department. And I strongly advise you to seek legal counsel, you're going to need it. Good day, the detective will see you out."

Evening 6:00PM
365 Maple Row, Eastgate, the suburbs

Karen was speeding. The dials on her dashboard pushed hard over and she didn't care. Getting stopped for a speeding ticket right now, ranked as the least of her worries. Her black SUV was throwing dead leaves twirling wildly in the air behind her as it streaked down the roadway. All she could think of was Internal Affairs. She couldn't figure out how Matt's problems landed on the desk of the police commissioner. For Internal Affairs to suggest she was delinquent in her job by trying to shield her husband was laughable. She ran the case over and over in her head. Searched for any area where she might have missed something or screwed up badly enough to get suspended. Nothing. She did everything just as she should regardless of her husband's problems. *Whoosh, whoosh,* Karen passed cars as if they were standing still. *Buzz...Buzz...Buzz,* the ringing of her phone buried in her purse brought her back. Easing her heavy foot from the pedal, she tried in vain to reach her beckoning phone. *Buzz...Buzz...Buzz,* dammit. She pulled over to rummage in the bottom of her bag.

"Hello" she abruptly yelled into the innocent device.

"I'm sorry. Did I get you at an inconvenient time?"

"Who is this?" Today wasn't the day for some annoying telemarketer to be bothering her.

"This is Marg, Margory Taylor, from the bank."

Remembering Marg Taylor, she was embarrassed with herself. A few years ago, when she was in uniform, Marg had approached her looking for some help with a rowdy neighbor problem she had been experiencing. Ever since then, Marg showed her gratefulness towards Karen whenever Karen ventured into the bank.

"I'm sorry Marg. Forgive me, it hasn't been a very good day for me."

"That's all right, but I'm afraid I might make your day even worse."

“Has Matt overdrawn his business account again? I’ll speak to him when I get home. If you need to, move some money from my saving account over to cover it.” This wouldn’t be the first time Matt’s accounts had been on the lean side. The normal course of affairs had Karen backfilling Matt from her savings as he struggled between customers.

“No, it’s not that, Matt’s accounts have been amazingly flush for the last while. I’m not supposed to tell you. It’s supposed to remain confidential, but you’ve been so good to me.”

Karen had no idea what in the world Marg felt she had to tell her so secretively.

“Early this morning, two policemen came into the bank to talk with the manager. Apparently, they took copies of both yours and Matt’s accounts for over the past year.”

An eerie wave ran through Karen, “Do you remember who those officers were?”

“I overheard one of them tell the manager they were from something called Internal Affairs. That’s all I heard before they shut the door. I thought it might be important, so I wanted to let you know.”

It was a little late to be telling her now, Internal Affairs had already accused her of being guilty of Kick-back. “Thanks Marg, I appreciate this.” She ended the call not waiting for any response from her confidant. She knew why they would be interested in her bank account. You combed through a suspect's bank records if you were looking for dirty money from bribes or payoffs from a cop working on the dark side.

She pulled into the driveway just as Matt stepped down from his truck. With a spring in his step and a broad smile on his face, put there from his successful day, he reached over and opened Karen's door. Leaning in, he planted a surprising kiss on his wife's tight lips. "What was that for?" she asked.

"Nothing. I'm just in a really good mood. You were right about going to the lawyer Cohan and laying it all out for him. He was so thrilled to receive the blackmail picture, he told me not to worry. It might take him a few days, but he'd get all the bogus Fraud and Theft actions against us dropped. In fact," slyly with eyes twinkling, "come inside and I'll show you what a good mood I'm really in."

"Now's not the time. It's been a hell of a day and I've got a lot on my mind." she said walking into the house leaving a disappointed Matt still holding her car door open.

Chapter 21

Thursday November 21 st
Early morning
Roxworth Towers, Apartment 10B.

It was that eerie time of sleep, when the last vestiges of night start to be choked off by the birth of the new day. Gray pallor draped the bedroom as morning light from the window fought for dominance over the retreating black of night. Ken, buried deep in his covers, was cold. Curled in a tight ball, with his knees clenched up against his chest, he could not get warm. It had been a tempestuous night of tossing and turning, of sweating and freezing and of dreams. Dreams that wracked his body and pummeled his brain. With his head pressed down hard into his pillow he was now travelling in that space that lies in-between sleep and waking where nightmares grow stronger.

From inside of his bathroom, he could hear the faint whimper of tears drifting out towards him. Struggling out of bed, his legs cramped causing him to stumble towards the closed bathroom door. Fighting to hold his balance, with his ear held against the cool wood, the whimper floated through his brain and enveloped his body. He had never felt so cold. Chills ran freely up and down his spine. The chattering of his teeth behind trembling blue lips didn't drown out the unmistakable sound of a girl crying, coming from the other side of the door. Slowly cracking it open, he saw her. Nearly exactly as he had first seen her, lying in a puddle of blood on his white tiled floor. This time her blood-streaked hair was pulled back showing her bright green eyes filled with tears and her small breasts heaved as she sobbed, gasping for breath. Ken knew, buried somewhere deep in the far reaches of his fog filled mind this couldn't be real. It had to be a dream. She was dead, he had found her, stepped over her, dead. She should've been long gone from here. He told himself he had to wake up. But try as he might, the nightmare wouldn't release him from its icy grip.

"Who are you? Why are you here?" He tried to make some sense of what the dream was trying to tell him.

"You know who I am. You found me here. This is where I belong" the girl replied, through lips that never moved.

"No...No...No" Ken answered, shaking his head. "I don't know you. I've never seen you before. You don't belong here. Go away. Leave me alone."

The dead girl raised her head from the red puddled floor, "My name is Rose, and I can't leave. I have to stay here with you."

"No...No...No" again Ken answered, furiously shaking his head. "Your name is Jane; everyone calls you Jane. Who did this to you?" Then with inquiring guilt, "Did I do this to you?"

The thought gained strength as it swarmed round and round him, 'Did I do this to you? Did I do this to you? Did I do this to you?' He collapsed on the floor beside her. Ken joined in her crying with his chest heaving in time with hers as he too gasped for breath.

The sunlight of the clear crisp November morning found Ken laying prone on his bathroom floor, drenched in sweat.

Morning
365 Maple Row, Eastgate, the suburbs

There was no urgency to get out of bed this morning. In fact, if she wanted, she could spend the whole day snuggled deep inside her blanket cocoon. She had nowhere pressing to go and nothing special she had to do. Exhausted, after she spent most of the long night tossing and turning, unable to quiet her mind while Matt, blissfully asleep sprawled beside her, snoring away at top volume. It wasn't his snoring, that had aggravated her. She was used to his nightly tune. It was the fact he slept so peacefully after his actions had plunged her into this turmoil.

"Here, I brought you a coffee." Matt dressed, ready to begin his day, placed Karens' cracked 'State Fair 02' mug on her bedside table. "You're going to be awful late for work today. You not feeling well?" It was unlike his wife to call off going into work. Matt often joked that if she was on her death bed, she'd be telling the doctors to wheel her into the station.

Karen hadn't told her husband there'd be no going to work today, or any other day until Cohan's changes worked through the bureaucracy of the force. How was she expected to tell him or explain to him her suspension when she herself was unable to understand or accept it. Struggling with herself, she had to get up out of bed. She couldn't wallow away the day being consumed by self-pity. "I'm not going in today. This past week I've worked more than enough overtime hours. I'm burnt out. Think I'm going to take it easy today for a change." This might work for today; she didn't know what excuse she'd use tomorrow. Maybe she'd get lucky and develop a case of the measles or something.

A little dumbfounded at his wife's unusual stance, "Okay, as long as you're alright. I've got a job on the other side of town today; I won't be late. If you need anything you can call me." With a kiss to her forehead that she fleetingly accepted, Matt was gone leaving her alone in her silent house.

Lying in bed, Karen's thoughts travelled back. Her early years had not been easy. A little too much to drink at one of her high school's after-football game parties. True love, or so she had thought at the time, with one of the team stars, and bang! There she was, seventeen and pregnant, alone, and scared. Karen's mother had been the strength and help she needed. She loved helping Karen, supported her through her daily struggles of diapers, feedings, bouts of colic. Encouraged her that things would be okay, that the future was still there. And no one had loved Baby Joyce more than Grandma. Karen's mother was so different than her father. He was disappointed, standoffish, not wanting to be involved in any way or at least any more than he had to be. Karen could see it in his eyes: he couldn't wait for her and that kid of her's to move out.

And now again her life had changed. Yesterday she lived life as a homicide detective, but today, that had been ripped away from her. Yesterday she had been determined, but today she just really didn't care. She looked into the future, saw her day's consisted of moping around the house instead of racing through streets chasing bad guys.

No longer needing to dress in one of her smart business casual outfits that filled her closet, she summoned the energy to pull on a pair of grubby sweatpants and a baggy top. In the mirror she shrugged, this had become her new Sergeant's uniform.

Morning
Police Services.

"Alright, settle down, I have an unfortunate announcement" the lieutenant called out to get the attention of the group. "For reasons I'm not at liberty to get into, Sergeant Langdon has been suspended from active duty." Receiving this information brought an immediate hush to the assembly. Each one of them had heard Internal Affairs had been poking around in homicide and each one had invented their own reasons why. Of all the motives in their thoughts, few had picked Sergeant Langdon as the cause. As a twinge of guilt swept over him, Detective Cravers was one of the few.

The lieutenant briefed his team on the events over the last number of days, being careful to steer clear of any mention of Sergeant Langdon and her problems. Sharing copies of the infamous photo he walked through the ramifications it brought to the surface.

"We can see our Mr. Harris is totally unconscious, so the likelihood of him being able to commit murder is slim. But there is still a chance he could have woken up in the night, and in a foggy stupor, killed Jane, returned to his bed and not remember doing it. So, despite his lawyer's assurances of him being innocent, I'm not ready to completely rule him out.

"And then there's this piece of slime, Jeff Hughes. He's a blackmailer and he's up to his eyeballs with Bernie Habers. He says he doesn't know the girls in the picture. He claimed they were friends of Harris's, and we know that's not true. Hughes claimed he left the apartment the night of the murder with the larger girl, a Rochelle, one of Habers' girls, and Jane was left in the bed passed out beside Harris. We saw him and this Rochelle leaving the apartment in the background from the building lobby camera, but that doesn't mean he didn't kill Jane before he left. And just to make it harder on us, I'm sure Habers' has put Rochelle in hiding so we can't get at her."

"That leaves us with the mysterious contractor. The neighbor from apartment 10A, Eleanor Upton, claims she recognized the lone man sneaking into 10B the night of the murder as the contractor who did some work for Harris during the summer. We now know that contractor to be Matt Langdon."

At the mention of Langdon, a hushed rustle of whispers circulated throughout the group. 'That's the sergeant's husband', 'My God, do you believe that?', 'No wonder she's suspended', 'I met him once, he didn't appear to be that stupid'.

"Alright, alright, settle down. As I was saying," the lieutenant continued, "the contractor was Matt Langdon, and yes, he is the husband of the sergeant. And although the lawyer Cohan won't confirm it, I think it's pretty clear he's the one who took this picture. Now, I can't see why he'd be the one who committed the murder, but he could have. Jane might have woken, startled to find Langdon standing there taking pictures, maybe started screaming and

Langdon in a panic killed her." Looking to Russ, "Detective, we need to talk with Matt Langdon. Take a couple of uniforms and pick him up."

"Lieutenant, can someone else pick him up? I've worked with the sergeant, and it'd be a little weird going to her house to pick up her husband right in front of her." Russ pleaded.

"Detective, not everything is easy. It's your job. Get on with it" the lieutenant ordered his reluctant underling.

Back at his desk, Russ ponders his approach to the uncomfortable task given to him by the lieutenant. This needed to be thought out or it could very easily get out of hand and turn nasty. Actions taken now could come back to plague him later in his career. He didn't want to be spending the next ten years working under the sergeant with a solid wall of animosity between them.

Morning
Jeff Hughes Apartment

Jeff woke with a splitting headache, again. Rummaging around in his bathroom medicine cabinet he found the bottle of aspirin wedged in the back and downed a couple of the white tablets. He was caught between the police, who were constantly pestering him with questions and Bernie threatening him with serious physical violence. The stress was causing him to drink far too much. Jeff was trying to hold the annoyance and worry at bay using the numbing effects of alcohol. It wasn't working, it just made things worse.

He had to go to work this morning after already missing a day earlier this week. The last thing he needed on top of his growing mountain of problems was to have his workaholic boss Simon think of him as a slacker who couldn't be depended on. So far, with quick thinking, he felt he had managed to successfully lie his way out of the fallout from the Ken murder disaster, but he knew he was spreading his luck pretty thin.

As he leaned into the mirror for a closer look, it revealed his tired worried face staring back at him. He looked terrible. The purple shading of one eye had just about faded away, but now two bloodshot eyes took center stage complete with the sullen drawn-out skin from sleepless nights and too much alcohol. He searched around his bathroom cabinet, thinking some strategically applied makeup might help improve his appearance. He found none. His apartment was seldom visited by any female guests leaving trifles behind. He was sure if he asked Betty, she'd have some and would be more than thrilled to help him. Confident that if he pressed her, Betty would easily succumb to his charms he thought half chuckling out loud. But with his quest to shortly be the boss, he felt it wasn't a good idea to have a romantic affair with one of his soon to be underlings. When he was in charge, he'd be running a tight ship. Being the master of trickery, his employees wouldn't be pulling any of the fast ones like the ones he pulled on Simon.

Morning
Roxworth Towers, Apartment 10B

Buzz…Buzz…Buzz

Buzz…Buzz…Buzz

Buzz...Buzz...Buzz

Sprawled out on the cold tile floor of his bathroom Ken struggled to wake, roused by the incessant sounds emanating from somewhere in his bedroom. His ears could hear the ringing, but after his night filled with dreams and nightmares, he couldn't be sure what the noise was.

Buzz...Buzz...Buzz

Buzz...Buzz...Buzz

Buzz...Buzz...Buzz

Staggering to his feet, he looked around to see if he was alone. She was gone. The blood was gone. Reassuringly clean, white floor tiles shone back at him. The clear light of morning had chased her back into the shadows.

Buzz...Buzz...Buzz

Buzz...Buzz...Buzz

Buzz...Buzz...Buzz

His phone, that's what the noise was. His phone was ringing.

"Hello" Ken said meekly, hoping that it was a real person calling. He was unable to leave his nightmare.

"Baby, what's the matter? You sound so weak, are you okay?"

Relieved, it was Vivian, with a heavy sigh he plopped down onto his bed.

"I'm okay, I've just had a terrible night." Ken answered.

"I wanted to stop by tonight on my way home from work, I haven't seen you in so long."

Ken really didn't want to have to deal with the pleasantries required during an evening with Vivian right now, not when he couldn't think straight. "Not tonight, Viv, I'm too wrecked right now. I didn't get much sleep last night and I have a lot on my mind." He thought of the troubling thoughts, Rose or Jane, or whatever she was called, had stirred up inside of him. He needed to dig deep to try to remember his actions from that fateful night. He couldn't do that with Vivian hovering around him. He needed to be alone.

Not wanting to give up Vivian countered. "How about tomorrow night?" Then with a hint of desperation in her voice, "It'd be Friday. We could spend some much-needed time together."

"Call me tomorrow and we'll see." Ken replied as he abruptly disconnected.

Small tears stared to form in Vivians eyes as she put down her phone. She was now reduced to begging. She didn't deserve to be treated so badly, but she couldn't help it. It was difficult being in love with a man like Ken Harris.

9:00am
Spirling World Supply

'*Bing*' "Betty," Jeff paged on the intercom, "Is the old man in yet?"

"Not yet, and it's unlike him to be so late." Betty replied, thinking back to all the times her boss chided her for when she came in even 5 minutes past 8:00am.

"Let me know the minute he arrives; I need to talk with him before anyone else does." Jeff, with a sour stomach now added to his hangover from the four cups of black coffee he'd downed this morning, had made a decision. He was going to have to go on the offensive. He'd been debating what action to take ever since Matt Langdon had threatened him with a revealing picture he claimed to have taken the night of the murder. He needed to find out how much his boss Simon really knew. If Simon was already aware of the picture, it could be disastrous. If he didn't know just yet, there was a chance. With some fancy talking, he felt confident he'd be able to turn it around in his favor. Jeff knew Simon to be too old and set in his ways to be tech-savvy. He'd be able to convince him the photo was a fake. A doctored picture, photo shopped by that criminal Matt Langdon, trying to blackmail both Ken and him. He'd remind Simon it was Ken who was taken advantage of by Langdon, and it was him who uncovered the crooked dealings of Langdon against the company. This was the act of a desperate man trying to use a phony picture in another one of his criminal attempts to get back at the two of them. He'd maneuver the old fool Simon into bringing an end to the delay. Simon must launch the anticipated Fraud and Theft charges against Matt Langdon right now, before it was too late.

'*Bing*' "Jeff, Mr. Spirling has just come in. He seems to be in a really foul mood. Are you sure you want to talk with him now?"

"I'll be right there."

Buzz...Buzz...Buzz

The phone on Jeffs' desk rang.

"Hello, Jeff Hughes here." he hurriedly answered.

"Jeff old buddy. So glad I caught you in."

Jeff recognized the sickly-sweet voice as Bernie Habers. "Bernie, I'm really busy right now, I was just going out the door" Jeff stated, not wanting to get into any kind of conversation with Bernie. He had to get to Simon urgently.

"Now Jeff, is that anyway to talk to an old friend like me? I really think you could spare a moment of your valuable time to speak with your new business partner, don't you?"

Jeff was starting to feel faint. With his sour stomach and pounding head, he couldn't fathom what Bernie was talking about. There was no business partner. In fact, there was no business. "I don't understand. What do you mean, Business Partner? You and I aren't in any kind of business." Bernie had to be losing it, Jeff thought, as he watched the minute hand of his wall clock slip around the dial. Precious time was being wasted with this foolishness.

"That seems a little strange to me," Bernie snidely replied. "I spent most of Tuesday afternoon with my good friend Lieutenant Melnyk of Homicide. Not something I planned on doing, but Tom had a very interesting picture he was determined to share with me."

At the mention of a picture Jeff's ears perked up and his eyes shot open. "The police showed you a picture?" Jeff asked in disbelief. How did Matt Langdon's picture end up in the hands of the police? Why would Langdon give up his insurance picture against him and Ken?

"Oh yeah, it was a very interesting picture in full living color. It clearly showed you and the girls working over your poor passed out friend. Of course, I told the lieutenant that it was all news to me, but as I see it, it looks like you were setting up for a sweet blackmail deal."

"But Bernie," Jeff, with a touch of pleading now appearing in his voice, "You know that night ended up in a murder. The murder wiped out any chance of working a blackmail scheme. You told me you didn't want to be linked into the murder scene in any way."

"It's not the murder that interests me, that's your problem. I want my fair share of the blackmail. Afterall, you did use my club, my drugs, and my poor innocent girl Rochelle. I think I'm entitled to be compensated, don't you? I'm guessing I'm owed, let's say, ten grand. I think that's fair. I want ten grand by Monday morning."

"That's impossible, I told you the blackmail never happened. I don't have ten grand. You got to be reasonable Bernie. I'm up to my neck with problems as it is with that dumb girl letting herself be killed."

"Like I said, old buddy, the murder is your problem. I want my fair share of the blackmail. You have till Monday, so I strongly suggest you get moving on it."

With that, Bernie hung up. Jeff, now pale white, covered in sweat, started to shiver.

'*Bing*' the intercom chimed, "Jeff, I told Mr. Spirling you wanted to see him. He's mad enough as it is. What's keeping you?"

Jeff never answered, he was frozen in thought, trying to think of a way out of the quagmire engulfing him, swallowing him up whole.

9:00am
365 Maple Row, Eastgate, the suburbs

Karen couldn't figure out what to do with herself. She'd already made the bed and tidied the house. That took less than two hours out of her day. Now what should she to do. She had grown used to being out in the world, active, thriving in the organized bedlam of the second-floor cop shop. Wandering alone, from room to room in this silent house was killing her.

She had tried calling Joyce, her daughter, just to maybe hear some small words of encouragement. Some small words that might help get her back on the road to reclaiming herself. But Joyce never returned her calls. The years of Joyce growing up while Karen thought she had been lovingly protecting her daughter from the dangers of youth had driven them apart. It was a mother's love and care made over into a wedge between her and her daughter. Her overbearing protection had robbed Joyce of her teenage years of growth and discovery. School dances, youthful romance, all denied. Joyce had seen the calls from her mother. Had it been her father she would have returned them, but for her mother, she had no time. She had her own life to live. Karen's love was returned by silence, at a time when she really needed someone.

Ignoring the Internal Affairs order, in desperation she called...

"Detective Cravers"

"Detective, this is Langdon, I've got some ideas I think you should be following up on." By being so unceremoniously removed, Karen had left unfinished work. Trails she thought shouldn't be allowed to slip.

“Sergeant, you shouldn’t be calling me, I don’t know if I’m allowed to be talking with you.”

“Listen to me. Even though I’m not there because of some mistaken screw up of the Commissioner, I’m still your Sergeant. Don’t you forget that.” Karen was trying to regain her sense of authority.

Russ listened to the sergeant, “I’m really sorry, but until you’re re-instated, talking with you about the case could land me in a lot of trouble. I have to go.”

Russ heard the audible ‘Choke’ reply from the other end of the phone as he hung up. Karen sat with her eyes stretched open and her mouth gaping. This had to be some kind of evil joke the lieutenant put Russ up to playing on her, and it wasn’t very funny.

9:30am
Spirling World Supply

As he entered Simon’s office, Jeff instinctively had a feeling that lady luck was about to close her embrace against him. Simon sat behind the well-worn desk with his eyes focused on the papers scattered over the top and never acknowledged the entrance of his employee.

“Hum. Hum.” Jeff cleared his dry throat to gain the attention of the bulky figure. Still no movement from Simon. “Mr. Spirling?” Jeff tried again.

Slowly the eyes raised and the disgust they held blazed out towards the creature standing on the other side of the desk. Eyes that were unable to even attempt to disguise the intense feelings boiling inside of Simon.

"Mr. Spirling" Jeff started his canned patter, "I can see you are upset about something, is there anything I can do to help? You know how much this business means to me. If there's anything I can do, all you have to do is tell me and you can consider it done."

Simon kept his eyes locked onto Jeff, and without saying a word shuffled the papers around on his desk, revealing a glossy full colored picture. A picture that he moved forward for Jeff to see. Although this was the first time for Jeff to see the ill-fated picture, he recognized it immediately. Inside, he had to admit, it was a very damning picture, but he was prepared and began his act of innocence.

"What's this?" Jeff picked up the photo and pretended to examine it carefully. He turned the picture this way and that. "Where in the world did this come from?"

In a slow deliberate voice Simon answered "Don't tell me you don't know about this picture. It's a picture of you."

Jeff took his time, drawing it out, "I've never seen this picture before. It's certainly not of me." He held the photo closer to his face, pretending to be able to scrutinize it better. "I don't know where you got this picture, but someone is trying to trick you." With an outstretched arm towards Simon, "Here, have a close look at it yourself. Anyone who knows anything about computers can create any picture they want. This clearly is a fake. It's been photo-shopped by a computer."

Simon never moved. He left Jeff standing awkwardly with the photo held out in his raised hand. Retreating his arm Jeff continued with his planned approach. "This had to have been done by that criminal Matt Langdon. It looks to me like the last act of a desperate man trying to strike out against your nephew Ken and myself. If you remember sir, Langdon was the contractor who took advantage of your nephew and our company, trying to get away with fraud. And if you also remember, it was me who caught onto the theft and alerted you so that our lawyers could investigate. They found clear evidence Langdon is an out and out crook. I think we shouldn't delay any longer. A criminal who would attempt to pull this kind of deceitful act, trying to lash out at Ken and myself is dangerous. We should file the charges of wrongful Fraud and Theft at once. He needs to be stopped."

It took all of Simon's strength to contain himself from breaking out into a fit of roaring laughter. If he had been forty years younger, he knew he'd be leaping over the top of the desk, squeezing his hands tight around Jeffs' neck to throttle him to silence.

"Jeff, I've done a lot of thinking," Simon said in a steely voice, "In the past it pains me to admit that I believed in you. I thought of you as a true trusted employee who could be counted on to always be acting for the good of the company. Now, considering everything that has happened, I realize that this whole caring for the company routine you pulled was nothing more than an act. You were always only looking out for yourself. I now know you'd go to any devious length to try to darken the reputation of Ken. The murder and now this revealing picture of your true intent is the final straw."

"But Mr. Spirling" Jeff hurriedly interrupted. "It's not true, none of it is true. I've told you the photo is a fake by the criminal Matt Langdon. As for your nephew Ken, it's him who has always taken advantage of his position in the company as your nephew. You know that's true. I've only ever acted to protect our company."

"You can stop this wasted effort. Yes, I know Ken has had his share of problems, but he's not the one guilty of murder. And there's one more important piece of information you seem to have forgotten."

In desperation, he saw his whole future collapsing around him, "And what is that?"

"No matter what schemes Ken has pulled in the past, he's family, and I can forgive him. You on the other hand are now done. I want you out of here right now and I never want to see you on company property again. Betty will send you what's owing to you. Now get out."

"But Mr. Spirling," Jeff tried to plead for his life.

"Out. Now!"

Slamming Simon's door, he passed by Betty's desk, "Jeff what's the matter. What has Mr. Spirling done to you?"

"The old fool has fired me. That's what he's done to me. But it's not going to be that easy. You just wait and see."

1:00pm
365 Maple Row, Eastgate, the suburbs

From her kitchen window, Karen watched as Russ and a black and white squad car pulled into the driveway, parking beside her large black SUV. Figuring this to be more of the lieutenant's plan to harass and humiliate her, she decided she'd make them wait. She ignored the tentative tapping on her door. She chose instead to take the time to wash and dry her morning coffee mug. Opening her fridge door, she wasted more time looking inside. She wasn't hungry, it was just part of the stall tactic. '*Tap...Tap...Tap*' a little firmer. Karen headed over to her living room. She cranked the radio on at near full blast. The afternoon news blared, filling the room, drowning out the increasingly strong tapping on her door. Tapping turned to knocking turned to full on pounding, and she still ignored the intruders.

"Sergeant," Russ yelled through the door. "I know you're in there. You don't need to be doing this."

"Go away, you didn't want to talk to me earlier. Now, I don't want to talk with you."

"It's not you I'm here for. It's your husband Matt."

That changed everything. She flung the door open. Stood proud in the doorway. "What do you want with Matt?"

"The lieutenant sent me to bring him in for questioning. Sergeant, I have no choice, I have to bring him in. Where is he?"

"I'm not sure. He left this morning for a job, I have no idea when he'll be back. Why does the lieutenant want to question him?"

"Sergeant, you don't need to play the role of an innocent wife with me. We all know he's the mysterious contractor you were supposed to find. We also know it was Matt who snapped the murder scene photo. There's no point in denying it. He needs to come in to be questioned. I have a couple of uniforms here if it's necessary to take him, but I hope it doesn't come to that."

"I'm telling you he's not here. The best I can do is bring him down to the station myself first thing in the morning. If that's not good enough for the lieutenant, that's too bad."

Russ didn't like the thought of having to return empty handed to the lieutenant. He debated searching the house, but without a warrant he knew the sergeant would surely stop him. He could wait outside for Matt to turn up, but lord knows how long that would take, and he had enough problems going home late at night as it was. "Alright, first thing in the morning, you promise?"

Karen shut the door without answering. The detective had no right questioning her word, and the hell with the lieutenant.

Chapter 22

Friday November 22 nd
Morning
Police Services.

Picking up her ringing phone "Carol here."

"This is Sergeant Omily down at reception. Sergeant Langdon and her husband, a Matt Langdon are here wanting to come up. She says her husband is to be interviewed, but there's a notice on my wall saying the sergeant is not to be given access. What do you want me to do?"

"Just have them wait for a couple of minutes until I can locate the lieutenant."

On hearing the instructions to sit down and wait Karen's pulse started to raise, "What do you mean wait? Did you tell Carol I was down here? This is ridiculous. Get her on the phone again."

"Sergeant, just sit over there, Carol has gone to find your lieutenant. I'm sure it'll only take a minute."

Begrudgingly, she turned and sat on one of the chairs lining the wall. She pointed to the seat beside her. Matt obediently took his place. While his wife had accepted this decree to appear for questioning as little more than an unnecessary annoyance driven by a spiteful lieutenant, to Matt, the thought of the questioning process was terrifying.

Matt remembered late last night, when he arrived home, tired from a long day of back breaking slogging, he was surprised to find his wife still up waiting for him. When she told him of the visit she had from Detective Cravers, and his need to go to the police station in the morning for questioning, his back pain left him, being replaced with a sense of dread.

"What do they want from me?"

"Come on Matt. Don't be so bloody stupid" Karen snapped back at him. She was on edge from her drawn-out day filled with annoyances with her husband now adding more and more to her irritation. "Of course, the team needs to question you. You were in the apartment the night of the murder and you were the last one to leave the murder scene. With the threat of legal action hanging over your head from the lead suspect Ken Harris, you have a strong motive."

"But I did as you said. I went to the lawyer Cohan and explained it all. He said everything was going to be alright. He was going to take the picture to the police. He promised to keep me out of it. How do the police even know I was there?"

"That's what we do. We find people who for whatever reason don't want to be found, and I can tell you, you were an easy one to find. The building superintendent, Bert Morrison, claimed it was the contractor working on Harris's renovations that disabled the building loading dock camera. Then there was the busy body old lady, Eleanor Upton, who lives across the hall in apartment 10A who recognized you sneaking into 10B the night of the murder. Then to top it all off, you kept playing right into the hand of that weasel Jeff Hughes."

"But I had nothing to do with the murder. I didn't even know there was a murder committed until I saw you on TV news that night. What are we going to do?" Matt worried that circumstances were pointing a huge finger his way.

"In the morning we're going down to the station. I'll be there with you if the lieutenant tries any of his tricks. All you have to do is keep quiet. Let me do the talking. You got that?" Karen said, determined not to let the lieutenant attempt to steam roll right over her guileless husband to get to her.

"Mr. Langdon," Matt wakes from his thoughts. "If you follow the officer, he'll take you upstairs to the homicide division." Sergeant Omily directed.

"Wait a minute" Karen protested, "What about me? My husband isn't going anywhere without me."

"I'm sorry Sergeant, but they just told me only your husband. You're to remain here. I was told Internal Affairs has locked you out."

Karen slumped back into her molded chair, defeated. With the phrase 'Internal Affairs' she knew there was no point in arguing. Matt was going to have to fend for himself.

Matt looked questioningly at his wife for direction, not knowing quite what to do. He had counted on having her at his side.

"Go ahead, and for God's sake, just tell the truth."

Interview Room #1

Matt sat alone waiting for someone to come and interview him. He didn't understand why he had to be here if no one was going to show an interest and show up. His project that he had just started on the other side of town needed to be complete by the end of the weekend. He was wasting prime working time sitting here alone. He looked around, the room was empty, save for the stark wooden table and a few plastic chairs. On the walls on opposite corners, he noticed the two cameras with their red lights blinking and realized he was being watched. On TV he had always seen the interview rooms with large two-way mirrors so the suspects could be observed as they were made to wait. Strange this room didn't have any mirrors, only blank pale colored walls.

The opening of the door startled him. In walked solemnly, two men and an older grey-haired woman who carried a large bundle of official looking papers under her arm.

"I'm Lieutenant Tom Melnyk, this is Detective Russell Cravers from Homicide. Joining us for this interview is Lieutenant April Kirby from Internal Affairs. This is being recorded, please say your name," the lieutenant directed towards Matt.

In a cracked dry voice "Matt Langdon."

"Please say it a little clearer for the recording."

Matt cleared his throat and blurted out, "Matt Langdon."

"Mr. Langdon," the lieutenant continued, "You do understand that you are here to be questioned in an active homicide investigation as a possible suspect?"

Matt's fear level took a sudden leap, "no one told me I was a suspect. My wife said I was to be interviewed as a witness. She never told me I was a suspect."

Lieutenant Kirby glanced towards Lieutenant Melnyk with a knowing nod, eager to drive Matt's statement home. "You're saying your wife, Sergeant Karen Langdon, of the Homicide Division, has been actively discussing the ongoing murder investigation with you? She has told you outright that you are not a suspect in that investigation. Is that right?"

"Hold on Lieutenant, we're jumping a little ahead of ourselves," Melnyk cut her off, causing April to slump back into her chair, cross her arms over her ample breasts, clearly annoyed to have the morsel abruptly snatched away from her. "Mr. Langdon, as a suspect, you have the right to have a lawyer present for this interview. If you want, we can postpone for a short while to give you time to contact one."

This was getting all too serious for Matt. The only lawyer he knew was Jonathan Cohan. Matt didn't know what to do. "I need to talk with my wife" he stated.

"Your wife is not a lawyer. Do you want us to postpone until you obtain legal counsel?" the lieutenant countered.

Matt remembered all the times during this dragged-out murder case he'd done the wrong thing by listening to other people tell him what he should be doing. "I don't care, I need to speak with my wife."

Melnyk again started to reply, "Mr. Langdon, as I told you, your wife—"

This time it was Lieutenant Kirby's turn as she leaned forward to cut off Melnyk mid-sentence. "It might be interesting to have him consult with his wife. I'd really like to know what advice she would give to him." Then to add weight to her suggestion, "It could be very helpful in our Internal Affairs investigation, Lieutenant."

Detective Russ sat quietly observing as the two dogs jostled for the bone. Lieutenant Kirby wanted to take advantage of the situation and pursue her investigation of Sergeant Langdon. Lieutenant Melnyk wanted to pursue the investigation of Jane Doe's murder with Matt Langdon. By playing the trump card of 'helpful in our Internal Affairs investigation'. Lieutenant Kirby easily won the duel.

Reluctantly, Lieutenant Melnyk directed his detective to call downstairs and let the sergeant come up. He chided himself. He knew it was a mistake to allow Kirby to 'sit in and observe' the interview. Internal Affairs never just sat and observed.

Morning
Jeff Hughes Apartment

Jeff sat on his couch with his living room drapes pulled tightly shut, holding out the morning sun as he took the last swig from his now empty whisky bottle. He'd been sitting there swilling down the amber liquor ever since he came home yesterday afternoon after being abruptly fired by Simon Spirling. Fired by the old fool he thought he had complete and total control over. Fired from the future he had mapped out for taking over the company and rising to be someone important. All his plans were crushed, summed up by the one word ... Fired. That's all he could think about as he relished in the warmth of self-pity. Being fired and getting revenge. As last evening wore on through to morning, the stronger the desire for revenge grew, fueled by the steady drain of the whisky bottle. The biggest insult of all still rang true in his ears, 'Ken was family, and he could be forgiven'. Well Ken, the manipulative, self-focused incompetent, wasn't going to get away with it. Jeff wasn't going to let Ken steal the future that rightly belonged to him. Stumbling, on wobbly legs, he grabbed his coat then lurched out the door. He was going over to teach Ken who was the better man.

In the back seat of the taxi, his steady ranting and raging for revenge against Ken drew the worried attention of the driver. It was much too early in the morning for someone to be this drunk and be so consumed with anger. It was a dangerous recipe for disaster. He looked in his rear-view mirror. He could tell his passenger had no idea of his surroundings or where he was. There was just the constant steady rant, laced with foul curse words, slurring forth from his lips. The driver decided there was no way he was going to be involved with this drunken warrior. He quickly turned the cab around and headed towards the cop shop. He'd let them deal with this. He wanted this mess out of his cab.

Morning, 10:00 am
Police Services.

"Lieutenant," Carol called out across the floor towards Lieutenant Melnyk and Detective Cravers as the two mulled around Russ's desk, waiting for Sergeant Langdon to finish counseling her husband upstairs in Interview Room #1.

Melnyk strolled over to Carol's workstation as she continued, "I just received a call from the downstairs holding cells. They wanted you to know they have Jeff Hughes in one of the drunk tanks. They've read from the morning reports that Homicide has been having an ongoing interest in him. Apparently, he's totally blotto and is ranting at the top of his lungs how he's going to get even with Ken Harris. They're holding him on Drunk and Disorderly, Public Nuisance and Uttering Threats."

The lieutenant stood, stone faced. He stared out into space as he drifted off into deep thought.

"Lieutenant, do you want me to tell them anything? They'll have to release him once he sobers up."

Still focused out into space, "Tell them to hold him until they hear from me. I have a phone call to make."

Seated behind his desk, the lieutenant grabbed a pen and started jotting down a series of points. He would need to get this right and didn't want to sound unprepared. He picked up his phone and dialed the number for the Assistant County DA.

"Assistant DA Faroe's Office" the professional voice on the other end of the line answered.

"Is she in? Tell her Lieutenant Melnyk of Homicide wants to talk with her."

"Hold on while I see if she's available. May I tell her what this is about?"

"Tell her it's about the Jane Doe #6 murder. I want her agreement to lay charges." Sounds of elevator music floated across to Melnyk as he was put on hold.

"Lieutenant Melnyk, this is Sharon Faroe. I thought we had discussed this matter a few days ago. Didn't we agree we wouldn't proceed with the laying of any charges until you had solid evidence." This being an election year, Sharon knew a good juicy murder case with solid winnable evidence would bring a lot of badly needed press her way, but a maybe case with shaky evidence, could prove disastrous. "Do you now have that solid evidence?" she asked hopefully.

Melnyk looked down at the hurriedly scribbled points he had just written and began his tale. " .... and we're in the process of interviewing Matt Langdon. If he confirms that he was the one that took the picture showing the blackmail setup of Hughes with Jane Doe in the photo, minutes before her murder, then I'll have the solid evidence you're looking for." The line sits quiet for a while, "Did you hear me, I'll have solid evidence."

"Sorry, I was thinking. Be careful, this Matt Langdon must freely admit to taking the picture AND," she emphasized, "AND he must admit that he knew what the picture was about. He must say, on record, that he truly believed the scene to be one of blackmail. If, and only if, you get those two statements from him I want you lay charges. Against Jeff Hughes, charge him with 'Complicity to Commit Murder'. Also against him and Matt Langdon charge them both with

'Felony Murder'. I believe Judge Hendriks is sitting this week. The minute you get the statements from Langdon, call my assistant and we'll notify the judge of the need for an Arraignment Hearing first thing Monday morning."

Pleased with himself, the lieutenant sat back in his chair, and absent mindedly put his feet up on his desk. "Carol, call downstairs and tell them to hold Jeff Hughes. He's not to be released. We're going to be laying charges shortly" the lieutenant said, confident that he'd get the required statements from Matt Langdon.

He headed out to Russ's desk, "Ok, Detective, let's go finish this interview with Langdon" he said with an almost skip to his step.

"Should I call Lieutenant Kirby?" Russ asked.

With a broad smile, "No Detective, this interview is for us. Do you have your cuffs with you?"

"Always" a puzzled Russ responded.

Chapter 23

Friday November 22 nd
Morning, 8:30 am
Subway System

"Ken, we really need to talk." Vivian implored as she called from the subway on her way to work. She'd been thinking about what to say all yesterday evening. For her, it had been a long night of reflection. She spent the time curled up on her couch. Slowly and methodically, she worked her way through her relationship with Ken. Her thoughts reconfirmed her love, while at the same time questioned the cost of that apparent one-sided emotion. For each plus point in her relationship analyses, there was an equal and more damaging negative point. And each negative point revolved around the uncertainty of Ken's feelings. "Since your release, I've tried several times to get together with you and each time you come up with some reason or other to put me off."

"But Viv, you need to understand, I don't know what's going on. I'm at my wits end. I still can't remember the night of the murder, or if I had any part to play in it. That's driving me crazy. I can't eat, I can't sleep, and I'm being plagued by a reoccurring nightmare that won't leave me in peace. I don't know, maybe my hidden memories are slowly torturing me for something I've done. My apartment, my sanctuary, has been invaded, everything has changed. And I recently learned Jeff was out to try to undermine me with my uncle. It was him, on the night of my birthday who had set up to blackmail me by bringing the girl who ended up being murdered to my apartment. I need to be alone. I have to figure out what's happening to me." This quagmire of uncertainty and guilt was unfamiliar ground for the once super confidant and self-centered Ken.

Vivian could hear his pain reaching out through his shaken voice. In the past, that would have been enough to cause Vivian to back down and quietly slink away, but not this morning. She had thought this all through and was prepared for this standoffish stance from Ken. "This is too important to me, and too important to us, if there is going to be any us" Vivian replied. "I'm stopping by tonight, right after work to talk. Whatever problems you're facing, we need to figure out if they're problems we can handle together." She never gave Ken any time to respond. Tonight, they would talk. Tonight, she would find out her future. One way or another, tonight a decision was going to be made. She just prayed it would be the right decision for both her and Ken.

Morning, 10:30 am
Police Services, Interview Room #1

"Sergeant," Russ said, as he stuck his head inside the room, "Are you done? Can we continue with the interview?"

Karen said nothing. Only nodded her head.

As the lieutenant and detective took their place, Karen had an uneasy feeling. This was the first time for her to be sitting on the opposite side of the bare table.

The lieutenant started, “Sergeant, if you could leave us now and return downstairs to wait, I’d like to get on with this interview.”

Karen in her most forceful voice stated, “At the request of my husband I’m staying.” eyes locked firmly on the lieutenant to make sure he got the message.

Thinking quickly, the lieutenant realized this could be to his advantage. If Matt Langdon wanted to substitute his wife in place of a lawyer, he might be able to get the information he was seeking easier. And as an added advantage, by having the sergeant be a witness to her husband's statements, he could avoid the messy need to inform her once the arrest was made.

“All right Sergeant, it’s a little unusual, but as long as your husband has no objections, and you don’t interfere with the questioning, you can stay.”

Melnyk turned his attention towards Matt, “Mr. Langdon, I ask you again, for the record, do you want to obtain legal counsel before we continue?”

Matt, glanced for reassurance from his wife. “No, I’m happy to answer any of your questions.”

“Mr. Langdon, can you tell us in your own words the events that took place on the night of Saturday, November 9th through to the morning of Sunday, November 10th. Please leave nothing out.”

Again, Matt looked to his wife. Karen gave a gentle nod for him to begin his story. "I need to start before the night of the murder so that you get the complete picture and understand why I did what I did."

Both the lieutenant and his detective settled back in their chairs.

"It all began much earlier, during the summer, when I was hired to do a large, major renovation to the bathroom in apartment 10B Roxworth Towers."

Russ interjects "This is the apartment of a Ken Harris. Is that correct?"

"Yes."

The lieutenant was annoyed with the interruption. "Detective, let's let Mr. Langdon tell his story in his own words." Turning towards Matt, "continue."

"As I was saying …." Matt carried on detailing all the events that lead up to the crucial night of the murder.

Russ couldn't contain himself, "You never mentioned anything about you disabling the building loading bay security camera."

Although frustrated by the second interruption, the lieutenant recognized it as an important point if they were going to try to prove intent later on.

"The security camera was an accident, I hit it while carrying some bulky materials into the building. I immediately reported it to the building super. He said he'd check into it when he had some time."

Russ made himself a note to check with the building superintendent. If the damage was reported, that wiped out any intent to conceal access to the building at a later date. Karen remembered back to her interview with Bert and Silvi Morrison. Although a worker, she placed Bert as a procrastinator who complained about the broken camera but never did anything about it.

The lieutenant, eager to keep the story moving along. "Ok, we've arrived at the night of the murder, what did you do?"

Matt sheepishly told of his pact with Jeff Hughes to attempt to retrieve some bogus records from Ken Harris's apartment. With the bogus records, Jeff had promised to stop the false charges of Fraud and Theft that Harris's company, Spirling World Supply, was threating him with. When he got to the part where he witnessed Jeff Hughes attempting to use two party girls to create explicit pictures with a passed-out Ken Harris, the lieutenant stopped him.

"Mr. Langdon, I need to stop you for a moment. You're saying you were there, in the apartment at the same time as Jeff Hughes and the two girls. One of which was later found dead in the bathroom."

Karen perked up at the lieutenants' question. What was he after? Why was he honing in on the fact that Matt was in the apartment during Jeff's setup? Matt had already admitted he was there. Something wasn't sounding right. "Lieutenant, my husband has already admitted to being in the apartment and explained why he was there. What are you after?"

"I'm just making sure we have a clear account of your husbands' actions for the record" the lieutenant replied. "So, seeing Jeff with the two-party girls and an incapacitated Ken Harris, what did you believe was going on?"

Matt was falling right into the lieutenant's trap. "It looked to me as if he was setting up to blackmail Harris."

"At the time, you were convinced the makings of a blackmail was in progress."

"Yes sir, no doubt about it, any fool could see what Jeff was up to."

"And what did you do during this blackmail scene?"

Karen didn't like what was going on. It was clear to her that the lieutenant was after something, and the way he was chasing it meant it was something important. "Hold on Matt. Don't say another word. The lieutenant is prying. He's looking for something." Then to the lieutenant, "We're not saying anything else until you come clean. What are you after?"

Melnyk was so close he couldn't stop now, "Sergeant, I told you, you could stay if you didn't interfere with the interrogation. If you open your mouth again, I'll have you forcibly removed."

Karen read this threat as a conformation of her fears. "You already know exactly what my husband did. He took a picture of the blackmail scene. We turned the picture over to the lawyer Cohan who gave it to you personally."

"Sergeant, we're not here to interview you. That's a job for Internal Affairs. I need to hear your husband say what he did."

Matt, not sure what was going on, in spite of his wife's direction, piped up, "I did exactly as my wife has said. I took a picture of the event, and we gave it to the lawyer Cohan."

The lieutenant wanted more, as he leaned halfway across the table. "You gave it to Cohan later, but that's not the reason you took the picture, is it?"

Karen was about to jump in when the lieutenant held up his hand to her, warning her to be quiet.

"No," Matt foolishly admitted. "I took the picture to protect myself from Jeff Hughes in case he didn't keep his end of the bargain with me."

"You admit taking the picture for your own gain."

"I guess so," he muttered. A lamb walking right into the slaughter.

"Thank you, Mr. Langdon." Melnyk said.

Cavers had his eyes focused on the sergeant, watching her as she finally realized what had just happened.

"Detective, read Mr. Langdon his rights, then cuff him. He's being charged with Felony Murder" the lieutenant directed triumphantly.

As Matt, reluctant to be taken, was half lifted and half dragged from the room by Detective Cavers. Karen seething with rage screamed at the gloating lieutenant. "You bastard. It wasn't enough to attack me, you had to go after my husband when you know he's innocent."

The lieutenant stared directly into the sergeants flame red eyes. "I'm not after you, that's the job of Internal Affairs. Your husband just admitted he was at the murder site during the commissioning of a major crime, and he did nothing to stop it. Had he stopped it, an innocent girl might not have been killed. What he did do was for his own selfish profit. Add those two together and that's textbook Felony Murder.

It's time now for you to get out of here and start looking for a good lawyer for your husband. He's going to need one."

Back on the second floor, in the homicide area, the lieutenant strolled over to Carols' desk. "Phone downstairs to the holding area and tell them I want to be personally notified when Jeff Hughes sobers up. Make it clear he is not to be released."

The ever-efficient Carol picked up her phone and carried out her lieutenants' directive.

Noon
Offices of Peters, Peters and Cohan

"Mr. Cohan," his desk intercom chimed, "There's a call for you on line two. It's a Sergeant Karen Langdon who says she needs to speak with you urgently."

Jonathan was curious. The last he heard from his sources was that the sergeant was under suspension. What could she be wanting from him? He had told Alister to call off the Police Commissioner since her husband Matt had freely given him the Hughes picture.

"This is Jonathan Cohan. What can I do for you Sergeant?"

Karen wanted to start off clean and lay her circumstances out for the lawyer before she got to the real purpose of her call. "Mr. Cohan, I'm not calling you as part of the police organization, in fact, right now I am under suspension, wrongly I might add. I'm calling you on behalf of my husband, Matt. He needs your help."

Jonathan instantly felt uneasy with this open-ended request. Ethics are a troubling sword. He already had allowed himself to be pushed once, flaunting the rules for his own gain, by being involved in the murder as legal counsel to Ken Harris. He didn't feel comfortable being drawn across the ethics line again. "Sergeant Langdon, before you say anything, I must remind you that our firm is the legal counsel for Spirling World Supply, and I am personally the council for Ken Harris. I don't think it wise that you should be talking to me on matters concerning your husband."

Karen had no time to be playing word footsie with the lawyer. She needed help and she needed it now. "Do I have to remind you it was my husband Matt who came to you with the photo that cleared your client, Harris? Matt didn't have to do that. He did it because it was the right thing to do. And it's partially the reason why my husband is in trouble. The least you owe him is to hear me out."

"I'll hear you, but I can't promise you anything."

Karen slowly went through all the details leading up to Matt's arrest. She made sure to add her feelings of contempt for Lieutenant Melnyk. "The lieutenant is using trumped up charges against my husband to get at me. Getting me suspended wasn't good enough for him. He has a vendetta against me and is trying to destroy my whole life."

Jonathon knew it wasn't the lieutenant that caused the Internal Affairs investigation onto her, it was him. He was part of the plan to get her discredited for the good of his client Harris. Now, with the queasy element of guilt stirring in his stomach, he started to do some thinking of what he could do to clear his conscience. "Sergeant, if everything is how you say it is, it sounds like your husband definitely fits the requirements for a Felony Murder charge. Like it or not, Matt was in a partnership arrangement with Jeff Hughes. Jeff Hughes, in setting the scene for blackmail, opened the door for the murder to happen. At the time, your husband did nothing to try to stop or alter either of the two crimes but chose to act in a way that he believed benefitted himself. That being said, felony murder is a complicated charge that is often difficult to prove. As I said, I can't promise you anything, but let me make a few phone calls then I'll get back to you."

Now that he had held off the sergeant, he needed to figure out what he could possibly do that would ease the feeling of guilty that had clamped onto his stomach. It wouldn't be easy, he knew he could have no real direct involvement, but he had to do something. He had an idea. It would be risky and could very easily blow up in his face, but he had to try it.

*****

"Sharon Faroe here"

"Hello Sharon, it's Jonathan Cohan. Do you remember me?" he asked hopefully.

"Why of course I do, how could I possibly forget my first real college crush," she replied with a slight lilt in her voice. "It's been a long time. How have you been doing?"

Jonathan took some time to bring her up to date on his life story. Told her of his marriage to the southern belle Dolly, and of their son, David.

"That's wonderful, I'm pleased to hear it. I haven't been so fortunate; you might say I ended up being married to my job, but I guess that's life. Now what could possibly make you call me after all this time? I'm sure it's not just to get caught up on our life stories."

Jonathan hesitated for a second, gathered up his courage, "Sharon, I hear by the grape vine that the DA's office is in the process of laying charges in the Roxworth Tower murder."

"Yes, we're laying charges against two individuals. I'm handling the cases myself." Then being cautious, "Why do you want to know? Do you have an interest in these two? You know I'm not supposed to discuss items like this with people outside my office."

"I understand, and I certainly don't want you to break any of the rules, but I am very familiar with the case and thought I might be able to help you." Before she could stop him, he delved into his involvement. Explained the role he played in representing Ken Harris, who at the beginning of the investigation was considered the prime suspect, leading up to Matt Langdon and Jeff Hughes.

Now was the time to get to the point of the call before she lost interest or cut him off. "You and I both know that the charges you are laying, Felony Murder and Complicity to Commit Murder, are complex and could be difficult to prove. With a critical election on the horizon, I wouldn't think you'd want to get tied up into a long, drawn-out court battle that you might not fare so well in."

He had her interest, "I'm listening, go on."

Not wanting to get into his actions that resulted in Karen Langdon's' suspension, he focused on Hughes. "From my knowledge, the king pin in this whole affair is Jeff Hughes. He's a manipulative, self-serving blackmailer. It was him, for his own selfish gains, who put the whole plan in motion that ultimately led to the murder of the unsuspecting party girl. Matt Langdon was just a simpleton pawn who get sucked into the crime by Hughes."

Faroe had done her homework and knew everything Jonathan was saying was true. "You're not telling me anything I don't know. I've read all the reports."

"Now wouldn't it be better to go into court with a sure thing that would result in some good press of you convicting a truly despicable criminal. It would read better rather than possibly getting some negative press about trying to convict a hard-working, simple family man who was taken advantage of?"

That was a valid point. The last thing Sharon wanted right now was to be portrayed as a mean witch beating down a poor peasant. Her whole campaign was based on 'Justice for the Common Folk'. "Okay, what are you suggesting? And remember, I'm not interested on anything with even the slightest hint of impropriety."

"What if I could guarantee that Matt Langdon would be willing to turn state's evidence against Hughes. It would make your case against Hughes a sure thing. The papers would eat it up. The common man helps the state get a conviction in a complex case and a murderer is taken off the streets for good."

Sharon liked what she was hearing. "Langdon would have to plead guilty."

"Understood, but there would need to be an agreement of a lenient sentence."

"If he can deliver Jeff Hughes to me on a silver platter, I'll suggest to the court he be given a probationary sentence with community service. Say something like 3 to 5 years."

"Agreed" Jonathan happy with the outcome of his pleadings.

"Now Jonathan, this conversation never took place. You should brief Langdon what to say when the time comes. The two of them are being arraigned in the county courthouse Monday at 10." Then added, just to relieve some of the tension of the call, "And next time, don't wait so long to call. It'd be nice to get together sometime."

6:20 PM
Roxworth Towers, Apartment 10B

"This is Vincent the doorman, there's a woman here," he paused, "What is your name again?"

"Just tell him Vivian is here. He's expecting me."

"She says her name is Vivian and that you're expecting her."

Ken wasn't looking forward to this. He hated when people, especially women, said they needed to talk, or they wanted to have a 'Heart-to-Heart'. In most cases he thought of it as code for 'You've done something wrong and I'm going to correct you.' With all his problems spinning wildly out of control in real life, the last thing he wanted to do was listen to some strung out woman trying to unload her make believe 'feelings' onto him.

"Okay, let her come up, but listen Vincent, I want you to do me a favor."

Vincent waved Vivian toward the elevators.

For most residents of the building, Vincent was only too happy to do the odd favor, that is for most residents that were good tippers and had him on their Christmas bottle list. But the smug, wannabe Harris certainly didn't fall into that category. "Excuse me, what do you mean 'do you a favor'? I'm pretty busy down here right now."

"Don't worry, I'll make it worth your while." Ken recognized Vincent's hand reaching out through the intercom for a reward.

"What do you want me to do?"

"In about ten minutes, call me again with something that's very important."

"What do you want me to say?"

"Don't worry about that. Just make the call." Ken set in place his escape from Vivian's expected upcoming drawn-out whining about her 'feelings' episode.

When she stepped from the elevator Vivian noticed the large wooden door of 10A creep open just a sliver and a pair of watery eyes focus on her. She had noticed them many times before, but this time they seemed to be more poignant. This time she felt the sad loneliness behind them. It reinforced her determination to take the steps required in her life, so she didn't become a lonely old woman sneaking peeks out as the world passed her by. As she walked down the hallway, for some reason, she gave a little wave and a smile. The door quickly and quietly closed.

When she entered the apartment, she was shocked. Her Ken, the always sharp dressed, well-groomed hunk stood looking more like a street living homeless soul. His clothes were disheveled, his face unshaven topped with a head of hair that hadn't seen a brush in days. Plus, to make matters worse, he emitted a sour smell that made her want to step back out of the fragrance zone. She looked around the apartment, and saw it wasn't in any better state than its owner. An apartment that had always shone clean and spotless, with the style and grace of wealthy elegance, now looked worn and dried out. "My God! Ken, you look terrible. What's happened to you? You've only been home for a couple of days, but you look like you've been lost on some deserted island for months. And this place is in shambles. Where's your cleaning lady? You shouldn't be living like this."

Ken stood, looking at her through glazed eyes that screamed for sleep, "I had to let her go." He pointed at the blood-stained footprints on the crème-colored carpet, "She couldn't clean my carpet." He walked back, and collapsed on the couch. "My beautiful carpet destroyed."

Vivian started to panic, unsure about what to do. There'd be no point trying to talk relationship, commitment, or future with this shell of a man. He needed help, professional help. Far greater help than she knew how to provide.

'*Ring*'...The apartment intercom chimed.

Ken rose and took the call. "Yes, yes, thank you, I'll take care of it."

Turning to Vivian, "You have to go, I have some important things I need to do."

In disbelief Viv questioned the remark, "What important things do you have to do? I just got here. For god's sake, you're barely able to function. I can't leave you like this."

"I said you have to go." Ken was growing weary of the intrusion. In his fog filled head he could start to hear the low moan coming from his bathroom. "She's here."

Vivian looked around, "Who's here Ken? There's no one here but us."

"Get out" he screamed. "Get out now!"

"Ken, if I leave, I won't be coming back."

"Now" he pointed to the door undeterred. No woman ever left him. He's the one that left them. She'd be back.

In the elevator Vivian's knees buckled and she dropped to the floor. Her body racked uncontrollably with stomach wrenching tears. She couldn't do it. She wouldn't leave a dog in the miserable state that Ken was in. She had to do something. She reached for her phone and put through perhaps the most important call of her life.

"Hello"

"Is this Molly, Molly Spirling?" Vivian murmured between sobs.

Yes, who's calling?"

"Mrs. Spirling," she tried to collect her breath. "It's Vivian Mooney, Ken's partner."

Detecting the anguish in the voice, "What's the matter dear? You sound troubled."

"I am. I'm very troubled. It's about Ken."

"What's happened? Has Ken been hurt? Is he in trouble? Tell me" Molly frantically demanded.

Vivan described the details of her short horrific encounter with Ken. At the end, both women are sobbing, Molly for her wounded boy, Vivian for her missing man.

"I'll be there as soon as I can" Molly told the weeping Vivian. Abruptly turning to her maid, "tell Henry to bring the car around and call my husband at his office and have him meet me at our nephew's apartment as fast as he can. Tell him it's urgent."

His aunt had never been to his apartment, Ken had always preferred to keep his single life independent from his past family upbringing.

At the entrance to the towers, Molly burst through the front doors, only to be confronted by a startled Vincent. "Excuse me, who do you wish to see" he inquired.

With a broad sweep of her club sized arm, she pushed past him. "Get out of my way you silly man," and was four steps ahead of him, as she charged towards the elevators, before Vincent was able to say a word. At the elevators Molly saw the lone woman with a tear-stained face waiting for her.

"Vivian?" she asked hurriedly.

"Yes, he's upstairs in 10B."

As she climbed into the open elevator, Molly questioned, "Are you coming up dear?"

Reluctantly Vivian replied, "No, I've done all I can do." As the elevator doors close to whisk Aunt Molly to her boy, Vivan turned to leave. With a wish for Ken, she embarked on a new journey forward to an unknown future, alone.

At the door with large decorative 10B letters she pounded, "Ken, Ken, let me in. It's Aunt Molly."

As Ken opened the door, Molly threw her arms around him and pulled him into her heaving bosom. "It's alright dear, Aunt Molly is here now, it's going to be alright."

Downstairs, Simon arrived. Striding over to where Vincent, still shaken, was standing, "which way to Ken Harris's apartment? Has my wife already arrived?"

Vincent started to ramble, "a huge woman just pushed past me—"

Simon cut him off mid complaint, "Never mind that" He reached into his pocket and pulled out his car keys along with a sizable bill and pushed them towards the gaping doorman. "Here, go park my car."

Once he saw the freely splash of money, Vincent instantly succumbed to the demanding authority of Simon. "Yes sir, the elevators are over there, Mr. Harris is in apartment 10B."

When Simon reached the apartment, Molly had Ken, cuddled to her breast, gently rocking him back and forth as he slept in her arms peacefully for the first time in days. "SHH" Molly motioned with her lips.

Simon reached for his phone, "I want an ambulance to Roxworth Towers, Apartment 10B right away"

Across the hall, Fredrick, disturbed by all the commotion and the constant running back and forth to the door by his wife Eleanor, "What's all the damn noise? I can't even hear the news."

"It's across the hall dear," the wispy voice replied. "It looks like 10B is having another party."

Fredrick tense in his chair, tightened his fists. “Get away from the door.” he demanded of his shrinking wife.

Chapter 24

Monday November 25th
Morning, 10:00AM
County Court Room #3

The first thing Jonathan sensed when he quietly slipped into the court room to take a seat in the back, beside Karen, was the smell of damp. Although today had turned out to be a brisk fall day, the steady rain of the past weekend had left its mark inside the aged building. The large room, with an amazingly high ceiling, was awash with dark worn wood. The old wooden bench that he sat on creaked and snapped back at him from his weight. A quiet under his breath "Morning" towards Karen drew an equally soft "Morning" reply. With the absence of windows or fans, the stagnant air inside the room left the slight taste of musk in the back of his throat. On the bench that Jonathan was sitting on, he noticed some bored participant from maybe years ago had carved 'DTH + CRY' deep into the seat. For a moment he wondered who they were and what had drawn them to be sitting here.

Karen, dressed in a black jacket, white blouse with black slacks, had been sitting staring out into nowhere for some time. With Matt under custody in the county lock-up, sleeping didn't come easy for her. She rose early, had only a dry piece of toast and black coffee. She had her dark SUV pointed towards the courthouse just as the sun had begun to rise. In the course of her career, she had been to many arraignment hearings and knew them to be a swift process, but she felt she needed to be there when Matt was ushered in. A commotion near the front of the room drew her attention as someone wearing an oversized baseball cap was ordered to remove it by one of the security guards. Words were exchanged. Warnings were given. The hat disappeared.

As he looked around Jonathan estimated approximately twenty to twenty-five people had chosen, or had been ordered, to spend their morning here. A few gray-haired seniors, outnumbered by the majority of young to middle aged males, were all sitting patiently waiting for something to happen. A small scattering of females were sprinkled among the group. Some were chattering, some were adjusting their makeup, some idly played with their hair. Everyone was growing restless with the wait. Jonathan thought he should say something encouraging to the sergeant sitting beside him. "Don't worry, this all is just a formality. We need to let it play out. The Assistant DA has promised Matt will coast through this with no problem."

The back doors flung open and a parade of briefcase carrying lawyers strutted down the center aisle to take their place in the front row. Propping their cases open, they started to spread an assortment of colored papers out, each one getting ready for their new clients. For some of them, it would be the first-time meeting face to face as they had been randomly chosen to be here, through the Public Defender's Office.

With a flourish, and the tasty smell of almonds surrounding her, the Assistant County DA Sharon Faroe made her entrance. Seeing Jonathan, sitting in the back, next to a rather attractive woman, trying to go unnoticed, brought a faint smile to her broad lips. Her heels clicking on the worn floor echoed up towards the vaulted ceiling, as she took her place. Quickly scurrying behind her, her entourage of assistants followed. Taking a moment, allowing her team to get settled, Sharon then gave a nod to the court bailiff indicating she was ready to begin.

In a practiced loud voice, the bailiff hailed "All rise, the Honorable Judge Milton Hendriks presiding."

On cue, from a side door, the judge, wearing a loose flowing black robe and thick lensed glasses took his seat behind the raised wooden podium.

"Be seated"

When the rustling of people trying to get comfortable subsided, the judge looked around his attentive court. "Ms. Faroe, it's nice to see the Assistant DA grace us with her presence this morning."

Sharon couldn't tell if it was a sarcastic remark or a genuine welcoming, either way she politely replied, "Thank you, your honor."

Then addressing the entire assembly, the judge gave a few opening remarks. "Since this is an Arraignment Hearing we will be informal, but at the same time, I will tolerate no outbursts or disturbances. Is that clear? We have a full docket of cases we need to work through, so let's get started. Bailiff, bring in the first case."

A large, bearded man in his late forties wearing handcuffs was escorted into the front. One of the group of lawyers rose to stand beside his new client. Sharon stayed seated as one of her underlings stepped forward. Quickly and efficiently the man was dealt with and ushered out, back into custody. This process continued for over an hour, one by one suspects are brought in, dealt with and removed. And after each one, the judge called out, "Next case." The whole time, Assistant DA Faroe, remained unconcerned.

"Next case," the judge directed.

This time two men are led in, both handcuffed, both wearing bright orange prison jump suits. The judge glanced down to have a quick read of his script, "Who have we here?" He noticed the movement of the Assistant DA, who for the first time had risen from her seat causing her juniors to fall back giving her room.

"Your honor. This is Mathew Langdon and Jeffery Hughes."

From the back of the court room, two reporters from the local papers clamored in, drawing a terse scowl from the judge and a smile from Sharon. Her campaign manager had made it a point to notify the media of the not to be missed performance happening today in the County Court House. For the good and safety of the community, Assistant DA Sharon Faroe was personally going to remove two dangerous criminals from the streets and bring justice for the innocent young girl murdered in Apartment 10B Roxworth Towers.

Finding Jeff and Matt on his score card, the judge took a moment to read the short blurb hand scribbled under their names. “Oh yes,” he said to himself, “Our main event for today.” Judge Henriks looked towards the two, “Gentlemen, I see the Assistant DA is intending to lay some pretty serious charges against you two.”

Sharon wanted to make sure the reporters heard the charges come from her lips, not the judges, butted in. “Your honor, we are charging Jeffery Hughes with Complicity to Commit Murder, along with Felony Murder. We are also charging Matthew Langdon with Felony Murder.”

“Thank you, Ms. Faroe,” the judge said annoyingly. “Gentlemen, in light of the seriousness of these charges, I want to make sure you both understand your rights in this proceeding. You have the right to legal counsel. Has the Public Defender's Office supplied you both with such council?”

The lawyer standing beside Jeff stated “Yes your honor, David Price, representing Jeffery Hughes.”

And the lawyer who stood beside Matt stated, “Harold Bohm representing Mathew Langdon your honor.”

The judge, who was trying to look as wise as possible, adjusted his robe and leaned forward to address Jeff and Matt. “Let’s take a minute so I can explain the meaning of these charges. I’ll start with the greater charge of Complicity to Commit Murder. That charge is being levied against you, Mr. Hughes. In a nutshell, complicity is the encouraging or the facilitating a person to commit murder. The second charge, which the Assistant DA has applied to you both, is Felony Murder. Now this is pretty straight forward. If a murder occurs during the commissioning of a crime, then all who participated in anyway with that crime can be held equally libel for the resultant murder." The judge, pleased with himself, took a deep breath and sat back in his chair. "I'm sure as you move forward through the justice process, your lawyers will be explaining a lot of new terms to both of you."

Jeff could no longer hold back and exploded. "Your honor, I shouldn't be here. I did nothing wrong; I'm being made out as a scape goat for other people."

The judge held up his hand, signaling Jeff to stop, "Mr. Price, perhaps you can start off by controlling your client."

The lawyer Price placed his arm around the shoulder of Jeff to try to calm his client down, but Jeff, not to be deterred, shook the arm off. "This isn't fair," he continued, "the real criminal here is Langdon. He's guilty of Fraud and Theft. I tried to stop him. You can ask anyone, I'm the innocent person here. You've got to believe me." He looked around in desperation at the court room audience. He spotted Jonathan and a stoic Karen seated in the back row. Jeff pointed with his cuffed hands, "There, there, in the back, his wife, a disgraced, suspended police sergeant along with the real killer's lawyer, Cohan. He'll tell you I'm innocent and it was his client Ken Harris, along with Langdon and his crooked wife, who are trying to frame me."

Matt, in a meager attempt to defend his wife, "You keep my wife out of this, or so help me God, I'll make you pay."

The judge, started to lose his patience. In a firm loud voice, "Mr. Price, Mr. Bohm, I won't ask you again. Control your clients."

There's little the lawyers could do. Jeff was beside himself with self-righteous anger. Matt, looked towards his only hope. He called, "Cohan, for god's sakes, you've got to do something to stop him."

"That's it" the judge declared, "Take the accused out and we'll have a ten-minute adjournment to allow Mr. Hughes and Mr. Langdon to collect themselves." Then he looked at the Assistant DA, "Ms. Faroe, Mr. Price, Mr. Bohm, I'd like to see you all in my chambers, now." Then thinking for a moment, "And Mr. Cohan, you seem to have an interest in these accused, I'd like you to join us, if you don't mind." This was exactly what Jonathan didn't want, He was here only as a courtesy to Karen, not to be personally involved.

By the time Jonathan arrived at the internal chamber, the judge had already removed his robe and was perched behind his desk, actively drumming his fingers loudly. He pointed for Jonathan to join the trio of lawyers standing in front of him. "Ms. Faroe, what the devils going on here. I was told by your office that this was going to be a simple process of the defendants entering their pleas and scheduling a preliminary hearing. Now I find there's accusations of Fraud, Theft and worse of all Police Corruption." Then turning to Cohan, "and Mr. Cohan, you, a known business lawyer, to hear you were acting as legal counsel to a murder suspect? A clear case of abuse of your sworn legal ethics." Then to round out his lecture, "And you two, Bohm and Price, you should be furious to have your clients dropped in the middle of this mess."

Sharon took the lead, "Your honor, this is as big a shock to me as it is to you." Quickly thinking it would be disastrous if it got out she was planning to make a deal with an accused involved with fraud and theft. And, if the public ever learned her deal was with a husband of a crooked cop, well, she wouldn't stand a chance to be elected dog catcher. Getting on her high horse, she proclaimed, “there will be no deal made with either of the accused. I plan to vigorously pursue justice in this murder case. And if I find the accusations of Police Corruption to be true, so much the better, I’ll clean that up along the way.”

Jonathan’s mouth fell open, “You can’t change your mind on the basis of wild accusations from a criminal manipulator like Hughes. All his claims are on him. Don’t fall for his lies or you’ll have egg on your face that you’ll never be able to wash off.”

Sharon was on a charging white horse and couldn’t be stopped. “Jonathan, if I were you, I’d be very careful Judge Henriks here, doesn’t report you to the State Bar Association on ethics charges.” She firmly planted the idea in the judge's mind.

With court resumed, the judge declared, “I will tolerate no more interruptions. Mr. Langdon, how do you plead to the charge of Felony Murder?”

Matt unsure of what to do. He had been told to plead guilty and join the assistant DA as a witness against Jeff. “I don’t know. There’s supposed to be a deal for me?”

Assistant DA Faroe jumped in for the good of the reporters in the court room, “My office will never make deals with accused criminals.”

The judge said, “I’ll accept a plea of ‘Not Guilty’ and your lawyer can work things out.” Turning his attention to Jeff, “Mr. Hughes, how do you plead to the dual charges of Complicity to Commit Murder and Felony Murder?”

Jeff, not wanting to give up, "I'm innocent of everything, you've got to believe me, it's Langdon, not me."

"I'll take that as a 'Not Guilty' plea" then added "since there is no bail allowed in this state for Murder charges, you both will be held over in custody until a suitable date for a preliminary hearing can be scheduled. Some other judge can try to make sense out of this mess. Bailiff, return the accused back into custody." With that, Matt and Jeff were led away, Jeff screamed his innocence all the way out of the building.

As they leave, Karen, furious with the outcome, lashed out at Cohan. "You promised, Matt helped you and you just sold him down the river for your own client Harris. You, more than anybody knows that Matt is innocent, but you still let this happen. You should be ashamed of yourself."

Jonathan was ashamed of himself, more than Karen could ever realize. He was ashamed he had managed to get himself dragged down into this whole mess, just to protect his and his family's comfortable life. He was physically sick to his stomach as he answered Karen, "I'm so terribly sorry, I tried my best."

Karen turned her back to the now hapless lawyer as she responded, "Well your best, along with your word, wasn't good enough."

Chapter 25

Tuesday November 26th
Morning, 6:30AM
Hedge Street, Eastgate, the suburbs

Russ sat quietly downstairs as usual, in his bathrobe, engrossed in the early morning paper. It's raised bold headline screamed out 'Assistant County DA charge two in recent Roxworth Tower Murder'. His coffee sat, growing cold, as he slowly read through the article, not wanting to miss any detail. It was clear to anyone in the know, the reporter was taking great license with the facts. The paper focused on the brilliant work of Assistant County DA Sharon Faroe and her tireless efforts in bringing justice to the brutal murder of an innocent young woman in Apartment 10B. Never once did the article give any credit to the homicide group and the long hours he suffered through, at the expense of his home life. Instead, it briefly hinted at possible Police Corruption in the investigation, and reassured its readers, Assistant County DA Sharon Faroe would leave no stone unturned in the pursuit of justice. If corruption existed, it would be rooted out and exposed for all to see.

Morning, 6:30AM
365 Maple Row, Eastgate, the suburbs

Karen hadn't slept a wink during the night. Worry about her husband Matt had kept sleep from reaching her. Matt was helpless in dealing with stress filled situations. It had always been her who made any critical decision. How was he going to handle the impact of being locked away? He was an innocent who would be ripe for the picking by any overpowering prison mate. She'd have to see him, daily, if necessary, to keep his spirits up. With a sleep deprived mind, she stepped out onto her front porch to fetch the morning paper. She glanced at the headline, and with pure rage, she heaved the offensive bundle out across her lawn. Determined now more than ever she wasn't going to give up. She'd find the real killer and get Matt freed.

Morning, 6:30AM
Downtown, City Apartments

Stepping from her morning steamed shower, Sharon Faroe, wrapped herself tightly in one of her plush white bath towels. Crossing to her empty bedroom, she gave a sigh. It would have been nice to renew her ancient affair with Jonathan. She would have enjoyed his bedroom company for the evening. But that wasn't to be. She made her decision for the good of her career rather than the call of her libido. Sharon picked up the morning paper. Reading it brought a satisfying grin to her makeup free face. The expensive dinner and endless drinks with the reporters after the court adjournment had paid off.

Thinking to herself, 'Who says you can't buy good press.'

Morning, 6:30AM Cohan Household

Alone at his morning breakfast table, Jonathan sat with the morning paper spread out in front of him. The headlined article made him cringe inside.

Mrs. Dodds asked if he was feeling alright. "You look awfully pale. Did you not sleep well last night?"

"I'm alright, just a little heartburn I guess," not wanting to get into a discussion with his housekeeper.

"I know what will bring you around, a nice hot bacon and eggs breakfast."

"No, not this morning Mrs. Dodds. Just some black coffee and make it strong." His sour stomach couldn't hold any food. Disgusted with himself with his head cradled in his hands, he lowered it down to rest on the table.

Morning, 6:30AM Habers' Penthouse

"Okay darling, get yourself dressed." He tossed a frilly 38DD bra across to the occupant of his bed from last night. "I've got a lot of work to do this morning."

With a whine "but Bernie, it's still dark outside. Come back to bed."

"Never mind that, it was fun, but it's over. Maurice will give you a ride home. Now get that cute little tush moving."

He reached for his paper on his breakfast tray. "Well, well. Will you look at that? Old Jeff has managed to get himself locked up." Reading through the article, he searched for any bad press about him or his club and found none. "At least he's learned to keep his mouth shut."

"Who are you talking about?" his companion questioned.

"I said, get moving, I've got to figure out how I'm going to get the ten grand owed to me from a prison cell."

Morning, 6:30AM
Roxworth Towers, Apartment 10A

"Where's the morning paper? You know I like to read the paper in the morning," Fredrick called out to his wife Eleanor who was tucked away in the bedroom. Drawn by the headline she scurried to her room to read as much as she could as rapidly as she could.

"It's right here Fredrick, I was just bringing it to you."

"And make me a coffee," he demanded. Startled by the headline, he threw open the paper on the table in front of him. Reading the article twice, needing to make sure... Jeff Hughes ... contractor Matt Langdon ... crooked police sergeant. It was over. He sat back in his kitchen chair and broke out into a roaring laugh that had his rotund belly bouncing.

"What's so funny?" Eleanor asked, depositing the coffee on the table.

"It's all here. They got that party boy Hughes along with his partner the contractor Langdon. And get this, they're going to be looking into that nosey police sergeant that wouldn't leave us alone.

"I thought Karen was a very nice person. She took time to have some tea with me. I wouldn't want anything bad to happen to her."

"You stay away from her, you hear me. She's being charged with Police Corruption. And what'd you do with those blood-stained slippers I told you to get rid of?"

"Fredrick, if you were involved with that poor girl's death, you really should tell Karen. She's a good policewoman who will help you."

In anger Fredrick grabbed his frail wife by the arm, sinking his fingers tight into the soft tissue. "I told you, when I went in there, she was already dead. I stepped in the puddle of blood oozing out of her head. If the police ever got hold of my slippers from that night, they'd railroad me with the murder. Now, did you get rid of them?"

"I always do what you tell me, you're hurting my arm." Eleanor lied to her husband. Her insurance was hidden under her bed, and if Karen needed them, she'd give the slippers to her. Knowing most people considered her senile, she smiled to herself. Her friend Karen was the only one who treated her well, and that deserved to be rewarded.

Morning, 6:30AM
Glendale

She staggered out of the bathroom, after vomiting the remainder of last night's party into the toilet. Housed in the one room flat that Bernie had hidden her away in, Rochelle was a wreck. Not knowing anyone at the Glendale club, she was forced to do her partying with a wide assortment of losers. Losers of every type. She missed her friends and the true party atmosphere of Club Envy. There she was a star. Everyone knew her as the queen of partying. But she couldn't go back until Bernie called her back. She had to wait until the police stopped looking for the killer of the stupid skinny hanger on who got herself killed that night in the bathroom. She hadn't meant to push her so hard, but when the fool laughed at her and mocked her, it just happened. It was an accident. A push, a loud crack and the pool of blood. As long as she kept it a secret, the party could go on, and that's what was important, the party and her friends. Not the accidental death of a nobody.

Roxworth Towers
Apartment 10B

Rose lay on the bathroom floor, naked, cold, alone, surrounded by blood. She had to wait. Wait until her killer came back so she could apologize to her for the mean things she had said. It might take a long time, but to Rose, time now had no meaning. Until she apologized, she couldn't move on. She waited.

Bonus Preview

The Secret

In

Apartment 3A

Bonus Preview

Chapter 1

October 3rd.

Something was wrong. More than that, something was very wrong. For Joyce Treacher, she had a decision to make. The kind of decision that if you're right, then all your fears and pent-up anxiety kept you safe, but if you're wrong, there would be no second decisions, ever. Did she ignore what her gut was telling her and walk right in, or did she listen to her body and call for help. Standing at the doorway to her apartment, winded from having climbed the three flights of stairs, juggling two bulging paper bags of groceries in her arms, she had to do something. The weight of the bags seemed to be growing and her arms seemed to be cramping. If she didn't do something soon, her bags would fall to the floor and spill out all over the darkened hallway.

When she had left her apartment a little over an hour ago to do her weekly grocery run, she was sure she had locked the door behind her. Now, arriving home, leaning on her door, as she fumbled between holding her bags and trying to slip a hand into her jacket pocket to root for her keys, she stopped in her tracks. Her door moved. No longer locked, her weight caused the door to nudge open a crack. She lived alone. Only the aged building super had a key, and he rarely expended the energy required to climb the steps.

Bonus Preview

Alarmed, she cautiously looked inside. All the lights were off, and she always left the small light above her stove on, so she didn't come home to a dark apartment.

The light cinched it. Backing away from the doorway, she quietly eased down the still hall to her neighbor's door, Mr. Fernandez. Martin Fernandez, or Marty, as he told her a hundred times to call him. Still struggling with her load of groceries, she quietly tapped on the door with her foot. No answer. *Tap ... Tap ... Tap*, this time a little harder.

"Joyce, here, let me hold those bags." Not waiting for a reply Marty snuggled close and grasped the heavy bags in a single swoop.

"Mr. Fernandez," Joyce started.

"Come on now, I told you to call me Marty," he interrupted her as a huge grin filled his face.

"Marty,"

"That's better," looking at his neighbor he saw the sharp sign of fear in her eyes. "Joyce, what's the matter, you look as if you've seen a ghost."

With a glance over her shoulder towards her open door, "it's my apartment" she said with a tremble in her voice. "I know I locked the door when I went out for groceries, and see, it's open. It shouldn't be open, and my lights are all out."

In a relaxed fatherly voice, "You sure you locked your door? You didn't run out in a hurry, thinking you locked it? I know I do it all the time."

"I'm positive, I always lock it, and my stove light in the kitchen is off. I never turn it off."

"Well, I'm sure everything's ok, the light probably just finally burnt out." He looked over his shoulder and called back to his wife, who was busily preparing dinner, "I'm going over to Joyce's for a minute."

"Don't be long, dinner's almost ready and the kids need to be fed."

With a content smile, he breathed in the aroma that wafted out from his wife's cooking, "You want to come in and join us for supper? Maria always makes more than even I can eat."

Joyce knew the wonderful spicy food Maria cooked, so much better tasting than the frozen prepared stuff she usually microwaved for herself after work. Often, little Manuel would bring leftovers from his mother for her to savor. "No, thanks. I need to get these groceries put away."

"Alright, your loss," he cheerfully teased, "Wait here, I'll go in and turn on your lights for you."

"Wouldn't it be better to call the police?" Joyce was nervous, her muscles tightening, her gut pounding in her ear, 'Police...Police'

"Don't be silly, just wait here." as he strode down the hall, with the confidence of a man helping a damsel in distress, through the door, into the dark kitchen, still clutching the bags in his arms. "What?" was all he said as the practiced hand reached out to drive the blade deep into his soft belly, twisting it home. Collapsing to the floor, the bags flew in the air, before they rained their contents down beside him. A gasp, a gurgle, as blood trickled from Marty's open mouth. Smashed ripe red tomatoes, mingled with the pool of blood that formed from the gaping wound in Marty's stomach. Eyes, bright, shone at the ceiling in disbelief, then slowly dimmed.

Hearing the commotion that came from her kitchen, Joyce stepped up, filling her doorway. "Marty, what's happening? Are you alright?" The dark figure, undeterred, plowed right through her, slashing at her arm, tossing her backward across the narrow hallway. Her head banged on the wall with a loud thud. She slipped down. The last thing she heard as the black wave swept over her was Maria, calling, "Marty, I'm putting supper on the table now."

*****

Don't miss what happens next in ....

<u>The Secret in Apartment 3A</u>

Bonus Preview

Dear Reader:

I hope you enjoyed this added preview bonus from ***The Secret in Apartment 3A****, the second novel in my three novel series titled*

The Apartment Murders.

David Tylor

davidtylor282@gmail.com

Joyce Treacher is a free drinks hostess at the local casino. Working one night she meets Fred Conti, a pretentious but inept office clerk who works in one of the most successful lawyer's offices in the state. Through Fred, Joyce is thrown into a political storm of corruption, blackmail, organized crime and murder. Little does she know, her only hope of survival lies in discovering the Secret that is hidden in her apartment.

The Apartment Murders

The Girl in Apartment 10B .... September 2022

The Secret in Apartment 3A ...

The Killer in Apartment 2F ....